BOWIE

Forge Books by Randy Lee Eickhoff
Bowie
The Fourth Horseman
The Raid

Other Works
A Hand to Execute
The Gombeen Man

Nonfiction
Exiled

BOWIE

A Novel

RANDY LEE EICKHOFF
&
LEONARD C. LEWIS

A TOM DOHERTY ASSOCIATES BOOK
NEW YORK

This is a work of fiction. All the characters and events portrayed in this novel either are fictitious or are used fictitiously.

BOWIE

This book is printed on acid-free paper.

A Forge Book
Published by Tom Doherty Associates, Inc.
175 Fifth Avenue
New York, NY 10010

Forge® is a registered trademark of Tom Doherty Associates, Inc.

Design by Maura Faddea Rosenthal

Library of Congress Cataloging-in-Publication Data

Eickhoff, Randy Lee.
    Bowie / Randy Lee Eickhoff & Leonard C. Lewis. —1st ed.
        p.   cm.
    "A Tom Doherty Associates book."
    ISBN 0–312–86619–4 (alk. paper)
    1. Bowie, James, d. 1836—Fiction. 2. Alamo (San Antonio, Tex.)—Siege, 1836—Fiction. 3. Texas—History—to 1846—Fiction.
    I. Lewis, Leonard C.   II. Title.
    PS3555.I23B6   1998
    813'.54—dc21   98-23449
                                                                    CIP

First Edition: October 1998

Printed in the United States of America

0 9 8 7 6 5 4 3 2 1

To Jesse Everhart,
who traveled the "wilds" of Wisconsin with me
—RLE

To my family for their patience
and to my friend Randy for his.
—LCL

— ACKNOWLEDGMENT —

This work owes a special debt of gratitude to our editor, Robert Gleason, who first suggested its unusual format in Chumley's in Greenwich Village while we were visiting old haunts. May your glass always be full.

"By Hercules! The man was greater than Caesar or Cromwell—well—Nay, Nearly equal to Odin or Thor. The Texans ought to build him an Altar!"
—THOMAS CARLYLE

Mine honour is my life; both grow in one;
Take honour from me, and my life is done.
—WILLIAM SHAKESPEARE
RICHARD II (I.I.L77)

Quod non pro patria.
—BOWIE MOTTO FROM FAMILY
COAT OF ARMS

BOWIE

A. J. SOWELL

According to the fashion of the day, I am obligated to take pen in hand and explain why I decided to write this book. The answer is quite simple: We need heroes more than ever now and I don't believe we can spare Jim Bowie. Of course, the heroes we need now are not the heroes that the dime novels and some of those "yellow journalists" are trying to cram down everyone's throats. No sir. We don't need those robber barons and such who think that making a pile of money makes them worthy of admiration. Money is nice, I don't begrudge a person for wanting it, but there are other things more important—especially for our young people today who don't seem to have those models to measure up to like I had when I was a youngster. Of course, I'm quick to admit that most of those heroes were real people and we knew their faults as well as we knew their qualities, and in the measuring we did, the latter greatly outweighed the former.

Strange, now that I am an old man, I am more aware of the value of having heroes than I did when I was growing up. I suppose that is a license of age. Too bad that it is wasted upon the old and not lavished any more upon the young. All too often, nowadays, I see people hustling and hustling their way through life without paying the slightest bit of attention to their children. They do not tell the stories that are necessary for children to hear, they do not read to their children anymore, and because of this, we are losing a vital part of our history as well. We can't afford to do that. We can't afford to lose men like Jim Bowie.

My family knew Jim Bowie since around 1829. But that's not so unusual. I reckon every person who lived in Texas prior to his death at the Alamo in 1836 knew Jim Bowie if not personally, then by sight, since people were prone to point out Bowie as he walked along the streets. But in our case, well, our family roots, like all family roots on the frontier, are very important, and the Sowells, like the Bowies, came from Highlander stock and Highlanders have a habit of sticking together. Bowie spent many a night discussing politics and Texas with my grandfather, my father, and my uncles.

I wasn't privy to this since I wasn't born until twelve years after Bowie's death, but I sure heard the details of some of his adventures from my kin who got it straight from the quiet man's mouth. They all delighted in filling my head with those wonderful stories. And stories were very important to a young man growing up on the edge of the frontier. He needed heroes to help him decide which road he was going to take when he became a man, and manhood came early in those days out of necessity, what with Indian problems and the renegades and outlaws thick as fleas before the Rangers took to combing them out of the Thicket and Hills District. Fact is, it seems like there was more opportunity for a young one to go wrong than to remain right those days. So heroes were important. Very important.

To know a man one must know something of his roots. James Bowie was a limb of a fine family tree. His ancestors on his father's side were Scots, Highlanders. The name "Bowie" might even be from an ancient Scottish word, buieclaiomh, *which could be translated as "the big man who carries the claymore," a claymore being a huge, two-handed broadsword. Though sometimes the clans cut down the sword or put a new hilt to it, the originals had a blade as long as six feet. The sword was traditionally carried by the clan's biggest warrior and used against men in armor. If the man was big enough and the claymore strong enough, it could cut the armored man in half.*

The Bowies were Scottish nobles and on familiar grounds with heroes like William Wallace and Rob Roy. In fact, Bowie was fond of saying that his family could trace its roots back to both Rob Roy and his wife, Helen

McGregor. *In fact, there seems to have been a strange parallel between James Bowie and Rob Roy, but to see that, it is necessary to explain a little about Rob Roy since heroes seem to be of little interest anymore among those who have become infatuated with the antics of villains.*

Rob Roy was a bit of a rogue, but there was goodness in him: depending upon which side of the Jacobite rebellion one supported and whether he was transporting your cattle to safety or simply to his own herds.

Sir Walter Scott wrote about him and the Highlanders still tell folk stories about Rob Roy McGregor Campbell. Those stories seem to be all that are left of the man and history has built him into a legend, but James Bowie's ancestor, John Bowie, knew the man, fought with him, and was, for a time, outlawed with him.

One day, John Bowie said to Rob Roy, "Rob, we'll do no good fighting the English. They don't know the old ways, nor follow the Highland code. We'll lose if we stay."

"Aye, you're right, John Bowie, but I'll do my best to rule my land," Rob Roy replied. "But you leave with the seal of your family, and I'll wager you'll keep the Highland honor alive."

Though some uncharitable souls did speak of the certain death of a dissolute rogue who had betrayed a clansman, the fact is John Bowie moved to Northern Ireland. An uncle named John Smith asked him to move to the New World, and in 1705 or '06, Bowie immigrated to Maryland.

John Bowie had a son, John Junior, who in turn had three sons. James Bowie, who was the grandfather of the subject of this book, was one. This James Bowie lived in Edgefield, South Carolina, and married a woman named Mirabeau. Though he died young, James and his wife had five children. One of these was named Rezin Pleasants. Rezin had a twin brother named Resa. I suppose it's hard for those not raised on the frontier to realize the hardships incurred by those who have lost a father. The male children are forced to become men even faster than usual. Backbreaking, mind-dulling labor combined with sudden Indian attacks does that.

Rezin Bowie was a "man" when he joined Col. Francis Marion—the "Swamp Fox"—during the Revolutionary War. He was only fifteen at the time and seventeen when he was injured and captured by the British.

In the 1700s, Dismal Swamp covered much of South Carolina. Oh, the people were making progress in taming the land and establishing plantations, but the Cherokees often raided the towns and plantations, and the border was slow in advancing. A maternal great uncle of mine, John Carpenter, also one of Marion's men, said that the swamps were the most dangerous spot on earth. Besides pools of mud and quicksand that could trap an unwary person, the swamps were mosquito-infested and filled with poi-sonous snakes, alligators, and wild boar. A man could easily get lost in those swamps and if he did, he died.

My mother's family knew both John and Rezin Bowie. In fact, he spon-sored them when they enlisted with Marion. For two years, they lived in or around Dismal Swamp. They fought many battles, but the one that was Rezin's downfall was Marion's attempt to take Savannah in 1779.

The Southern colonies were less inviting to the British than the North, so the British did not concentrate efforts at capturing the South until around 1778, when they moved into Savannah and effectively conquered Georgia with its capture in December of that year.

In September 1779, Maj. Gen. Benjamin Lincoln led members of the Continental Army against the British forces. They could not take Savan-nah, so Lincoln lay siege to the city, trying to starve the defenders out. But the British general, Augustin Prevost, refused to surrender, waiting for the arrival of British troops led by Lt. Col. John Maitland. Meanwhile, Marion brought his forces to link up with Lincoln's soldiers. For some reason, Lin-coln did not attack the city until Maitland's arrival. Then, he planned a three-pronged attack against the city. First, he feinted at the enemy's left, then led a strong attack at the British rear, through Sailor's Gate, and at Spring Hill Redoubt.

His plans might have worked, but Sgt. Maj. James Curry of the Charleston Grenadiers deserted Lincoln's forces and took news of the plan to Prevost. The British were waiting for the attack. Marion, my uncle, and Rezin all attacked the Redoubt on October 9, 1779. The fight lasted for hours. The British laid down a hellish fire from cannon and muskets, but Marion led his men straight to the parapet and raised the flag. Two officers were instantly killed and a Sergeant Jasper tried to save the flag, but he was killed.

Maitland counterattacked and the hand-to-hand battle lasted for well over an hour. Rezin fought well for only being a boy of seventeen. He used an old saber he had rescued from a junk pile after it was broken by a musket ball during a skirmish with Tarleton's men. He reground the point and with its basket-hilt it became his favorite weapon.

At the Redoubt, Rezin killed three soldiers when suddenly he sensed someone behind him. He whirled and found an officer swinging a saber at him. He had no time to block the blow. He caught the blade with his left hand. The sword nearly severed it. He swung his short sword into the officer's belly, then dropped to his knees, tearing off a hunk of his homespun shirt and staunching the pouring blood with it.

Meanwhile, the Swamp Fox led his men back, leaving Rezin wounded at the Redoubt. He was taken to a field hospital in Savannah, where he was treated by Elve Ap-Catesby Jones, the daughter of John Jones, a recent Welsh immigrant. Elve was immediately taken with the handsome Rezin, and in 1782 they married. She was a calming influence on Rezin, soothing his fiery temper when it threatened to explode, as it frequently did during those frontier years. They had ten children: twin girls who died in infancy, Sarah, Mary, Martha, John, Rezin Junior, James, Stephen, and David, who drowned in the Mississippi when he was nineteen.

The Bowies moved from Georgia to Tennessee, then Kentucky, Missouri, and finally, in 1802, to Louisiana, where they first took up land on Bushley Bayou near Rapides. At the time, Louisiana was a Spanish possession struggling to make itself civilized. I heard many stories about how Rezin, Elve, and their children fought the renegades who tried to take advantage of them.

One adventure in particular happened when a gang of rogues tried to squat on Bowie's land. The leader, Garreoux, I think his name was, had three others with him. He was confident that he and his men could handle an old war veteran and his brood of young children, so he camped on the Bowie plantation and began logging the ash, oak, walnut, and maple, floating it downriver to New Orleans to sell.

Rezin took his son John with him when he went to speak with Garreoux, but Garreoux only laughed at him. He insulted Rezin and Rezin's temper flared. He pulled his pistols and told Garreoux and his men to get off his land. Garreoux's response was to draw his knife and throw it at Rezin. I suppose he thought he could scare Rezin away, but Rezin was far beyond scaring by then. He shot Garreoux in the chest, handed his gun to John and told him to reload while the other three rushed him. He pulled out his knife and slashed one across the chest and shot another in the leg. John had reloaded by this time and the others decided that discretion was far better than valor—especially since the old man had just put three of theirs out of commission. They took off running.

Now, the parish sheriff was no friend of Rezin's. He came out to the plantation to arrest him and took Rezin back to the town, where he put him into the wooden jail. Elve knew Rezin had fought in self-defense, so when word leaked back to her that the sheriff—Barnett, I think he was called—was a cousin or something to Garreoux, she decided this nonsense had gone far enough.

She ordered one of the Negroes to saddle three horses while she loaded four Lancaster horse pistols that fired .50 caliber balls. She took the Negro with her and rode into town, where she confronted Barnett and told him to let Rezin out of jail. When Barnett tried to laugh at her, she handed two pistols through the bars to Rezin and pointed the other two at Barnett. Now, that may not sound like much, but those .50 caliber bores look as big as cannon when you're looking down the business end. The sheriff promptly opened the door and let Rezin out.

They worked the land along the bayou for quite a few years, always trading for better land when it came up for sale. When word came back about Texas land, Rezin began to talk about moving the family there, but he died in 1819 without ever seeing it.

I'm an old man, now, and I can see how those stories might have been embellished, but somehow, that doesn't seem to be such a bad thing. Good should be stronger than Evil. I can remember Grandpa telling me the story about how the first Bowie knife was made. I could only have been about five years old at the time.

We lived in a one-room cabin, but it was snug and warm as my family took pains to show craftsmanship in all they did. The fireplace was made with cut stone all carefully placed so as to have no chinks to let smoke back into the cabin. My father and uncles were already discussing the extra rooms that would be added come spring, but right then, at night, in the dead of winter, the atmosphere beside the fire was perfect for a story of high adventure.

Grandpa spoke like a Tennessee hill man. He never did lose that even though the rest of us had developed a Texas drawl, and his voice was always slow, the words evenly spaced, so you didn't really notice the depth of his voice or the quiet authority of his words. He was an educated man who still worked with his hands, a rarity on the Texas frontier. When he told his stories, the images just jumped and danced in your head and it didn't take much in the way of a youthful imagination to draw yourself into the picture, too.

That night of the Bowie knife story, Grandpa rocked in his chair, staring at the fire, while he slowly honed a Bowie knife, eleven inches of mirror-bright steel an inch and a half wide. The rasp of steel against the Arkansas white rock matched the creak of his rocker. His voice startled me.

"You know what this is, boy?"

"A Bowie knife, sir," I answered.

"You know how it came to be called that?"

"No, sir," I said anxiously. I settled myself on the floor beside his big feet because I knew a story was forthcoming.

"I had a little shop in the Hill Country. It was pretty wild back then. A forest primeval, hills and trees—darkness caused by shadows. I dug my

shop into a cave. It seemed so much more fitting to make iron into steel while tucked within the earth itself. Just as the old craftsmen did at the dawning of the world."

He handed the knife to me. I took it gingerly, turning it over in my hand, watching the tiny lights from the fire dance off its wicked edge. He pulled his pipe from his vest and took out his little buckskin pouch of Eagle Claw tobacco and began to patiently fill his pipe. He watched me carefully as I handled that knife. When he was comfortable and his pipe drawing well, he began.

"I was working late in my cave-shop. It was much drier there than outside. A big Texas storm was raging. Lightning turned the dark night into day for brief seconds and the sound of thunder was like a mountain falling upon you. Those kind of nights are best spent inside where you can forget the hobgoblins, but I had work that needed finishing.

"I had the forge at its hottest and the cave had taken on a warm, red glow, when a particularly loud blast of thunder startled me. A dark figure stood in the cave's mouth." Grandpa's hand closed into a huge fist and I felt the hairs begin to prickle on the back of my neck.

" 'Who be ye?' I called out. But the figure didn't answer. Slowly, it raised its hand and removed a rain-sodden hat. It was Jim Bowie himself, a big man, red-haired and fair of face. His words were soft, but when someone made him angry, thunder clapped from him.

" 'Mr. Sowell, I need somethin from you. There is not another man I can trust. Only a man whose blood has been replaced with steel. Only a man whose ancestors were the armorers of William Wallace and Rob Roy himself could do me this favor.'

" 'What favor, Jim?' I asked.

" 'I need a new knife. War's coming to Texas, and I need a knife that will cut the heart strings of thousands of enemy soldiers.'

" 'Well, can you give me an idea about what you want?' I asked.

"He reached beneath the serape he wore against the rain and pulled out a knife he had whittled out of loblolly pine. The blade was like this," Grandpa said, reaching down and taking the knife from my hand. "The blade longer than most, short for a sword, though. Single-edged, but with a weighted back so the power of a slash would be increased.

" 'I have business elsewhere and won't be back this way for a month or so. Could you have it ready by then?'

"He knew the answer before he asked, for a Highland master armsmith always did his best work for the laird who goes to war. Especially when the laird is the greatest knife fighter of the day.

"For a month, I worked steel. Some was too brittle, some became pitted.

Knife after knife I threw back into the melting pot, working back, tempering it time and again. I reformed the point to make it look like an old clipper ship and sharpened a bit of the front so that it could be used for ripping. I put on a D guard and an eagle's head pommel, invoking the old Scottish symbol. It was a miniature saber, but in the hands of a man like Bowie, it was death to the enemies of Texas."

Granddad stopped and stared right at me. "Finally, on a night just like the night of the request, the proper elements formed."

He fell silent, rocking and staring into the coals of the fire, seeing the coals of his forge in his memory. I stayed quiet, letting him remember, knowing that he would tell me when he was ready.

"Maybe, it came from the fires of Hell. I don't know if Heaven or Hell was in that knife. There wasn't another like it. Steel like a mirror, bronze the color of lightning, an ebony handle bright and checkered so it wouldn't slip in the hand, with a cross guard and the pommel like a Highland eagle.

"Jim entered as I finished edging it. He took it and looked at it closely, turning it in his huge hands. I watched him anxiously because I had made a few changes from the model he had given me and I didn't know how he would take to them. Then he looked at me and said, 'It's the finest knife ever made. What do you call it?'

" 'I'll call it the Bowie knife, if that'll suit ye,' I replied.

"It suited him just fine and all the other knives that came after that are still called by the same name I gave to him that night in my cave."

Today, Grandpa's words seem a bit far-fetched, but he modeled his stories after those told by Sir Walter Scott in the books he kept on a shelf above his bed. But I called for all the stories I could get on Jim Bowie and never tired of hearing Grandpa slip into his storytelling voice. When I got older and traveled away from the homeplace, I kept a sharp ear out for other stories about Jim Bowie from oldtimers sitting in bars or around potbellied stoves whittling and chewing while they remembered when. But I always remembered Grandpa's best.

And what adventures Jim Bowie had! Riding alligators in the swamps, hunting wild cattle with a knife, duels, Indian fights, lost treasure, these fabulous tales became my favorite fare. In the daytime, I reenacted those stories, becoming in my youthful imagination Jim Bowie, while my playmates became the villains that I would dispatch with swings of my whittled Bowie knife.

I needed somebody like Jim Bowie. I needed a demigod who fought because it was the right thing to do. Later, I even joined the Rangers because I felt it was something that Jim Bowie would have done, because the frontier needed men who were willing to protect those who couldn't protect themselves.

One of the stories that was a particular favorite of mine was the story of the "Grass Fight." It seems Bowie and Fannin fought an action against a vastly greater force of Mexicans. Bowie yelled out, "Keep under cover, boys, and reserve your fire. We haven't a man to spare." I have no reason to doubt this because Uncle Andrew was there and he never tired of telling how Bowie handled the battle. But the real point that needs to be mentioned here is that what he said is still true to this day. We haven't a man to spare. Certainly not a man like Jim Bowie.

Today, it seems to be popular to point out another's weaknesses. I don't know why that is so popular. Everybody has a weakness or two. That doesn't matter. It's what a man does with his life that matters. And that's the reason why I decided to write this book. To set the record straight about Jim Bowie.

One of the first interviews I conducted was with Black Sam, who was a slave of Bowie's sent out of the Alamo just before its fall with a letter for Sam Houston. Unknown to Black Sam, the packet he carried also had his letters of manumission setting him free. Apparently Bowie knew that he would die in the Alamo and was performing one of his wife's last requests, to set their slaves free before both died.

Black Sam was ninety-eight years old when I found him in Los Angeles, where he was living with his great-grandson and wife. His memory was sharp, for the most part, but the picture Black Sam could give us of Jim Bowie is incomplete.

BLACK SAM

Black Sam was one of Bowie's slaves who was sent out of the Alamo at the end with his papers of freedom and a message for Sam Houston. It was one of the last acts of Bowie, who had remembered his dead wife's last wishes to set Black Sam free. Black Sam had been with Bowie for over twenty years and had served him faithfully during all that time, even to caring for Bowie when he went through the dark depression following his wife's death. —**A. J. S.**

Mars Jim? Well, he buy me oncet while I was lying in a shed down by the wharf in Naw leans, him. Aint nothing for it but that, you see. I was a rascal then, me, and the white trash who owned me was gonna take me to the Breakerman after I refused to work the cotton without water. Breakerman he wrap chains around me sos I couldnt run—heavy chains them like the swamp loggers used up in the loblolly pines—and then whip me with a blacksnake that curled the hide right off my back.

Mars Jim, why, he had come down to Naw leans to find a buyer for the lumber he and him brothers—Rezin and, well, I forgets just now, but I tries to remember, me—they cut trees in the sawmill they had in the back bayous somewheres.

I dont rightly remember much about Mars Jim, now—course, that all be good forty, mebbe sixty years ago he send me out of that place with a message for his brother Rezin. Ifn I know what coming down to happen, why I stay with him. Dont know what I coulda done different from the others once them Messicanos come down upon them, but who knows? Maybe one more gun make the difference in the right place at the right time. Happen before, it did, on San Saba—you know bout the silver mine out where the Caddos they kill the Spanish soldiers and take the silver for themselves? Thought so. It pretty much part of Mars Jims legend now.

Now, that whole thing start when Mars Jim get to seeing what the Injuns bring into San Antonio to trade once a year. Silver. But it not the silver that they dig from the ground. No sir. It the silver what already been dug from the ground and melted down into tiny bars. Oh, they tries to hide it but it dont take no smart mans to see what it was before they break it up into chunks or work it up into bands and such. It come from a worked mine.

Mars Jim take his time. He talks to the old chief and makes good friends with him. Goes back with them to theys village. Hunting, he says. Takes me alongs with him. They never seen nigger before although theys heard about one that came through many years before. Supposed to be a witch. You know, one of thems who can make sick peoples well and well people sick. Aint one of them but they dont knows that so they think it good luck to have me along with thems. Dont know what I do if I have to do something with the magic, but luck comes with us and I only have to cure a boy with the bellyache— which I do with a little bicarb of soda that Mars Jim bring along to make into breads. They mighty pleased with me and Mars Jim for that. Think it sorta breaks through this wall somes have around us.

Anyways, not long after this, Mars Jim come back from hunting with the old chief and he all excited and can hardly wait to get back to San Antonio. Seems that the old chief finally shows Mars Jim where they gets the silver. Mars Jim he tell me about this as we go back to San Antonio. Seems some missionaries—Franciscans, I think he calls them—sets the Injuns to working for them. Make them dig ore outta the ground and melt it down. That not bad, cept they treat them bad like some white mans treat niggers. Like the dockman and the Breakerman treats me, you understand. Yes?

Now, Mars Jim, he promise the old chief that he wont tell nobody nothing about the silver mine. He tell me, course, but that aint like telling someone. I his and it like talking to hisself when he do that. Sort of having another ear. But it only another year pass and when the Injuns come back to San Antonio, they aint friendly no more. Gotta new chief, too, they does. Mean mans who Mars Jim nearly fought with oncet in the village cept the old chief tell him that aint mannerly. Dont know quite what manners have to do with Injuns, but somes aint bad just like somes white mans aint bad, but on the whole I rather stick with niggers like me.

Well, Mars Jim married now with the governors daughter and he and the governor get to thinking that nows the time to go back to that silver mine and bring out a load of silver and make everyone richer than they already is. The governor and Mars Jim already rich, but funny thing about that is I aint never seen a white man who have enough. Always wanting more. Messicans the same way. Always wanting more than theys already has. Cant spend what they do has but that aint making no matter.

Except in Mars Jim it was different. Mars Jim didnt care as much for the money as for the getting of it. He likely give it away oncet he gots it when he gets it.

Not long after the Injuns leave San Antonio, Mars Jim has a party together and we a-heading off to the West after them, not sos to make them suspicious—though I thinks they had those suspicions anyways—also think that new chief of theirs knew Mars Jim was coming after him cause he manage to get an awful lot of Injuns together when he finally finds the place where he wants us—but that wouldnt have made Mars Jim any less determined to go. He just naturally that way. Long with us comes Jim Coryell, Dave Buchanan, Bob Armstrong, Jesse Wallace, Matt Doyle, Tom McCaslin, Caiaphas Ham, and Mars Jims brother, Rezin.

The sun shining bright like the Lord coming down on Judgment Day. Hotter than a griddle. Sweat already soaking through my homespun shirt before the mule I was riding and me get out of the plaza. Course I back among the pack animals along, but it clear to all there that I aint just nobodys nigger to be doing whatever it is they wants. Mars Jim see to that. I his nigger and aint nothing to nobody else.

But that day sure enough be a hot one. I cussing at it long before we clear the town. Aint much of a town, either: just a few mud shacks. One look pretty near like another cept some bigger than others and fancier inside. Should of not tempted the Lord, though, with all that cussing because it weren't long before the water came down in sheets that put Noah's flood to shame. We dont dry out no more than down it come again. And again.

Finally, about two weeks out, it stop raining for good and then I wisht it was back a-pouring as much as it want.

Took us bout a month or so—leastways it seemed so to me—to get across that land. Terrible land, it was, too. Dry most of the season cept now when we thought over again that none of the gear would dry out. Plenty of oak and mesquite for good cooking and Mars Jim and the others kept the larder filled with deer and turkeys.

Reckon it must have come somewheres north of the Llano when we run into a couple of Comanches and a Messican they used to speak for them. Seems like some younguns had stolen some horses that belonged to folks back in San Antonio and wanted to return them fore folks decided to go hunting Comanches.

Mars Jim, now, well he tell them no hard feelings by folks back in San Antonio held against the Injuns for what been done. They mighty grateful for what Mars Jim tell them and after Mars Jim give them some tobaccy and powder and shot, they ride away.

Next day, though, the Messican he come riding back, wearing out his pony like the devil at his heels! Seems they run across over a hundred Injuns following after us. Tehuacanas, Wacos, Caddos. A bit of everything.

Well, Rezin—Mars Jims brother—ast him what them Injuns might want with us and he tells us they Injuns after our hair. Dont know what they want with my woolly hair, but I get this funny feeling deep down in the pit of my stomach bout what I hears. Mars Jim, though, his eyes lit up like new silver dollars and he grins and allows how things were sounding mighty intrasting. Mighty intrasting.

The Messican he tells us that Ysayune—he the chief of the Injuns what was friendly to us?—gets to thinking bout all this and he sends the Messican on to tell us to come back and he help us him. But Mars Jim he figgers it not far to the old Spanish fort built by the mens when the Franciscans mining the silver to protects them. Mars Jim says that it best if we go there cause them adobe walls can stop a lot more arrows and bullets than a bunch of willows and mesquite bushes.

But we dont get there fore we begins to lose our horses cause it too stony and rocky and theys pulling up lame. Well, the river aint got no place to defend, sos we leave the river and rides north to where theys a bunch of oak trees with a thicket on the north. A small creek runs by it and Mars Jim decides this be the place to camp.

We dont sleeps much that night. Next morning, we pack up to move when Rezin spies the Injuns coming towards us. Injuns! he hollars and we ducks into the thicket till Mars Jim can decide what to do. Over a hundret Injuns they was.

"Well, boys," Mars Jim says. "Reckon weve got our work cut out for usns."

"Looks like it, Jim," Mars Rezin says. "But fore we do, I think wed better go and have a little talk with them. Wont do no harm and ifn we can get out of this fix without fighting, so much the better."

Well, Mars Jim allows that wouldnt be a bad idea, so Mars Rezin, he and Mars Dave goes off to talks with them. Mars Dave he speaks a little Caddo lingo and they making a bit of friends when one Waco man waves a scalp and shouts out, How-de-do! Then, well, them Injuns begins to shoot and Mars Dave he hit in the leg.

Mars Rezin picks him up and begins to run back to the thicket and them Injuns try to run Mars Rezin down. But Mars Jim he leads a bunch of the others outta the thicket and they keep the Injuns off til Mars Rezin makes it to the trees.

Then they settles down and gets to shooting like the devil, leading his apostates at us. Yessir, I there, too, loading up Mars Jims pistols fast he could shoot them and between times keeping his rifle handy, too. When they gets in close, why that to Mars Jims liking with that big knife his. That terrible to see it. Dont know what come over Mars Jim when that knife in his hand. Seems he possessed by the devil. Face gets all white and tight like he shoes pinching the corns on his feet and his eyes, mad. I sees that once in Naw leans I. House there where Mars Jim he send this woman . . . but that story dont belong here no.

Mars Tom he killed when he try to gets a good shot at an Injun and fore long, why, they aint much left of us. Most all been shot and all been shot at so many times that no one pays any attention to balls whistling by like quail singing.

The Injuns set fire to the thicket and some try to get in on us, but Mars Jim take that knife of his and kill them. Some nights, I still hears them screaming when Mars Jim fall upon them and sees that knife of his streaming blood from it.

They runs from the thicket and bout that time a chief he tries to get the Injuns to charge back into the thicket. But Mars Jim, he shoot him dead and the Injuns pull back to think about coming into the thicket again. Ifn they only knew that most of our guns was out of bullets cause we dassnt open a powder horn to reload what with all them sparks flying around us, we be dead now.

While theys talking about they plans, Mars Jim he gets us building a fort by throwing up piles of dirt and stones wherever we cans. We works on this through the night, thinking the Injuns come upon us at first light. But, no, they aint coming. They have enough and pulls out and leave usns alone. We return to San Antonio. Mars Jim, why, he most disappointed, but he figgers maybe the next year we try again. We never do, though.

I dont talk bout things that hurt Mars Jim no. Not that man. I dont care for some of the things he do, but he save me from the Breakerman.

Pay top dollar for me then. Happen down Naw leans way. Long time ago. Long time. Old mans mind plays tricks on him do. But I be sold at auction offn Mars Beauchamps death when his daughter sell everything and move back to Franch she. I trained for house duty, not fields. Can read some, too, I. First man buys me try to put me in cotton fields, but I dont take to that and next thing I know, Im back on the block, me, and dockman he buy me and tell me tote bale that I aint no house nigger no more and I try to tells him I that not good way to spend moneys him, but he lay that blacksnake cross my shoulders and carve his initials with it in my back him.

I try; aint no way no man not try with that snake coming fast cross his shoulders him. But aint no way I can work like others time. No way. Not brought up used to work like that no me. I house nigger. Field nigger cant do no house nigger work; house nigger can do no field nigger work no ways. Happen be that dockman—Wilson he name—he get the Breakerman who happy with the blacksnake and take his cut at me each morning sometimes noon, too. Time today it bother me and my daughter she put the linament on it but it hurt no how anyway.

I make up my mind that I run away. They catch me they hang me good, but I dont care no more.

I remember the day, now. Remember it well although it do slip in and outta my memory at times. Memory aint what it used to be. No sir. Time was I could remember most everything, then I married up with Dulcie after Mars Jim send me back home and we free and monied, then, so we move down into Naw leans and open a restrant down in Storyville. That another story—maybes I tell it and maybes I dont. But we work that fifty years fore Dulcie she die and I works it another five before my son take over after he gets the lolapoloozing out of his system.

No, I remember that day. All I gotta do is twist wrong when the rain coming and I can remember that day. Cept there no rain that day, no sir. Just hot old sun shining down like a fifty-dollar gold piece, making the sweat run right down my back and stinging where the salt rolls into the cuts made by the Breakerman's whip. I remember that sun. And I remember them mosquiteers and horseflies buzzing around the blood on my back and biting till I thought I go mad.

That when Mars Jim come down, redhaired and gray-eyed he, and the dockman he try to impress the big white man with what he can do with the blacksnake and he curl that lash along my shoulders and knock me down. The cotton bale I carry fall into the water and he start to lean into the whip across my shoulders see me. I dont pay him no mind, though. I just trying to keep the Breakerman whip off my back. But I aint no field nigger, I a house nigger, and that why I cant work as fast as others and that make the Breakerman mad and before I knows it that old blacksnake curling around my back again.

Mars Jim dont say much. Just pick up that Breakerman and toss him into the Mississippi down where the slops sloshing against the pilings. Sure funny enough to see that but it aint good for me, Im thinking, once that Breakerman get outta that water it gonna be me that pays for Mars Jim throwing him in among the slops and the others laughing at him while he hanging onto a piling and puking his breakfast up among the slops. No sir.

I gives Mars Jim a long look and he stares back. I dont do nothing but stare at him and slowly he nods and walks over to the dockman and they begins talking and I can see that Mars Jim is working mighty hard on what he saying, but the dockman he just keeps shaking his head like he got the St. Viters Dance or something, but then Mars Jim fold his arms like this and lay his head back and stare down at that dockman and the dockman, why he suddenly make up his mind and nod. He spit in his hand and shake Mars Jims hand and Mars Jim yells to the smith on the pier to knock my chains off cause aint no way his nigger gonna insult him walking down Bourbon Street with chains clanking around the cobblestones.

That was Mars Jim. He buy me from the dockman and I go with him for many years. But not always good these places we go. But I see him many times help others like he help me him. I see him happy and I see him cry from pain when his wife and babies die. I see him the day in Baratara when we go to buy niggers from Jean Lafitte. Fact is, we find out how to get to Lafitte's place when Mars Jim take me to Pierre Lafitte blacksmith shop and have the smith break the studs off my collar.

Where was I? Oh yes. We go to Barataria Island. Day cold and wet, gray like the bayou water for a hurrican come and throw it back up on the land. Stink, I tell you. Worse than the dock in Naw leans. Much worse. What make it so the gibbet where five men hanging and feeding the gulls and kites swarming around their heads, tearing strips of meat off them like they was prime beef hanging in a tree and forgotten. Bad.

Dont rightly know what one of Lafitte mans say to insult Mars Jim, but Mars Jim, why he knock him over loop-de-loop. One smack with Mars Jim fist and down goes pirate.

For a minute there I think that we gonna join the men on the gibbet, but Mars Jim step up to Lafitte cool as rainwater and say he buy all the slaves including the culls and Lafitte just narrow his eyes down over his suety cheeks and laugh. He gonna forget what Mars Jim do to—Diego, that he name? Think so—but the other pirates there they dont let him forget what Mars Jim do so they has to have an accounting. But Lafitte, he a smart man: he wont allow no accounting until he accounts paid in full which mean Mars Jim own the slaves but if he killed, why then Lafitte own them back again along with the money Mars Jim bring with him.

But Lafitte, by then he think to be fair with Mars Jim cause he know that Mars Jim might be buying more slaves if he live. But he have what he call the honor of the society to uphold.

Well, Mars Jim allow how that seem right to him, but I see that the excitement getting upon him by his eyes. He look across the sand and see this log half-buried where the big water bring it up on the fast tide. He walk down to that and get to studying it and the next thing I see, they pirates a-nailing both Mars Jim and this Diego to this log in the sand, driving them tenpenny nails deep through their pants into the log. They give a knife to each and the pirate he try to kill Mars Jim straight off, but Mars Jim too big and cut the pirate throat with one slice. Sand turn black from the blood gushing from his throat like a fountain.

We run the slaves for near two years. Mars Jim he smarter than other runners. No swamp sale for him. No sir. He take niggers to the mainland and then take them north and find the sheriff at Naw leans. He turn the niggers in to the sheriff, saying he find them him along the coast. Sheriff hold he sale and Mars Jim take half the money for his reward. Everything all up and up on the legal.

I know the sheriff he know what Mars Jim doing. Aint no man catch as many niggers that way alone along a coast. Maybe once in a lifetime all. But he can tell that he better not call Mars Jim a liar. There something about the way Mars Jim had at looking into another mans eyes that made a man think twice about calling him a liar even if he was a time or two.

Oh, that dont mean he not without honor. How you think the judges get rich in Naw leans anyways? Or the lawyers? Aint one of them without honor. But in the trade, why every man looks out after himself. That business. That all.

But that aint it either, Im thinking. No, sir. Not at all. Always something else about Mars Jim that make you want to believe him even when you knows you crazy for believing him. I guess that what bring up the big fights down at the sandbar. Yessir, that the one between him and Major Norris Wright except that ain't what it really is. A woman involved there, too. Seem like always in the big fights before Texas theys a woman involved. They flocks around Mars Jim like flies on a honey pot. Why somes even send him gifts—mostly married womens them. They the ones that aint gotta worry about theys reputations because theys husband gives them respecterbility.

Mars Jim send most of them back but always send along a little something extra sos not to insult them. He say a mad woman be the worst thing a man could have and he just didnt have the time to try and make things smooth with a mad womans. Besides, some of those womans come from pretty powerful family in Naw leans at the time. Oh yes. Mighty important some. But Mars Jim, why he play soft with them.

Cept one.

Sometimes I think she the one that make Mars Jim do crazy things like running niggers from Barataria. Seem like he always trying to get more and more moneys faster and faster. I think he have in mind making a wife of that one. But she bad. I know. Man not look at her beauty, look behind it, man can see the poison there. Bad poison.

Judalon de Bornay. Remember her name, now. No way I forget her. Mars Jim kill two men for her. Notice I says for her. Not on cause of her. That woman she likes to play with men. Make all mad for her then pit them together like buck niggers in the quarter, know what I mean? Way the owners used to bring theys big buck niggers in from the fields and fight them against each other in the quarter, back where theys a courtyard or two. Fight to the death, thems. But that aint for Judalon Bourney. No sir. She gets herself in with some bad mens and beg Mars Jim to take her out of her trouble.

First time that happen she courting this fancy fencing man and he get a little fresh with her. She tell Mars Jim the fencing man try to take liberties that only a married man should take—cepting we know that aint exactly true cause womens take the same liberties when they cans—and Mars Jim he challenges the man to a duel.

That a bad one and Mars Jim kill the man back of St. Somethings place—one of them gambling places where niggers exchange owners three, four times a night, sometimes. In an old storeroom it was. They puts both of them in there without lights, the fancy fencing man with a sword and Mars Jim with this big knife—I tell you about Dominique You, Lafittes man in Naw leans? No? Well it seems that . . . sorry. Old man rambles at times. Well, it his knife Mars Jim uses. Everybody laugh at that, knife against a sword. Nobody laugh when Mars Jim walk out without a scratch upon him and the fancy fencing man laying in a pool of blood on the floor of that storeroom.

Another time, years later and Mars Jim already married to Ursula he love so much who he send away to die. But Mars Jim and me on a riverboat that time, coming down to Naw leans after clearing up a old debts owed Mars Jim and he brothers from the time they in the land business up north. This Judalon Bourney married now to somebody who no good for her. A weak man who gambled away all theys money cept Mars Jim, why he know they aint no way that game straight narrowed. Crooked as a black cat's tail. He get into the game and catch them cheating. One man crazy enough to challenge Mars Jim and Mars Jim drive that big knife of hisn clean through his breast bone when the gambler try to shoot him. Strike so hard you could hear the bone break when the knife hit him.

She the reason, though, that we make maybe fifteen run with gang

---

Children of James Bowie and Ursula Bowie, née María Ursula de Veramendi

Maria Elve Bowie, born April 18, 1832, in Bexar
James Veramendi Bowie, born July 18, 1833, in Monclova

---

of niggers from Barataria and Mars Jim he get rich. But last time bad time. It all my fault. I sleep and the niggers get away and the niggers they get away after Mars Jim tells me not to chain them cause we far enough inland and away from the ocean that they wont run. But when I on watch, I fall asleep and the niggers take and creep away from the fire and run back towards the coast from which we just takes them. Stupid niggers. They run right into the Kronks, them. Cannibals.

When we catch up to them wasnt nothing left. The Kronks ate good they. Nothing left cept cooked bones and splotches of fat and grease and blood on the sands. Birds bellies heavy with what Kronks dont eat.

Well, Mars Jim, he look at what Kronks do and he shake his head and turn away. "Sam," says he, "aint no good come from all this. This a warning that we have made enough trips with slaves. We find something else to make money."

That what he tells me. But I think he just plain sick, him, of what he be doing to other men. Mars Jim never treat me like a dumb nigger and he never beat me. Never. I know what men say about Mars Jim, but he aint like that. He a kind and gentle man lessen someone push him too far. Never take sass, but never look for trouble either him.

We once down in Natchez and some mans—think his name Bloody Jack—well, he insult Mars Jim and they takes out their knives and goes to cutting at each other. Mars Jim coulda killed that man, but he dont. He cut him bad in the arm and the man just stand there looking stupid-like, blood dripping down his arm. Mars Jim, though, he just put up his knife and walks away.

Shoulda killed that man, though. Bloody Jack get some dock trash

together and send them after Mars Jim who riding back to Lous-
anna through the canebrake. They jump him and hes best friend
there. Hurt him bad, but he kill all three. Bad thing, he lose his best
friend who get killed in Mars Jim place.

Another time, why Mars Jim and me over Texas way. This after
his wife and children killed by the fever and Mars Jim, why, he take
to drinking. For a while, I think he bout to drink Texas dry, but one
day the man Houston come to him and say, "Jim, you nothing but
a damn drunk and I know what Im talking about for I been there,
too. Now, pull your head outta them jugs and get to work for us. I
need you. War a-coming with Mexico and we need men like you
bad."

Well, Mars Jim pull his head outta the jug and he get to work
for Houston. Lotta people they dont care for Mars Jim cause when
he drinking he not the most sociable one around. Fact being he once
throw Travis into a pond when Travis think he can insult Mars Jim
and another time he dry-shave a man with his big knife when the
man think he can take advantage of Mars Jim when Mars Jim drunk.

But Mars Jim he have a reason for acting like that and it a reason
that all men would have if they love theys wifes like Mars Jim love
his. He do anything for her. He even send her away when the fever
come to keep her safe. But he dint pick the best place. The fever
already there. She die, but she die only after her children they die.

I guess that make Mars Jim hate himself, knowing like he do that
he responsible for his wife dying. Her death leave a big empty hole
inside him that never fill back up. Never. Not even when Houston
ask him to finish with his drinking. Reason he stop cause he honor.
At the end, it his honor as a man that finally matter. He cant let
nobody see him die like that. Not a drunk. But the hole still there.
A deep dark hole.

ELVE BOWIE

Elve Ap-Catesby Jones Bowie was second-generation Welsh, a frontier woman about whom not much more need be said. She knew the harsh life of a frontier farm, how to work a plantation, and how to raise a family.—**A. J. S.**

So. You want to know about my son, James. I haven't said much: my one comment after his death at the Alamo has been widely quoted. I have been told it appeared in many newspaper articles. Jim's death caught me off-guard when my daughter Martha told me about it, but I knew something bad was going to happen. I had had a dream about Jim the night before and he was splashed red and around him burned a golden glow like you see around fireflies. I just knew that I was seeing my boy's spirit with a hero's halo spreading around it, turning gradually red, reflecting the fury that took over him at times. In a way, I guess you could say I was prepared for Martha's words.

"I'll wager no wounds were found in his back," I said to her. I meant that, too. Jim was never one to turn his back on danger. I don't mean that he went around looking for trouble. He was always somewhat reasonable, but when people began to push him, I would see that golden glow begin to rise up around him and then, well, it was better if you just stayed out of his way.

I didn't cry when Martha told me. Much has been said about that, too. But that's the way the Welsh and Highlander-Irish are. Death is just a part of life. The only thing that matters is how you live it. And Jim lived well.

He always liked his stories, did Jim. We came from a race of storytellers, you know, so Rezin and I always had one or two to entertain our children when it was raining outside and they got restless. The old stories are good ones and I never tired of telling them. There's a lot of wisdom in them and I'd hate to see them lost. Rezin believed that the more you knew, the better off you'd be, so he made sure that all of the children—me, too—were given the best education that was possible.

My husband was a man of vision. That's the reason our children were so well educated for the time. Every tutor that came through the country had to stop and give lessons to our future, as Rezin used to say.

It seems like Rezin was always thinking about the future and planning for it. No one who has not been there can imagine the hard physical labor that it takes to carve a plantation out of the wilderness, and fewer see the labor that goes into converting the raw produce from the plantation into saleable produce.

"Boys," Rezin would say, "the English lord would watch men work and the profit he would keep. That's why the English lost the American colonies. It will not be the cause of us losing our plantation."

He meant the boys had to know hard labor as well as civilized behavior. He made the boys work with the slaves and because of this, two things happened. First, the plantation prospered, and second, the boys grew very strong both physically and in character.

Rezin always said that the land did not belong to you until your sweat watered it. Or your blood. Our boys sweated over their land, and as any who work the land can tell you they scraped enough skin off to spill some of their blood onto that fine black land.

Much of the land we settled was covered with oak groves. The oak had to be cut down and then dragged to the pit for cutting into planks. Many of those old trees weighed a ton or more, and they had to be manhandled into a position so the horse could drag it, then moved into position over the pit.

Once they had that oak tree over the pit where they wanted it, one of the boys would climb down into that damp hole in the ground and pull down on a whipsaw. The person above would then pull the saw back up and then the boy in the bottom would pull it back down.

Up-down, up-down, while the sweat poured off them and the mites of sawdust clung to their skin and gritted into their eyes already stinging from salty sweat. It took special people to work like that. No one today is willing to do that kind of labor. Less'n they're nigras.

Jim seemed to be able to stand the pit longer than most, and one day, took to bragging about it. His father took him aside to speak to him about that. I was on the porch, shelling peas, and heard every word.

"Jim," Rezin said, "a gentleman is both born and made. It takes good blood, and you have that. But a gentleman must also learn the rules of behavior. A gentleman doesn't brag because that only gets him into trouble. If he brags, why then, he must prove himself over and over because there's always someone somewhere wanting to test him. A gentleman lets what he does stand by itself."

I think Jim was thirteen, maybe fourteen at the time, but he marked right up, saying, "Yes, Father. But when is it bragging and when is it just stating fact?"

Rezin turned away from Jim and looked out over the land. He chewed on his lower lip for a minute, composing his thoughts.

"I think, son, any time you are being asked if you can do something and you answer with the truth, then that's fact. If you are just telling people who have no need to know, then it's bragging."

Jim seemed to mull that over for a while, then he nodded soberly and went back to work. But I could tell that those words had an effect upon him. I think he kept those words with him for the rest of his life.

Yes, Jim's father had a major influence upon Jim. For example, Rezin was always talking about machinery around the boys, telling them that was the future of the country. He said even then that if machines could cut down on work, then we wouldn't need slaves and we'd be able to turn them free to start their own lives.

Well, Rezin heard about a machine that ground the sugarcane down in half again the time it took to do it by hand. He always talked about putting together a stake and going back East to get one of those machines. He died, though, before he could realize that dream. But Jim remembered it and in 1821, his brother Rezin and Jim bought a stream-driven cane machine and installed it on Rezin's plantation. It was the first one in the state and the boys were extremely proud of their accomplishment. But they weren't any prouder than their father would have been if he had lived to see what his boys did with his words. My husband died just a little bit before.

Now, I know this isn't what you wanted to hear, but I want you to understand that Jim was not a roughneck, not the wild man that folks and those newspaper fellows and magazine writers want you to believe. No, he was a man who was trained to be a gentleman. Rezin used the heroes out of Sir Walter Scott as prime examples of how a man should behave, and Jim took the lessons to heart. He never tired of hearing about Rob Roy and Ivanhoe, or the Irish tales of the Red Branch. Cuchulainn. Others. He was a knowledgeable man who had a keen insight into others.

Now, I don't mean that Jim didn't have a wild streak in him. He did. All my boys did. They were pretty rambunctious when out in the woods. They hunted and hunted well. Our slaves never went hungry, even during the lean years when drought hit. There was always food on our tables. That wasn't an easy thing to do, either, when you figure there were always six or seven children around and at least eight slaves and Rezin and me. Seventeen or eighteen mouths, sometimes more. All the boys learned to hunt and fish almost from the time they could walk. I suppose that's when people started calling them "the wild Bowie boys." But there was a restlessness in Jim that the others didn't have.

Jim used to ride alligators, you know. Can you picture that? He used to sneak up on a sleeping gator—there must've been a million of them in the swamp back then—and jump on his back. He held the gator's mouth shut and plunged his thumbs into the gator's snakelike eyes. (You ever look into a gator's eyes? Cold as death, they are.) Well, that gator'd run into the water and toss and turn, trying to throw Jim from its back. 'Course it couldn't see and besides, even if he could, he couldn't do much about it 'cause a gator's strength ain't in opening its mouth; it's closing it. A grown gator can snap a heavy board in two with one chomp, but a young child can keep it from opening it. Just has to watch out for his tail is all.

But I suppose the most dangerous thing Jim did was to hunt wild cattle with a knife and rope. Doesn't sound like much, I know, when you look at cattle these days, but back then, well, those cattle were mean. And smart. Jim used to climb a tree along a well-worn path and wait patiently for hours until one wandered by. Then he'd drop a loop over those horns, snub the rope around the tree, then drop down and cut his throat with the knife.

When he was young, I paddled his britches, I tell you that. Nigh to wore my hand out, I did. But, at the same time, I was pretty proud of what he did. Not many men would try to get under those hooking horns to cut the animal's throat, much less boys. Still, it was a constant battle between him and me. Eventually, he won. I just got tired of whipping him for not minding what he was told. Besides, we got to liking that fresh beef now and then. Made a welcome change from our other fare.

Fishing was something else, too. While most people would go after the perch and crappie, Jim always went after the alligator gar. You know those fish? A fighter with teeth like razors. Keeps fighting even while it's dying.

I remember another story about Jim. Once, we had a bear raiding our corn patch. Now, things were a bit tight at the time and we couldn't have our food being taken from us. I don't recall where Mr. Bowie was at the time, but young Jim decided something had to be done about it. Swamp bears may not be the size of those animals I hear about in the shining mountains, but they can still kill an ox with one swipe of the paw. There ain't as much room in the swamp, neither, as in the mountains, so it's kind of hard to take a long shot at one, you understand?

Well, this big black must've thought he was on easy street, taking corn from a woman and her little ones. What he didn't eat, why he just threw down on the ground and put his scent all over it to keep any others from eating it. Let his water on it, he did.

Jim found where the bear was entering the patch and he went out and got himself a cypress knee. He then hollowed out that log just enough for the bear to get his muzzle in, then hammered in big nails cattywampus so that when the bear stuck his muzzle in to get the honey that Jim used to bait his trap he couldn't pull it back out again. I didn't think it would work, but one night there was a fearful roaring from down at the corn patch. Jim flashed that big grin of his, took a gun and walked down and shot that bear.

I still have its hide under my bed. It feels rather nice on cool mornings when I climb out to get dressed. And I always think of Jim when I do.

When Jim was young, his favorite story was one about Mr. Bowie, his father, and me. I always told Jim I was pregnant with him, but this happened in spring of '95 and Jim didn't come along until April of '96 and I don't think he ever did arithmetic it out.

We had just moved out to a farm in Kentucky when some ne'er-do-wells came to squat. I guess they thought Mr. Bowie was too tame to shoo them off, because they were downright arrogant about what they were planning on doing which was to take our best pasture land. Well, Mr. Bowie went down to reason with them. John and David went along with him. He had decided that it was time that the boys learn how to deal with rascals. I remember I didn't want them along with him, but when Mr. Bowie set his mind on something it was near impossible to talk him out of it.

Those men were just plain stupid. Mr. Bowie was a big man. Close to six-two, he was, and broad and strong. He had a bad left hand from a saber cut during the War. That was when I captured him, you see. We used to joke about that. Savannah it was. . . . Where was I? Oh yes.

Well, Mr. Bowie gave each of the boys a pistol. David was preparing himself for sainthood and didn't want to take one, but Mr. Bowie was firm about it and each of the boys tucked one of those big horse pistols into the waistband of their trousers. Mr. Bowie took two for himself and this saber he had cut down along with the highland dirk he'd got from his father. The dirk had the family seal on the half. He used that seal to sign documents.

They rode down to the creek where the men had decided to squat. Mr. Bowie had a special leather belt that he wore around his waist. It had two loops for his pistols and a scabbard for his saber. He wore the dirk over his left buttock at the small of his back. He carried a double-barreled shotgun across his saddle as he rode.

I remember David telling me what happened when they got to the men's camp. He said it stunk to high heaven. The men had a rough lean-to built, but that was about it. They had a bunch of cowhides staked out, drying in the sun, and a pile of oak stacked and drying. It was our wood, too, that they'd hauled from where Mr. Bowie had cut and stacked it.

"What the hell do you want?" the leader said.

"I want you to explain your camp on my land," Mr. Bowie said. David said that his father's words were so soft-spoken that he had to strain to hear them. If so, that should have been the ruffians' warning. But when you get men like that who think they own the world, you can't tell them anything.

"Your land?" The leader laughed. "Why, I reckon this land belongs as to him who can take it."

Mr. Bowie shrugged then and dropped his reins across the saddle in front of him. He looked the leader calmly in the face and said, "Why, then I suppose you'd better get to taking. Or leave. Choice is yours."

Wouldn't you know they made the wrong choice? That man raised his musket, an old Brown Bess, if David remembered correctly, and pointed it at Mr. Bowie. But Mr. Bowie drummed his heels into the horse's side and it reared, startling the ruffian so much that he hurried his shot and missed. He never got another 'cause Mr. Bowie dropped that double-barreled shottie square into his face and pulled the trigger, blowing his head clean off his shoulders.

Mr. Bowie slid from his horse with a horse pistol in his hand. That .50-caliber ball nigh tore another's head off. One of the others snapped a shot at Mr. Bowie and he took a ball in the side. The boys were trying to stop their horses from rearing, but they couldn't and they were afraid to shoot for fear of hitting their father.

Mr. Bowie dropped his horse pistol and pulled two others from his belt. He fired at the man who was aiming at the boys, and knocked the musket from his hands. He didn't do that on purpose, you understand. He just missed, that's all. He dropped the pistols and drew his knife while he rushed at the fourth man trying to load his rifle. The man tried to brain him with his musket, but Mr. Bowie slipped under it and slashed him across the stomach. The man screamed and fell down, trying to hold his guts in.

At that time, David shouted a warning and Mr. Bowie turned as the man who had tried to shoot the boys rushed at him, swinging a big axe. Mr. Bowie ducked under the swing, lifted the man across his shoulders and ran him hard against a tree. He pulled that dirk out and swung it hard into the man's belly, pinning him against the tree.

Well, that was the end of that fight. Mr. Bowie loaded the bodies in the wagon and took them into town. He turned them over to the sheriff and kept the wagon and what little they had to pay himself for the trouble and for the lumber he figured they'd stolen. He came on back home, but that wasn't the end of the story.

It seems that the good people of Eliott Springs were beginning to feel themselves somewhat civilized although for the life of me, I can't understand why what with a killing a month going on somewhere in the area. Anyway, they got the sheriff to come on out to our farm and arrest Mr. Bowie. I remember when he arrived, standing there uncomfortable like, scratching his head, wondering if he was going to get out of there alive or not.

Finally, he spoke up, saying, "Mr. Bowie, there were four men killed and even though we ain't yet found out who they are, all this killing makes us look bad. Uncivilized like, you understand? Well, I sure would appreciate it if you'd come on back to my cabin and sit a spell while we try to figure out who they is. Leastways, it'd look mighty nice to the voters if they saw me bringing you in. Sort of send a message that we ain't taking their killing lightly."

Well, Mr. Bowie sort of hid this little smile he had at times when his fancy got tickled. Me, why I was hopping mad that the sheriff'd dare take in Mr. Bowie for defending himself and what was his. I lay into that sheriff something awful, but Mr. Bowie just told me to take care of the children and leave the rest to him. He got his horse and went into Eliott Springs with the sheriff.

I waited three days for Mr. Bowie to come home, then finally I yelled at Zeke, one of our Negroes, to hitch up the wagon and take me into town. It was about ten miles and the more that wagon bumped along that road, the madder I got until by the time we got to town, I was ready to shoot someone myself.

I had a couple of pistols with me when we got to the sheriff's cabin. I climbed down and looked that sheriff straight in the eye and told him that I wanted to see my husband.

"Why, of course, ma'am. Mizzus Bowie," he stammered. He opened the door and I looked in at Mr. Bowie sitting at the table.

"All right, Rezin," I said to him. "You've had your little fun. Now, it's time to come on back to the farm and get to work. You've got a family that needs you more than this sheriff needs a prisoner."

He smiled that little smile. Oh, he knew that I missed him and he knew that I meant what I had said. He winked at me and rose, saying, "Why, of course, Elve. I was wondering how long it would take you to come on in."

"Now, just a minute," the sheriff blustered, his face all red beneath this scruff of a beard he had. "This man's a prisoner. He can't go nowheres at all."

"Oh, I reckon he can," I said smoothly. "I reckon in this instance you'd be willing to make a little exception, wouldn't you?"

I pulled one of those pistols and jammed it deep into his belly. His face turned sort of pasty white—kind of like a catfish's belly—and he decided right then and there that Mr. Bowie must have acted completely in self-defense.

Mr. Bowie and I went on back home and never heard another thing about it. Ah, but Jim loved that story. Once he said to me, "Mama, we always have to do what's right, don't we? Weren't you wrong when you took Papa from the jail?"

"Maybe," I answered. "The law's right, Jim. But sometimes, people like to twist the law to suit themselves and when they do, why then you're right when you go against it. You just have to know when you're right."

"Yes," he said, his little face sober. "That's something I'll always have to remember, won't I?"

That was my son Jim.

Mrs. Bowie's story differs somewhat from the story my grandfather told, yet so many similarities exist between the two, that I am inclined to believe the story to be true.—A. J. S.

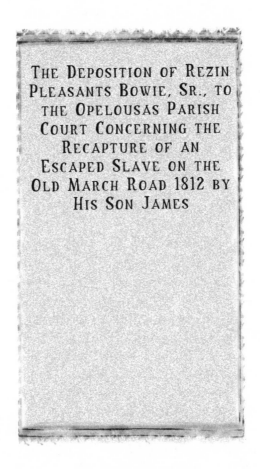

THE DEPOSITION OF REZIN
PLEASANTS BOWIE, SR., TO
THE OPELOUSAS PARISH
COURT CONCERNING THE
RECAPTURE OF AN
ESCAPED SLAVE ON THE
OLD MARCH ROAD 1812 BY
HIS SON JAMES

Rezin Pleasants Bowie, Sr., grew up fast on the frontier. He had not reached the age of seventeen when he joined Col. Francis Marion (the Swamp Fox) to fight the British. Shortly after the war, he married and began a new life, carving a plantation out of the wilderness. But he was never satisfied with his land and continued to move west until finally settling in Opelousas Parish, Louisiana, when it was under Spanish rule. He was a tall, big-shouldered man with red hair and high principles. He died in 1819.—**A. J. S.**

To the Opelousas Parish Court

Sir:

    Since this is a formal document for the court of this parish I will begin by introducing myself. I am Rezin Bowie, Sr., father of James Bowie. I am a freeman and legal resident of

William Micajah "Big" Harpe, and his brother, Wiley "Little" Harpe, were the scourge of the Wilderness Trail leading from Knoxville, Tennessee, to the uncharted West. The brothers were Tories in North Carolina until after the British surrender, when they fled to Tennessee, robbing and killing westward-bound settlers. The two giant, bearded, wild-eyed men were captured time and again but always managed to escape from the flimsy frontier jails.

Five murders have been documented in which the Harpes disemboweled their victims and filled the cavities with stones, sinking them in the Barren River.

After a $300 reward was placed upon their heads, they drifted up into the Ohio River valley and eventually made their way to the infamous Cave-in-the-Rock, a natural fortress honeycombed with subterranean passages so large that the Harpes hid stolen herds of cattle and horses in them.

Finally, the Harpes were trapped by a posse in 1799 in Ohio. Wiley escaped, but a volley of shots blew Micajah from his horse. The posse fell upon Micajah with long-bladed knives, attempting to cut off his head. As they were sawing away, the mammoth killer bellowed, "You are a Goddamned rough butcher but cut on and be damned!"

Harpe's head bounced along in a saddlebag as the posse made its way back to camp. Lack of provisions, however, led them to boil his head for supper one night. The skull was nailed to an oak tree as a warning to other highwaymen. Wiley Harpe disappeared, but legend has it that one winter after 1800 he was caught by a pack of wild wolves that tore him to pieces.

Opelousas Parish, Louisiana. My business is the sale of lumber and crops from my own plantation. My son, who was born in Logan County, Kentucky, in 1796, the year the Harpes were on such a rampage, is just fifteen, this year of 1812.

I have been asked to briefly explain Jim's character, and to relate the incident that happened to him when he was performing an errand for me. The first can be done easily. He has always been raised by the teachings of the Church, and what it means to be descended from nobles of the Scottish Highlands. He has had such schooling as my wife and I can give as well as what we could hire from private tutors. He speaks Spanish, Cajun French, some of the old tongue from Scotland, and, of course, American. He understands arithmetic and has read many of the Classics, and though he has not had the advantage of reading Greek or Latin, he has become acquainted with Homer and Virgil, as well as Walter Scott and the modern writers.

My son is now and will always be a gentleman. Albeit, he also understands the rough and tumble life of the frontier and the hard work involved in running a plantation.

The second question that I am to answer in this document is somewhat more difficult. I feel this questioning comes about because people have written about my sons. These writers have called them the Wild Bowie Boys, only because they do what others might want to do, but can't stomach. James has hunted gators, aye, and ridden them. He has hunted the dangerous wild cattle with only a knife and sometimes a piece of rope.

I don't hold with these risks taken by my sons, but I do understand the excitement of youth and I also know how many precautions my sons take before they do these things. Jim is a crack shot and can throw a knife like none I've ever seen. Though he's only fifteen, he's an uncommonly tall, strong man. He stands almost six feet tall and weighs about 160 pounds.

The difficulty for which he stands before this court is one that takes very little explaining, but cannot be completely verified. Jim was defending someone less fortunate than himself. What else could a gentleman do?

Jim was traveling by Old Marsh Road on business for the plantation. He chanced upon a Flatboatman who seemed lost but was traveling in the same direction as my son. This man had in his company two black slaves. A young buck of about twenty years, and a young girl of tender years, say four or maybe five. The young girl was deformed with a twisted and crippled limb. The crippled limb was much shorter than the other, making it somewhat difficult for the young girl to walk.

The Flatboatman was described as tall, thin and sinewy. He wore the uniform of his kind: a loose blue jerkin that reached to his waist, over a bright red flannel shirt, coarse brown trousers of linsey-woolsey that covered his nether regions, and on his head he wore a cap made of untanned skunk skin, with the fur side out and the red feather of the fighter proclaiming to one and all his nature. On his feet he wore moccasins of leather and he had a wide belt from which he hung, in a poorly made leather sheath, a wide-blade, sharp-pointed Spanish dagger. The blade was about eight inches long. He also had a tobacco pouch and a small pouch carrying bits and pieces, and a shot pouch and a powder horn. Behind the belt was a smooth-bore .52-caliber horse pistol of British make, following the military pattern of 1806. His final piece of equipment wrapped around his torso was a huge blacksnake whip, with a hardwood handle.

The man was in his middle years, and had obviously learned cruelty in a misspent life, for he was tingeing the air blue with his cursing of the slave. The young slave had been carrying the child, and was now tired beyond human endurance. The Flatboatman was issuing threats amidst the cursing.

The words were all of death to at least the young girl, and probably to the young slave. Jim was simply minding his own business, but the language was barely tolerable. Jim has been taught to mind his own business.

Jim could not make out much of the cause of contention, but the man said he would teach manners to the recalcitrant slave. Then he uncoiled the whip from around his torso, and straightened it with a snap of his wrist, so that it flew out behind him. His body was aimed at the young girl, not the man.

Jim told me he asked the man if that little girl wasn't a bit young to be whipped like a field slave.

The man cursed Jim and told him to mind his own business.

"Shouldn't all men be aware of right and wrong, and so be prepared to defend the right?" reasonably responded my son to the rather unreasonable man.

This haughty villain challenged Jim. He said, So you want to fight, do you? Well, the word he used isn't really worth putting into this document, but needless to say it was a word a man must not take from another man, especially such a specimen as Jim described to me.

But, because Jim had simply been attempting to catch the man's attention so as to let his temper cool, he was willing to let the insult be ignored. But, the man continued with a string of verbal abuse that insulted me, my wife, Jim's natural mother, and his other antecedents. He proclaimed that my son committed vile acts on his relatives and animals.

Jim has an easygoing nature, so he was willing to let this pass as well, again allowing for the fact that the Flatboatman was already roused and so was not really responsible for all the words he was so reprehensibly using.

But then he snapped the whip at Jim. What else could the boy do? He had taken words no gentleman should have to and he was about to see a child whipped because she had a God-given disfigurement.

When the man hit Jim with the whip, Jim caught it. While the man was strong, he was not expecting his strength to be matched by such a youngster. Jim pulled the man off of his feet.

Jim's temper finally snapped and he pulled the handle of the whip to him. "You have no call to use this whip on me" were the very words my son reported to me as he told me about this unfortunate affair.

But the man didn't see reason and tried to drag the horse pistol from under his belt. While he rolled over and searched for the pistol grip, Jim had time to rush forward.

"First you try to whip me, then you try to pistol me," he said. Surely this can be forgiven since it was a problem that could be settled no other way.

Jim hit the man's right wrist with the oak handle of the whip. Since the man could not hold the weapon with a broken wrist, he dropped it. The Flatboatman with his left hand then tried to draw his Spanish dagger.

Jim rapped the man's fur cap, knocking it off the man's head. The man tried to roll to his pistol, but the slave picked it up and he and the young child moved a bit away from the commotion.

The man, seeing that he could not use either gun or knife, decided on rough and tumble and raised himself to charge my son. Jim stood his ground. The man rushed in and Jim fetched him a blow with the fist holding the whipstock. There was a loud crack as the man's jaw broke. But the man's momentum pushed Jim back.

The pain of the broken jaw and the power of the blow made the Flatboatman lose his footing and he fell hard. Jim regained his balance and quickly reached for the Spanish dagger at the man's side. He flipped it away so that the melee would be handled without bloodshed.

The man got up slowly. There was no give in the man, and by this time Jim could do nothing but defend himself. The man took a very proper beating, with the outcome being that Jim left the man unconscious three miles from the village on the marsh road.

He said the man was dragged to the Gallows oak bend and was laid under the Spanish moss. Jim returned home to report these things to me, bringing the slaves and the man's weapons home with him as well. I took them along with my own weapons and went back to the spot where Jim had left the man. He was gone.

My sons do not lie to me, and so I believe the story as was told to me. And as a former justice of the peace, I knew that a proper record should be made of the incident. I reported to the Sheriff and am now making this statement for the Parish records. Of course, since the man had absconded, and a slave cannot be asked to testify, very little else can be said. Except repeating what I have said throughout. My sons are gentlemen, and gentlemen don't lie, especially to their fathers.

The last item that must be brought to the attention of the court is that after reporting to the Sheriff, I learned that the Negroes were stolen. If more details of how this was discovered are necessary, I can furnish details, but the fact that the court should be made aware of is that I communicated with the legal owner. I bought the slaves from said owner, who did not want the trouble of sending a bounty hunter to retrieve his property. The deed is on record, and can be viewed by the court.

Though this is a hearsay piece of information it should also be recorded. The Flatboatman was thought to be part of a group that stole slaves and sold them to new masters, convincing the slaves that they were slowly being moved to an area that would allow the slaves a chance to board the underground railroad and flee to freedom. I cannot attest to the truth of this last statement.

Signed,

Rezin Pleasants Bowie, Sr. (RUBRIC)

Addendum to the report by Mr. Rezin Pleasants Bowie of Opelousas Parish

Jim Bowie was sent a reward by Mr. Jean Paul Devareaux of the Picard Plantation. The U.S. Government also sent a reward for the capture of an escaped slave. In addition Mr. Bowie was allowed to keep the whip, knife and pistol of the man who stole the slaves.

Rezin Pleasants Bowie, Sr. (RUBRIC)

The conspiracy Mr. Bowie mentions in his report has surfaced several times, though generally it is not a flatboatman who is guarding the slaves.

The John Murrell of whom he speaks was a man of infamy who looted and plundered the entire southern United States. He tried to begin a slave rebellion by catering to dissatisfied slaves on selected plantations across the South, but financing his planned rebellion by stealing slaves from one plantation and selling them to another up or down the Natchez Trace.

*He owned several "sporting houses" in the Swamp District of New Orleans, the Pig-Gut District of Memphis, and Natchez-Under-the-Hill. Over the course of a few years, he managed to assemble an army of cut-throats and brigands such as has never been brought together by one man in the history of the West. Among his confederates numbered many notorious men such as Bloody Jack Sturdivant and others who terrorized travelers along the Trace and the Mississippi River. Some say Murrell alone murdered over a hundred men although there is no way of verifying those numbers. He died insane.—*A. J. S.

REZIN PLEASANTS BOWIE

Rezin, one of James's older brothers, was born September 8, 1793, and lived often in his baby brother's shadow. He was an astute businessman who owned plantations and different mills and twice was elected to the Louisiana State Legislature.—**A. J. S.**

Brother Jim was remarkable. I know you've corresponded with John—most people begin with the oldest and work their way on down—so you know that Jim was the gentlest of gentlemen and yet he seemed always to be around when someone lost his temper and pulled him into an argument. When people challenged my brother, well, there was nothing to it but to defend his honor.

That was a common enough thing in those days, so I really don't understand why so many people make a big set-to about the duels he fought and the men he killed. People take a look at a man's record and judge him by that without thinking about the times that made the man. Even Aaron Burr, Thomas Jefferson's vice president, fought a duel once or twice as did Andy Jackson and others. But you don't see anyone making much fuss about their doings. I don't know why they do about Jim's.

Well, that's not quite right. I guess I might add a bit more. You see, Jim had a natural curiosity that led him to always being near the center of these melees. But that came natural to him. We were raised as frontiersmen of sorts. We did well by the standards of the areas in which we resided, but we never became Southern aristocrats. Seems like people have a rather narrow view of the Southern man. He's either a Southern gentleman sitting on his porch between white columns and sipping sugared whiskey or else he's poor white trash. We were neither. We started poor, but we increased our wealth through our own labor, sweating and hauling logs out of swamps right beside our Nigras.

I guess you could say that put us in the unique situation of being betwixt and between. Father taught us the meaning of being a Highland laird, and this set us apart from others and caused a few stories to spring up about us that simply were not true. "The Wild Bowie Boys" were really not much different from other young men of those days. Everyone had a streak of wildness in him that had to be unleashed at times. Boys are the same now, twenty years later, except that it seems that wildness in the young ones is more directed at hurting others than simply giving leash to a restlessness of the spirit.

Personally, I prefer great literature and music. So did Jim, but his spirit was so restless that he seemed to want to experience the whole world as quickly as possible. I went hunting and fishing with him quite a bit, but I really prefer to be around people who stimulate me intellectually, so I have a tendency of staying in the background. People took to calling me "that other Bowie" and I guess I earned the name.

Jim's curiosity manifested itself in travel. He was always on the go. One moment he would be talking to a man in a shack on the Mississippi, the next he would be in a mansion eloquently discussing politics and modern machinery. He loved the wilderness, but when he returned to civilization, he would immediately seek large crowds, immersing himself in what had happened during his absence, de-vouring newspapers to keep himself up-to-date about what was happening in the world. He would go to low dives on the waterfront or to fancy balls. Made no difference to him and he treated people the same wherever he went.

In a way, that was his undoing, for people don't really like to be treated like other people. Everyone thinks of himself as better than someone else. I guess people need someone to look down upon to reaffirm their own place in the world. They resent it when someone reminds them of their place in humanity. Quite often, Jim's attitude would grate on people and eventually they'd toss a challenge out to him. That took some doing, for as long as his honor wasn't besmirched, why Jim would laugh and walk away from them. That, of course, often made the other man look a fool, which infuriated him even more.

I remember one time when a young Creole took umbrage at something Jim said to one of his friends. The young man really had no business listening to Jim's conversation, but, well, people are like that, too. What they dislike in others they often have in themselves. Anyway, this young Creole sent his seconds around to where Jim was staying, telling him that he demanded satisfaction. This, of course, gave Jim the choice of weapons and Jim laughed and said the weapons would be snowballs at ten paces the next time it snowed in New Orleans.

This sort of baffled those Creoles who had never seen snow and perplexed them because they couldn't understand why someone with Jim's reputation didn't leap at the opportunity to kill someone else. But Jim never saw the necessity of killing someone just to be killing someone. There always had to be a purpose for it and words, well, words that did not question his honor never hurt him.

I remember once we were almost robbed by river pirates. You never heard that? Well, one day a letter from Jim arrived at my plantation at Avoyelles. It was sort of cryptic: "Rezin, we've got a challenge. Jim."

Well, I told my slave, Jeb, to saddle my horse while I immediately packed a bedroll, took out two pistols and a knife my blacksmith had made for me with a crossguard across its handle. I took down my long Pennsylvania rifle, climbed into the saddle, and left for Jim's cabin.

The day was gray and gloomy. It had rained the night before and the red soil was slick like grease. I let my horse pick his own way while I watched the trees carefully alongside the road. We had been having a bit of trouble with highwaymen and I didn't need a surprise. I didn't know what Jim meant by a challenge, but I suspected that it had something to do with our business, which was floating logs down the river to New Orleans for sale.

When I rode into the clearing where Jim's cabin stood, I gave out a long hello. An answering call came from behind the low log cabin. I hitched my horse to a corner butt, settled my pistols in my belt, and walked around to the log pit that Jim, his slave Black Sam, and I had built to allow us to fashion planks. Jim was in the pit; Sam was up top. Even though he had sent for me and was expecting me, Jim still spent his time working. He never seemed to rest.

Jim laughed and pulled himself out of the pit in one smooth movement. An ordinary man would have had a ladder down there but Jim just jumped in and out of that six-foot pit like others get up and off a stool. He picked me up and spun me around like I was a child and told Black Sam that he could have the rest of the day off.

We went up to his cabin and had a meal of roasted boar, washing it down with a little corn liquor he had picked up from friends of his who had a still back in the swamps. Jim was about the only one I knew who was willing to go that deep into the swamps where some of those Cajuns lived. Not because he wanted or needed liquor—brother Jim was moderate in his habits and so drank only a little—but he went into the swamps to meet people, and to see the wild country. And Jim came back while other people who delved into the backcountry swamps didn't come back out. Gator meat, we called them. People who lived that deep into those swamps didn't want outsiders coming in. I don't know why; just the nature of some, I reckon. Anyway, all that rich meat and that liquor was making me sleepy. I yawned. Jim noticed and grinned.

"A bit sleepy," I confessed. "Might could use a nap, I reckon."

"Rezin," Jim said. "We've got to get my logs down to the dock at Gallows Bend. I've got a mortgage due and I can't wait any longer for a run-together."

What Jim meant by that "run-together" referred to the habit that we loggers had come to, bunching our logs into one or two massive float rafts and shepherding them downriver to keep the log pirates from stealing us blind. Normally, one or two men could easily make a float down to Gallows Bend, but to go any farther made it a bit chancy unless there were four or five in the party.

Now, I really don't know if Jim's note was that pressing or not.

Sometimes, Jim just took it into his head to clean out a nest of snakes and did it. Other times, he might just walk on past the nest and leave them be as long as they left him alone. I never could understand that. Whenever I came across a nest of snakes I always cleaned it out. The same with renegades and outlaws.

"Well, of course, I'll help you," I said. "We're brothers." But I was a bit puzzled. If he had to go only as far as Gallows Bend, then he and Black Sam should have been able to easily manage the float alone. I told him that.

"Rezin," he said quietly, "there are some river pirates working near where the Atchafalaya and Red rivers converge."

"They're moving up the river," I said quietly.

Jim nodded. A tiny smile played around his lips. "You don't look so tired, now, Rezin," he teased.

"I think I just woke up," I answered.

The problem was easy to see. Jim had to ride the current, keeping the logs floating straight and not jamming. That meant that he could not watch the bank as well as for snags in the river.

"How do you want to play it?" I asked.

He leaned forward, tiny lights dancing in his eyes as he outlined his plan. Black Sam would ride the current this time while he and I paralleled him along the bank, just inside the cover of trees. The river pirates would think Black Sam was a lone nigger that they could take advantage of, and when they made their move, why Jim and I would rush from the trees and take care of them.

It was a simple plan and I didn't see anything wrong with it except that at some places, the woods were mighty thick and the float could get on downriver ahead of us. Jim laughed and allowed he had thought about that, too, and there were only one or two places where that might happen. We would beach the float when we came to those places and have Black Sam rest a spell to give Jim and me a chance to work along the banks and get ahead of him.

We set off in early light the next morning. The forest was thick and the rains had left the ground softer than usual. We followed Black Sam without too much trouble until we got to Big Bend, which wrapped around the conflux of the Atchafalaya and Red. We helped Black Sam beach the float and Jim told him to give us two hours' head start to work our way overland before he poled around the bend.

Black Sam nodded and settled himself in the shade beneath a

loblolly pine. Jim grinned at me and we took off through the woods, cutting across the bend. We were about halfway there when we stumbled upon fresh tracks. Jim looked at me and leaned close, whispering, "I think they've got an ambush set up ahead."

"Now, what makes you think that?" I started to ask, but then we heard Black Sam singing a hymn like a young boy would walking past a graveyard at night.

Jim swore. "Damn it, he sure enough has a poor sense of time."

We moved forward a bit faster than we should have, but it was a good thing that we did for we came upon the ambush just as they tried to spring it on Black Sam. A shot rang out and for a moment, I thought they had hit Sam, but he just dropped flat on the float and picked up an old musket.

I pulled down upon one man and fired at the would-be assassin, but missed. The man rose and began running, but Jim shot him before he took more than three or four steps. Five others rushed for the raft, and Jim and I pulled out our pistols and fired at them. We both chose the same target, however, so we wasted one round although, as we later discovered, both of us had hit him dead center.

Black Sam rose to his knee and steadied his aim at the other four. They turned and ran for the woods away from the shore. In their panic, they ran right towards us. The one in front carried an axe that he swung wildly as he neared us. I caught his swing with my rifle and deflected it, coming up with the stock to catch him square on the chin. He dropped as if pole-axed.

Another had an old cutlass that looked as if it had sailed on one of Jean Lafitte's ships. He was swinging it at Jim, trying to cut him in half, but Jim danced back and forth, a grin on his lips, waiting until the man overextended a swing. Jim darted in and sank his knife deep into the man's stomach, ripping up and disemboweling him.

The other had had enough of us and took off running for all he was worth, weaving in and out of the trees, heading deeper into the woods. Jim took off after him, his long legs moving smoothly like a panther. I ran after him, reloading my pistol as I went.

We hadn't gone more than a mile into the woods when we suddenly came upon a clearing. I expected Jim to pause, but he didn't. He gave out that panther scream of his that like to near froze my blood even though I was half-expecting it. He leaped into that clearing and bounded across the clearing, catching the men as they emerged from the crude lean-to they'd erected. The first one tried to stop Jim, but he just swerved to one side and his arm flickered across the man's throat like a cat's paw, leaving a streak in its path that immediately flooded bright red.

The second one tried to raise a pistol, but Jim's huge, knotted fist struck him, knocking him flat on his back, his feet flying up higher than his head. The one we'd chased saw all this and turned to run back into the trees. I guess he didn't see me standing in the shadows, for he ran right to me and I clubbed him to the ground with my rifle.

We tied the two survivors up with strips of rawhide and took a look at their camp. They'd been making a haul, waylaying loggers and merchants traveling the river. We found a stack of hides that had been cured and stretched, a couple of bales of cotton, indigo, and a pouch full of rings and watches that belonged to those unlucky ones who had probably been thrown into a gator hole somewhere back in the swamp.

We took the men to the sheriff while Black Sam floated the logs on down to Gallows Bend. The sheriff was mighty unhappy to see us, saying, "Well, you catched them, now you can just hold them until the judge comes on around. I ain't wastin' my money feeding scum that'll soon be on the gallows tree."

Jim complained that our keeping those renegades for the two weeks it took for the judge to arrive was one of the most expensive things he had done, but the truth of the matter was that the judge gave Jim and me all but ten percent of the loot we had recovered from the renegades, that ten percent going to something he vaguely called court costs. We made enough for Jim to clear his mortgage and for me to take another arpent of land.

But the point was that had those rascals not tried to waylay Jim's raft, then Jim probably would have left them alone. Then again, maybe he wouldn't have. Jim was mighty unpredictable in those cases. One thing he did do, however, was return a watch that he found in the loot that had *W. H. Cade* engraved on the back to a young girl back in the bayou, Sibyl Cade, a beautiful, buxom girl who had most of the bachelors in the area panting at her doorstep.

Sometimes, I sit on my porch in the twilight, sipping and remembering that time we broke up the river pirates. I think now that Jim knew what had happened to Sibyl's brother and decided that those renegades had come close enough to him. Remember what I told you before: Jim had a tendency to leave people alone as long as they didn't bother him or his friends. Whether or not that was the case in this instance, I don't know. I did discover later that Jim had a clear month left before his mortgage ran due. And I know that Jim was one of those bachelors that kept coming around her cabin. I wonder what might have come of Jim had she been able to work her Cajun charm upon him.

SYBIL CADE

*Sybil Cade was the first woman that James Bowie loved. She gave the following when she was ninety-seven and living in a nursing home in Opelousas. She never married and had one child. She never revealed the name of the father.—***A. J. S.**

Jim.

Dont think a day gone by when I aint thought about him since he went down to Nawluns and fell in with that fast crowd.

And that woman.

Cant blame him for falling in love with her. She was everything Im not.

Everything.

Beautiful.

High society.

I dont even know what fork to use or how to dance them dances they dance down there.

She ruin Jim with her fancy ways. Before he go down there and fall in with that pirate Lafitte and find how much he like them fancy clothes and all, he plain folk like me. Good folk.

I meet him at a broom-jump. You know that? Minister or priest hard to find in bayou and time comes when man woman decide to marry, why something must be done. So they gets their friends and relatives together at a cabin. Lots of music and eat and drink big, and then at midnight, someone brings a broom to center of the room and hold it low about a foot off ground and the two take hands and jump over it together. That all. They married, then.

Course, some also get married again when priest or minister come around. Dont happen all that time, though. Last one through here stay one night and go away. Think he get gator bait. Not so wrong about that. One did get gator bait twenty, thirty year back.

No, aint much use for holy man in the back bayou.

Jim aint got much use for them, either. But when I meet him at broom-jump of Cousin Ellie he handsome. Head and shoulders taller than any man there. Red-gold hair and them eyes could look right through a woman and make her soft like butter.

Smell good, too. Like he rub sweet soap all over. But that man-smell there, too. Cant keep that away. Cept with Jim, why it not raw and strong like with others.

At the dance, man name Terchett try to take me out to the cypress when I tell him no. Others watch him dragging me away, but not Jim. He knock Terchett down. Bam! One smack with his big fist and Terchett stretched out like dead.

That night he kiss me down by the cypress. I remember that. Arms like iron bars, but gentle.

Gentle.

A softness in him that other men wont let a woman see.

We begin walkin out together. Down here, that mean hands-off to other men and most people on bayou know bout Jim and his temper and stay away from that side of him.

Once while we at a birthday people they talk about Jim and his gator-ridin. Most call that a lie. Jim get real quiet and go borrow old clothes and change and we go down to the water and sure enough, theys a gator floating there like a log. Jim he creep out on a branch and drop down on top of gator and grab that gator by the jaws, squeezing hard, and jam he thumbs into gator eyes. They flop and turn all over that water and other gators see this and come in, but Jim, well, he just hollar and laugh. Finally he come out, wet, like a god he look and my heart thump against my breastbone like it trying to knock a hole in it.

That night we make love like we invent it.

And Jim ask me marry with him.

We set for that spring, but then Jim he go to Nawluns with lumber he and his brothers cut to sell from they mill. I feel funny bout that. Almost like something tellin me dont let him go. Stay way. I get cold sweats at night and bad dream, always same bad dream bout a black rooster, and I know Jim aint comin back and I feel all hollow and empty inside. Cold like when sudden wind come down from the north and burn the trees.

And I know Jim aint comin back.

But I pretend everything all right before he leave. I know he stay if I ask, but they a restlessness in him and I know that a man with that need to walk it out of him and so I say nothin. A man have to have his freedom. Cant keep tied to the house and all because then he not a man no more. Spirit break and nothin left of the man. And Jim, well, he all spirit. Take that away and aint Jim no more.

So he go to Nawluns.

And meet that girl.

I see her once and she pretty. Black-haired and black-eyed. Tiny. Not like me. Delicate. But there a set to her mouth like in a person who suck lemon. And I know she a wicked lady.

Cruel.

And she no good for Jim.

But something like that a man have to see. Aint listening to no one tell him differently. So I stay quiet and watch Jim hang around her like she a bitch in heat. Maybe she be, cause she always whinin and complainin and Jim try to make things right but never can.

Jim's mama dont like her either. Say she not woman enough for Jim, but Jim dont listen to her. Finally Jim's mama tell Jim it time for the woman to leave cause she doin nothin but whinin and Jim take her and go back to Nawluns.

Next thing, he over to Campacino and Lafitte and kill two men and he . . .

*Here, Sybil's daughter interrupted, objecting to our interview. Sybil became confused and could not recall what had happened later.—*A. J. S.

Well, no man like Jim. No man.

John Jones Bowie

John Jones Bowie was born in 1785 in Burke County, Georgia. He was the oldest of the "wild Bowie boys" and became a prosperous businessman and plantation owner, as well as a state representative in Louisiana.—A. J. S.

Jim was a contradiction. There's no two ways about it. I suppose we all are to some extent or the other, but Jim more than most.

He was born in Logan County, Kentucky, in spring of 1796. But he spent the most important part of his childhood in Catahoula Parish between 1802 and 1809, embracing the years between six and thirteen.

He was young, proud, poor, and ambitious, without any rich family connections, or influential friends to aid him in the battle of life. After reaching the age of maturity he was a stout, rather raw-boned man, of six feet height, weighed 180 pounds, and about as well made as any man I ever saw. Taken altogether, he was a manly, fine-looking person, and by many of the fair ones he was called handsome.

People I know have a tendency to be dreamers or doers. Jim was both. Whereas most people found a passion in business or politics and used the woods for their amusement, Jim made the woods his business. I suppose if he had stayed in town and worked his charm on people he could have become president. Just about everybody who met him liked him—except those who thought his easy manner marked him as an easy man. There wasn't anything easy about Jim.

We lived on the edge of the frontier, back then. My father, Rezin Pleasants Sr., moved from the land south of Ohio, I guess in either Tennessee or Kentucky, around 1800 to a place around Bushley Bayou. He got two thousand arpents of land which he cleared with his slaves. It was hard, brutal work and very dangerous with ruffians and renegades hanging around in the woods, looking to waylay someone. A lot of people don't think about that because New Orleans was pretty settled and civilized, but the country outside the city was still frontier.

At night, Father taught us to read and write not only in English but in Spanish and some French as well. We balked at this, but he held firm, telling us that we needed to know all three languages if we were to get ahead in the world. At the time, we thought he was crazy, but we knew better than to argue with Father. Of course, he was a natural teacher, too. He knew when we had had enough of book learning for a while. Then, he taught us to shoot and hunt. Everything that appeals to young boys.

Jim was better than all of us. Smarter at his books and a better woodsman, too. He picked up things fast. He listened and then he knew and he never forgot anything he knew. He was good for us, too, for we had to learn to answer fast or else baby brother would make us look like fools.

We ran into many problems where we lived, so we had to learn how to deal with trouble without relying too heavily upon the law. Part of the reason for that was because we really couldn't trust the law. But that's not unusual. We still have that trouble today. People use the law for their own means, twisting and turning it until it represents only their own interests.

But you don't want to know about this; you want to know about Jim. Well, let me tell you a story or two.

One time we were out hunting wild cattle near Bayou Teche

when Jim saw a gator sleeping on the bank. Jim had been thinking about a story an old trapper had told us about how a gator's mouth was weak opening but real strong closing and he had figured out a way to have a little fun.

"John," he whispered, "I think I could ride that old gator."

"Quit it, Jim," I whispered back. "Ma would tan your hide proper if she found out what you're planning."

Jim ignored me. He usually did that when he had his mind set upon something. I never knew a person to change his mind once it was set and right then it was set upon riding that gator.

"Listen. I'm going to sneak up on that old gator and go for a little ride."

Well, Rezin was with us and he laughed at Jim. "Tell me, little brother," he said. "How you planning on getting off that gator once you're done riding him?"

Jim frowned and scratched his head, then just shrugged. "Well, I guess I'll just jump off and run."

As the oldest, I probably should have said something, but I didn't. Besides, I wanted to try it myself, but it was Jim's idea and so I thought I'd let him go first. It wouldn't have made any difference anyhow. I would've had to fight Jim in order to go first.

Jim crept up on that old gator sunning himself under a moss-covered oak and jumped up on his back. He grabbed hold of that gator's mouth with both hands and squeezed tightly.

That old gator woke up and took off running for the water. Now, a lot of people think that a gator is big and slow, but it just isn't so. We yelled, and that probably scared the gator even more. That gator hit that water with a big splash and swam for the deep water. I could tell Jim didn't know what to do; he hadn't figured that the gator would head for water and there he was. Rezin and I tried to draw a bead on the gator, but couldn't fire for fear of hitting Jim.

Jim kept cool, though. He jammed his thumbs into the gator's eyes, blinding him. The gator started twisting and turning in the water, and Jim took the opportunity to slip off his back and get away. That gator splashed around some, snapping its huge jaws, trying to find the thing that had blinded him. But Jim got away.

Well, Rezin and me, we figured that we couldn't let our baby brother have all the fun, so we took to scouting out gators for our own little ride. One day, some people spotted us riding them and word got back to Mother and we got one of the worst tongue-lashings we ever got.

I guess that's when people started calling us "the wild Bowie boys." Or it might have been the way we hunted wild cattle. That, too, was a bit of an accident, but necessary as well.

A drought had hit the South at the time and crops were pitiful. We needed meat but shot and powder was pretty expensive so Jim came up with this idea about how to get meat for the table. Actually, I think it was one of the Indians who told him, but he made out that it was his own idea.

We waited in a tree above a cowpath until one of those horned bulls came down the path. Then we dropped a loop over its horns, tied it to a tree, then tried to sneak in under the slashing horns to cut its throat. Mother undoubtedly knew what we were doing because no bullet holes were in the hides we brought home, but she didn't say anything.

One time, though, Jim tied into one that was too big, a big, mossy-horned bull well over a ton with a horn-spread of well over four feet. He yanked Jim out of his tree before Jim could get him close-snubbed. He swung those wicked horns at Jim and nearly un-zipped him from belly to chin, but Jim still had his knife and whipped it across the bull's muzzle.

The bull roared in pain and rage and started raking at Jim with his horns, but Jim rolled under its belly and reached up and slit his throat. Blood gushed down, near drowning him, then the bull fell down upon him.

Jim's pride was mighty hurt by that, but we can all use that a time or two in our lives. It took Rezin and me about half an hour to get that bull's carcass off Jim. Of course, we were laughing half the time while Jim wore out the Lord's name in vain at us, but finally we managed to pull him out from under that bull.

Jim was mighty red by that time, what with the bull having bled itself dry. It was only after we tossed him into the river to get cleaned up that we found out his knife had slipped when he went across the bull's throat, gashing his hand pretty deep.

Rezin took one look at that wound of Jim's and put his mind to work. That night, he saw Father's cut-down saber and reasoned that if a sword was built like that to save a man's hand, then a hunting knife should be, too. He talked Jesse Clift, our blacksmith, into mak-ing a knife patterned after a sword for Jim out of an old file and that was how the Bowie knife came to be made. I know a lot of people have been taking credit for it, but there's no romance to the story at all. Just plain common sense.

I told you Jim was a contradiction, and I think another story is needed to illustrate what I mean.

There was a time when Jim was seventeen that Father had to go downriver to sell lumber and he left Jim in charge of his Blue Leopard puppies. They were old enough to train and Father had told Jim to start them out while he was gone.

The next day, Jim took them out, but they still had enough puppy in them to ignore his calling. He lost sight of them and stumbled over a backwoodsman's cabin while looking for them. Turns out the man, Jean Lebeau, was beating his Indian wife with a rawhide whip when Jim came upon them. Jim knocked the man down, but the squaw ran into the house and came out with a musket and pointed it at Jim, telling him to get.

Well, that man's pride was a little hurt what with Jim knocking him down in front of his wife and all. When Jim came back that way with the pups leashed, Lebeau gave him a black look, but Jim ignored him. He'd done what he thought he should and if the woman wanted to be treated that way, why, then, so be it.

That night, Lebeau crept over to our house and took one of the pups. I forgot to tell you that Lebeau was pretty well known along the bayou for his mean streak. That was why Father had refused to sell him one of the male pups when he came around offering. I think he thought that he could get Jim in trouble with Father if one of the pups turned up missing.

Anyway, Jim trailed the man back to his cabin and told him that he wanted the pup returned. About this time, Jim was a stout, rather raw-boned man nearing six feet in height and weighing upwards of 180 pounds with shoulders as well-made as any man I ever saw. His hair was light-colored, not quite red—his eyes were gray, rather deep set in his head, very keen and penetrating in his glance. His complexion was fair, and cheekbones rather high. He was handsome, as many ladies such as Sibyl Cade called him. I suppose Lebeau thought that made him not quite a man, for he laughed at Jim and cussed him out in French and Choctaw, telling Jim he was illegitimate and that all of our family was the same. Jim got redder and redder, but when Lebeau said something about Mother being poorly paid for her favors, Jim knocked him ass over teakettle.

BOWIE

Lebeau went to Judge Beauvier over that, claiming that Jim had stolen his dog. He swore out a warrant for assault and battery against Jim and the judge fined Jim five dollars because Jim couldn't produce the pup that Lebeau had hid. That was a lot of money in those days and the more Jim thought about the injustice of it all, the madder he got.

Finally, he couldn't take it anymore and went back to Lebeau's cabin. He found the pup in Lebeau's smokehouse and when he tried to bring the pup home, Lebeau came out to stop him. Jim beat the hell out of the man, leaving his face looking like a rainbow, and brought the dog back home again. Then, he went to see the judge. He found him in town and confronted him. A crowd slowly gathered, listening, for everybody around there knew what had happened.

"Judge Beauvier," he said. "That dog belongs to my father. I found him in the smokehouse where Lebeau tried to hide him. I told you he had him, but you wouldn't go out to Lebeau's place to look for him. Now, I want my money back."

"Look, youngster, my ruling was final and that's that," Judge Beauvier said.

"Even though you were wrong?" Jim said.

"Who says I was wrong? You a lawyer, now? I could charge you with contempt of court and—"

"Now, wait a minute," Jim said. "You're saying that I'm wrong?"

"I'm the law around here," Beauvier blustered. "Until you study law, you have no idea as to what is wrong." He snorted and sneered at Jim. I suppose he thought that he had young Jim on the run, but he missed the golden mist that sort of rose up around Jim. And then he made a big mistake. "I could charge you with contempt of court, but because of your lack of knowledge and your tender age, I'll forgive that."

"Let me get this straight," Jim said. "You'll forgive me for demanding that you serve justice?"

"No young whippersnapper is going to stop me in the street and challenge me with some trumped-up story . . ." He broke off as he saw the lights beginning to burn in Jim's eyes.

"You're calling me a liar after treating me like a brawler?" Jim said quietly.

That's when he remembered that Jim was a yonker and decided that the high road was the right road. He also noticed that people were gathering around them, listening to the argument. He took heart in their nearness and straightened as tall as he could—which really wasn't very tall since he still had to crane his neck in order to meet Jim's eye.

"Yes," he said. "You are on the road to becoming a bravo and a scoundrel."

With that, Jim slapped him across the face, knocking him down. The judge yelled for help, but most there had run up against the judge's court a time or two and they ignored him. Jim reached down, hauled the man to his feet, then knocked him down again. When he pulled him back up, the judge figured he had kissed enough ground and put up a hand stopping him. He handed Jim five dollars and Jim left. The crowd cheered him as Jim walked away. The judge never did anything about the way Jim had treated him. I guess he didn't want to take on the rest of the wild Bowie boys.

Jim left home somewhere around 1814 and took up a new life on Bayou Boeuf, Rapides Parish. There, he cleared a small piece of land, but his chief means of support was from sawing plank and other lumber with the common whip-saw, and boating the wood down the bayou for sale. He was like many those days: young, proud, poor, and ambitious. He didn't have any rich family connections or influential friends to aid him in making his way in life. He made his own way. He had an open and frank disposition with rather a good temper despite what others say. He always had to be aroused by some insult, and then his anger was terrible to see and frequently terminated in a tragic scene. That judge was lucky, as was Lebeau. When Jim was possessed by anger, he couldn't be reasoned with. But I never knew him to abuse a conquered enemy or impose himself upon the weak and defenseless.

He was a man of very strong social feelings and loved his friends with a deep faithfulness and hated his enemies and their friends with all the rancor of an Indian. He was social and plain with all men, fond of music, and liked a glass in the merry mood to drive dull care away. But he seldom allowed it to steal away his brains or transform him into a beast. Except once, and that was his Dark Period that we Bowies don't talk about much on account of we feel that some things should remain in the family.

Well, you asked about Jim and I guess this sort of tells you something about him. Jim never was one to tolerate injustice whether it was directed to him or others. There was just something stubborn about him that made him wade right in and stand up against what was wrong.

In the end, it was that which killed him. That, and some other things.

EDWIN FORREST

Edwin Forrest was one of America's first actors to achieve international recognition. He was powerful, handsome, willful, and unschooled, his character molded in part in New Orleans during 1829, when he was thrown into a crowd that was at once gay, sophisticated, crude, and cruel. His puissant animal vigor and sonorous utterance, coupled with his vigorous style and love for characters of rugged, primitive heroism, made him quickly popular with theater audiences beginning to tire of worn melodramas and static Shakespearean presentations by untalented actors. He numbered among his friends James Bowie and became so enamored of the man that he modeled part of his persona after him, even to challenging his employer on one occasion to a duel in a darkened room, naked and armed only with knives in emulation of a duel Bowie supposedly fought against a man named Contrecourt. Bowie was amused at the younger man's hero-worship and went so far as to give Forrest a copy of his knife. Forrest used that knife whenever possible in his many stage roles, but most often in the play Matamora.

*He was most famous for his interpretation of Hamlet, playing him as a strong-willed, elemental character in revolt that mirrored his own unconscious revolt against the idealized classic drama. For that, his audience forgave him for his uncontrolled, egocentric passions, his vanity, and his arrogance.—*A. J. S.

Had Shakespeare known Jim Bowie—God! What an epic! A tragedy! A triumph!

I would have played him—who better?—as a Hercules, browbeaten by a tepid society unworthy of him and fearing him for knowing itself to be unworthy of him.

Yes, he was my friend. I even forgave him for a little impromptu medley that occurred between us at St. Cyr's gambling establishment when both of us were, shall we say, taken a bit with drink and momentarily infatuated with the same woman of rather tainted reputation who had gained entrance to the establishment on the arm of yet another gentleman.

Jim and I had begun our late-night carouse through Vieux Carré following one of my better Hamlets on a Tuesday night, I remember. After fortifying ourselves with a few glasses of absinthe at a small establishment near Pierre Lafitte's blacksmith shop on Bourbon Street, we began working our way through the Quarter, one establishment at a time, stopping for the rather thirsty business of progress at every, or nearly every, saloon along the way, arriving at last at St. Cyr's.

Jim was quite amiable but I, well I, flush from my triumph of seven curtain calls, still felt the fire of the stage in my veins, and stalked to the gaming tables. My muse still smiled upon me, triumph after triumph, coin after coin finding its way into my pocket. Yes, my night was rapidly becoming complete. All I needed was a gift from Aphrodite to fulfill my evening and launch me triumphant unto the new day.

Then, *she* walked in. A quadroon of especial beauty. Eyes smoky gray, skin of *café au lait*, hair black and gleaming like a raven's wing, her breasts full and copiously displayed so that when one stood next to her the hint of aureoles could be seen, tantalizing. She was Faustus's Helen and my head became light with desire. I ached for her. The very room suddenly became charged with male want. I sensed a low, barbaric growl simmering throughout the room.

"Ah!" I cried, standing erect and gesturing towards her.

*"Was this the face that launched a thousand ships,
And burnt the topless towers of Ilium?"*

I walked towards her, balancing carefully on the balls of my feet. I stopped, stage center, declaiming declining,

"Sweet Helen, make me immortal with a kiss."

She laughed and curtsied and gestured with her fan for me to approach. I slipped up and leaned down to kiss gently those rich, full lips. A hint of mint lingered on my lips, and I touched it with my tongue.

*"Her lips suck forth my soul: see where it flies.
Come, Helen, come, give me my soul again."*

I leaned forward again, but she interplaced between our lips her fan. I frowned and started to speak when a hand closed gently around my upper arm, tugging me back.

"Enough, Edwin," Jim said softly. "You are embarrassing the lady."

I looked back at him, flaring, "How dare you upstage me, up-start?"

"I apologize," he said, ignoring my outburst. He bowed to the young lady. "We have been celebrating his triumph at the St. Charles Theater."

A tiny smile spread her lips, lifting a tiny mole at the dimple of her left cheek, in a desirable manner. Her eyes looked frankly into his for a moment, then lowered demurely as he took her hand, bowing gallantly over her fingers.

"Thank you, sir, for your courtesy," she said, her voice like soft, tinkling notes from a French music box.

"James Bowie," he said.

The atmosphere suddenly seemed charged with heat between them and a pang of jealousy quickly swept into me. I stepped forward and pulled Jim back away from her.

"This is totally unforgivable," I said. "I do not need you to apologize for me."

He laughed and brushed my hand from his arm. "You're drunk, Edwin," he said. "Perhaps we had better leave."

A fury seemed to rise inside me. I slapped his face, regretting my action almost immediately, for he had done nothing for me to give him such an offense. A gasp went up around the room. I became instantly aware of the ticking of a clock somewhere, the lapse whirling of a wheel, the clink of chips. I felt the hungry eyes of the room upon me, waiting for Jim's response to this insult.

I threw my head back to stare into his eyes and felt my heart grow cold. I looked at death, a dark emptiness, watching the color change from blue to slate-gray, his lips thinning.

"You are a fool, Edwin," he said softly. "I could kill you for that."

"I'm at your service, sir," I said. My tongue felt thick in my mouth. I swallowed past the instant dryness. I knew then I was dead, but honor does strange things to a man, forcing him into extended moments of foolishness. I was young—that is my only excuse—and the lust of a young man often causes him to mistake honor for common sense.

"You may . . ." I started to say, "name your seconds," but his fist, the size of a boulder, crunched against my jaw, knocking me over a chair. Unfortunately, the blow also knocked common sense from me (or perhaps it was relief at being treated in this manner instead of a roasted Christmas goose ready for carving). I leaped to my feet and charged him, flailing my fists like a border ruffian only to be knocked back over the chair again.

Laughter ran around the room. Stung, I rose and remembered the lessons of Jem Mace, a pugilist friend who had given me a brief stint of training. I shrugged out of my jacket and raised my fists in the accepted style and advanced upon him. I caught his next blow on my forearm and lashed out at him, bloodying his nose.

"There, you rascal!" I panted. "I'm for you!"

He laughed again, stinging me into action. I leaped forward only to find my fist caught in his hand. I cried out as his other hand grabbed me in my private parts and then swung me high overhead. He threw me like a sack of meal onto a table, knocking the wind from me. I slid off onto the floor and looked wonderingly at the strange pattern in the Oriental carpet. Then, I pushed myself erect and stumbled towards him. He shook his head and gave a great sigh.

"Edwin, you are the biggest damn fool."

"Sir," I croaked, then I saw his big fist coming towards me and . . . nothing.

I awoke in my rooms with a cold cloth lying across my forehead. I ached all over and my stomach rolled from the wine and brandy I had drunk. Suddenly, a wave of nausea rolled over me. I rolled to the edge of my bed in order not to foul myself and felt a hand drag me over a basin into which I vomited.

"Thank you," I said weakly and rolled back onto my pillow. Jim's face swam into focus and shame burned through me.

"God," I moaned. "I'm sorry."

"All right," he said and rinsed the cloth and replaced it over my head. "You've made a fool of yourself. You're lucky that our seconds weren't visiting, now. None would blame me for killing you after that."

"I know," I said miserably.

"Do you?" he said sharply. "Look at me!"

I raised my head with an effort and tried to look at him, but his features swam in and out of focus. He shook me and I almost vomited again.

"You must control your temper," he said. "Any of those in the room could have and would have killed you in a minute for what you did. You are not in their caliber. They have blazed before and you have only pretended to it."

"I have my honor . . ." I began, but he interrupted me.

"You'd better learn the difference between honor and stupidity," he said sharply. "If you leave yourself open to insult by your actions, your honor has been transgressed only by yourself, not by those who insult you then. Your honor should be defended only when someone insults you of his own will, not yours."

"I'll remember," I said, closing my eyes.

And I have, although my temper has failed me several times, such as when I caught George W. Jamieson and my wife in compromising positions, or when Macready led his friends against my Macbeth in London. When that poor excuse for an actor brought his troupe to America, I returned the favor, but he would not let it lie there and, well, I regret that my friends became overzealous and many people died, but that, I insist, was not my doing. In all things, I have since

The incident with William Charles Macready to which Forrest refers occurred at the Astor Place Opera House in New York in May 1849. Forrest was acting at the Broadway Theater and had nothing to do with the disgrace that occurred on the eighth, when Macready attempted to act Macbeth and was howled down by a riotous mob of Forrest adherents who had packed the playhouse. Macready's friends convinced him to try another farewell performance on the tenth, refusing Forrest's friends admission to the theater. But they could not control the streets. A great angry mob gathered and began to stone the theater, smashing all the windows and beginning to tear down the structure to get at Macready, who had insulted their hero Forrest during Forrest's London tour. The 7th Regiment was called out to escort Macready in disguise to safety. When the ruse was discovered, the mob began to fight the militia until finally the word was given to fire. Twenty-two persons were killed by the militia in the riot and thirty-six wounded before the mob dispersed, leaving in its wake a wrecked theater and a black shadow upon Forrest's reputation.—A. J. S.

defended only slights that have been cast upon my honor through no fault of my own.

Jim surprised me a few nights later by giving me his knife as a gesture of forgiveness. I was touched and filled with awe as I held that weapon in my hands. It was the one with which he had fought duels, going naked into a darkened room with another, armed only with knives, yet another duel at Galvez-town, and the Vidalia incident. I have treasured that knife and used it several times on stage when situations called for it. I have it yet, in my house in Philadelphia in my private museum.

Yes, Jim was a friend. Nay, more like an older brother to whom I owe much that I never repaid.

Forrest had built a large home on North Broad Street, Philadelphia, and it was here where he had housed his memorabilia in a wing off the house. It was subsequently destroyed in a fire and the contents lost with the exception of the famous knife given to him by Bowie which he had fortuitously placed in another room.

HENRY CLAY

Henry Clay met Jim Bowie in 1832. Clay regaled many of his friends with the story of that meeting, which took place in a coach somewhere in the southeastern United States. Another traveler, William McGinley, wrote an article about the occurrence that was widely published in newspapers around the country. The famous statesman and great compromiser, who died in 1852, told this story to an acquaintance of mine. Here is the way it was told to me.—A. J. S.

I was traveling on the Cumberland Road by coach. It was an uncomfortable trip due to the fact that it was unseasonably cold, wet, and blustery. The ventilation in a coach is usually not that exceptional, yet with the weather being what it was we found no cause but to shut the leather shades to keep the inclemency out of doors.

There were three men and a very pretty little lady in the coach.

The man was Bill McGinley, a businessman who was of average height and build. Altogether a pleasant companion who spoke about the topics of the day with some knowledge. He spoke thoughtfully and was never angered by disagreement.

The lady was hardly more than a girl. She was quite petite, maybe just a tad under five feet tall and with a slender build. She was dressed in good clothes, though they seemed to be not quite new, colored in shades of blue which set off both her eyes and the yellow of her hair which spilled out from under her hat.

The third traveler was a huge man. More than six feet tall, it would seem, and very broad, though these things had to be guessed at because he was wrapped up in a huge black cloak, and he had a black slouch hat that he pulled low over his face. Mostly he sat quietly, either dozing or listening to our conversation, but when he made a comment, I looked into those firm gray eyes and heard a well-mannered, well-modulated voice, that showed Southern breeding and dignity. Those additions to the dialogue showed both deep understanding and quick intelligence. I was very much impressed with my fellow traveler.

I was, of course, the third man.

The first leg of the journey was entertaining and even a little enlightening. Even though the stuffy condition in the coach made us a bit uncomfortable, the cozy companionship made for a pleasant travel.

This was to change as another man joined us. The man, dressed in buckskin pants, a homespun shirt covered by a leather hunting jacket, and sporting a fur cap, was a raw-boned six-footer. Tall, lank, and unwashed, he bellowed in the close confines of the coach, "I'm half-horse, half-alligator; the yaller flower of the forest; all brimstone but the head and ears, and that's *aqua fortis*!"

The man was untutored and halted our conversation since we were forced to listen to his side of the issue which was based on his ill-perceived, nay, ill-conceived, knowledge of the world. The man had never been out of the forest, and never been in a city larger than a few hundred people. Though this in and of itself was not a hindrance to all backwoodsmen, this particular specimen was proud of his lack of thought. His philosophy seemed to be, don't think, do.

Our mysterious passenger just rolled himself tighter in his cloak and tried to sleep. He was soon able to, as conversation in the coach dried up like a creek bed in a drought.

The man, feeling that he had won over us poor thinkers, pulled out a pipe and began puffing. Soon the coach was as smoky as the common room in an ale house on Saturday night.

Our little flower began to cough. "Please, Mister, the air is too thick for you to add to."

The man's face was angular and had the appearance of an axe, and his words came out like cold steel chopping at her protests. "I paid for my place, an' if I want to smoke, nobody's gonna stop me, nohow."

Then in a blur of movement, our man of mystery threw back his cloak and pulled a huge knife from behind his neck. The blade was at least a foot long and had a brass handguard and backstrap.

"Stranger, my name is James Bowie, well known in Arkansas and Louisiana; and if you don't put that pipe out the window in a quarter of a minute, I'll put this knife through your bowels, as sure as death."

The pipe went out the window, along with his tobacco. The man did not want to incur the wrath of that fine Southern gentleman, the greatest fighting man in the Southwest, the patriot Jim Bowie.

JOHN BOWIE

In the early 1800s, there were two things that really stirred a man's blood—land speculation and politics. Texas was a new land and its new government conflicted with the older government, resulting in anger, frustration, and opportunity. For a population who equated wealth with the ownership of land, Texas was a dream come true. But problems arose.

Speculators invested money and, in some cases, risked their money against questionable titles. However, the settlers were in no mood to wait for the courts to decide ownership, so they bought land through speculators. If the courts overturned titles, the speculators would return the money to their clients and then lose their investment.

The Bowies used the money raised through Jim's slave venture to invest in land. The Bowies sold much of the land to other speculators, judges, lawyers, and politicians. This made a fortune for the Bowies and resulted in several court cases that damaged Jim Bowie's reputation.

Since he was the most visible of the Bowies, and because he was known as an adventurer, he became the villain.—A. J. S.

Since the time of the first Bowie, the family has always acquired land. My grandfather, my father, and finally myself and my brothers Rezin and Jim have always believed in owning land. We began purchasing land around 1820 and will continue purchasing land as long as the price is right and we have funds.

I have never spoken about our problems. It is best to keep these things to yourself. I know Jim always felt the same way, that's why he had so much trouble with the death of his wife, but more of that another time. Land is the question, now.

Major Norris Wright, as sheriff of Rapides Parish, Louisiana, introduced us to a certain friend of his who purported to be Bernardo Sampayreac. Señor Sampayreac offered us sixty thousand arpents of land left from a grant made to him by Governor Miro of Spanish Louisiana. Alfred and Carey Blanchard served as witness to this meeting.

In good faith, we purchased this land, though in working out the deal, we had to borrow from numerous banks, and one problem we did not think to have was that Major Wright would often do his best to block these loans.

This would infuriate James, especially because Jim had some other difficulty with Major Wright, and these led to Major Wright trying to commit murder, and then losing his own life to Jim in Natchez.

In 1828, we were vindicated by the Arkansas State Court. Jim had just gotten out of his sickbed, and decided to move to Texas and leave all the problems and notoriety of his battle with Major Wright behind him.

In Texas, he applied for one-quarter league of land on Galveston Island. This was his right as a single man and citizen of Mexico. He knew this island well when he had certain business dealings in Texas in 1819 and 1820 with Jean Lafitte. He was soon looking at the many possibilities in Texas and started planning where investments were best.

A lot of people are not aware that we Bowies were the first to bring mechanical sugar presses into Louisiana. This was only one of the advances we made, and Jim had even bigger plans for Texas.

He discussed the financial rewards the family could gain if we were to establish cotton gins and textile factories in Texas. Considering there was fine cotton being grown there and an available port for shipping, we decided that this would be a very good investment.

Add to this the huge tracts of land available cheap and Texas appeared to be the finest opportunity for Jim. This is why he went to Texas.

JAMES STEWART

The land in question purchased from Sampayreac was first placed in John's name, then sold to James Stewart.—A. J. S.

John Bowie sold me land that they had purchased on 22 October 1828. The land title was filed in the county records of Hempstead County, town of Washington, in the State of Arkansas.

I received title in December and applied for the land at the land office in Little Rock on 12 December 1828. The land coordinates were N.E. 13, 11 S.W., 26 W. and E. one-half, S.E. 17, 11 S., 26 W. and W. one-half, N.E. 13, 11 S.W. This was entered on the register on that day.

Much of our problem came about because we had to show how Señor Sampayreac received the grant. The court tried to prove he was deceased prior to Bowie buying the land, maybe even prior to receiving the grant, or that he was a foreigner and they also tried to prove he was a fictitious person. Though how he could be both fictional and real I am still unsure.

I believe it was these conflicting testimonies that lost the case for Sam C. Roane, the state prosecutor. The testimony of John Heberard was very important to the case since he swore to the legitimacy of Sampayreac and the grant.

In 1831, through some chicanery brought about through the Attorney General of the United States William Wirt and Roane, the verdict was overturned again and the state got my land. The Bowies made good the loss, but it still irritates me that they were able to take my land from me.

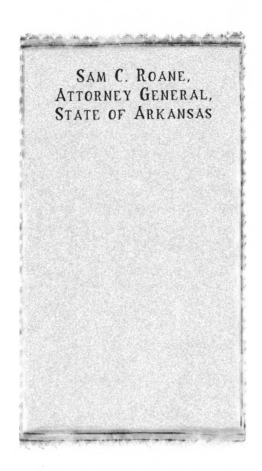

SAM C. ROANE,
ATTORNEY GENERAL,
STATE OF ARKANSAS

The Bowies were con men, plain and simple. There were more than
126 cases that were heard in the State Courts that had to deal with
the Sampayreac land grant. It is my belief that there never was a
Sampayreac. The name is incredible. In all my research, I could find
no such person in any Spanish documents, and the individual could
not be produced for cross-examination. Any way you look at it, the
entire business was simply a land swindle.

The first case was forced into court in 1827—the same year as
that scandalous duel near Natchez. The fact was that 126 land claims
were being held up while we tried to prove their validity. The case
went before Judges Johnson and Eskridge. I asked for a continuance
in order to study both evidence in the form of this Sampayreac and
Spanish law. For precedence, I cited *Soulard* v. *United States* where
Chief Justice Marshall ruled that attorneys for the state sometimes
need extra time to prepare for cases dealing with foreign land and
property laws.

Letter from Thomas F. McKinney to Stephen F. Austin

Permit me to introduce to you Mr. James Bowie, a gentleman who stands highly esteemed by his acquaintances, and merits the attention particularly of the citizens of Texas as he is disposed to become a citizen of that country, and will evidently be able to promote its general interests. I hope that you and Mr. Bowie may concur in sentiments and that you may facilitate his views.

The judges refused. I do not suggest that the real reason behind their refusal lay in the fact that the Bowies and their fellow speculators sold this land to every man of influence or power within the state, and that these lawyers, bankers, businessmen and judges stood to make a very large amount of money at the expense of both the State and Federal governments.

On December 19, 1827, the case was again brought to trial. Three days earlier, on the 16th, a subpoena had been issued, clearly stating the charges against the Bowies stemming from the fact that Sampayreac was a fictitious person, or was a foreigner and then dead, that is to say, he was dead before the land grant was issued.

A deposition was allowed into evidence from a Mr. John Heberard that swayed the judges into finding for said Sampayreac for four hundred arpents of land.

We filed a bill on December 28, 1827, that alleged due to surprise and fraud the court erred in its proceedings. We even declared that the papers used to prove the Bowie case were forgeries. Personally, I think they were drawn up by that master forger Bloody Jack Sturdivant. But I could never prove my suspicions.

On February 7, 1831, the ruling was overturned and the four hundred arpents of land were returned to the State of Arkansas and the United States of America.

Criminal proceedings against Jim Bowie were never initiated. I suppose it is because people were afraid of retaliation. Personally, if someone had been willing to file a charge, I would have been happy to prosecute the rapscallion.

I spent the better part of four years working on this problem while Bowie languished in the lap of luxury, married to a Mexican governor's daughter, an heiress by all account.

Still, we won despite everything and the government received its just due.

MARY WELLS

Mary Wells, sister of General Montfort Wells, Samuel Levi Wells III, and Thomas Jefferson Wells, was the victim of a rather sordid piece of gossip that Dr. Thomas Harris Maddox heard from one of his patients and took great delight in repeating upon his various visits to the taverns in and around Natchez. It was a scandalous tale that no gentleman would have dared repeat unless he thought himself invulnerable from challenge. Mary apparently was linked to Bowie following the death of her sister, Cecelia, two weeks before Cecelia was to be married to Bowie. Of course, the scandal became even more popular when people realized that the Wellses and Bowies were cousins. Major Norris Wright took a certain vicious delight in the scandal as he had been a contender for Cecelia's hand as well, only to be thrown over rather contemptuously by Cecelia when he pressed his suit. —**A. J. S.**

The man had absolutely no scruples at all. None. Dr. Maddox, I mean, and as for Major Wright I have only the utmost contempt.

The whole affair began when Cecelia died just two weeks before she and Jim were to be married. Jim was totally devastated by Cecelia's death.

I get ahead of myself.

Or behind.

I . . . loved Jim more than . . .

But it was Cecelia that he wanted. Then. And in that, there was a bit of scandal as well for I was the oldest and should have been the one first married. But it was frail Cecelia that Jim chose. Oh, I did not hate him for loving Cecelia. My love was too great. I wanted only his happiness. That was all that mattered.

Cecelia died on a Thursday and we buried her on a Saturday. Jim rode down along the river, after the funeral. When he did not return to our house that night, I rode out in the early morning, searching for him. I found him down by the willows on the lower quarter of our land along the river. I went to him and comforted him in his grief. My breast ached for him and I felt his sorrow and loss as harshly as my own, and when he put his arms around me and cried, I weakened. I went all hot under his hands, soft beneath their hardness. Maybe it was because I felt what was beneath his killer's hands, maybe not. By accident we kissed.

And we made love. Not from any sense of lust, but to find ourselves and our love for Cecelia in each other. It was an affirmation, perhaps an epiphany. By making love to each other, we confirmed our loss of Cecelia.

I cannot explain it well, but it was this one time and only once that Jim and I were together as man and woman. And it was enough for both of us to realize our loss.

But we were observed at the willows by someone. I suspect Wright. Why? He was always around, like a weasel trying to sneak into the hen house. Always ingratiating or trying to ingratiate himself within our family. But we knew him for what he was, a blackguard of the worst kind. He wanted Cecelia only because my brothers held title to a piece of bottom land that he needed to provide a docking and delivery for his crops. Otherwise, he had to haul his cotton into the Cotton House and pay the poundage rate for transfer.

But my brothers had no intention of selling the land and when he became abusive, even refused him the right-of-way across their land, doubling the distance that Wright had to transport his cotton.

And then there was the matter of his association with Colonel Crain, who had no honor at all in regards to his just and due debts, electing to challenge those who had loaned him money instead of paying them.

Wright did ask me to marry him after Cecelia refused him, but I knew that the only reason he sought my hand was for the leverage that would give him with my brothers to gain a right-of-way. I guess you could say I was partly responsible for leading him to believe I was interested in him. I was not and still am not the prettiest girl in Louisiana or Texas. My jaw is square and my brothers complain that I have a rather frank way of looking into men's eyes as if I were challenging them. That's how I knew what Wright was up to, for a man like Wright would not have paid any attention to me for my looks alone.

Wright pretty much had his own choice of women—for the most part, that is, for he had a penchant for married women—because he had that mysterious dark quality about him. Saturnine, or satanic, thin-lipped with the coldest eyes I have seen except on a snake.

I remember when he asked me to marry him. We had gone out riding together along the river road leading down to the Cuny Plantation. The day was hot and humid and I had removed my corset before riding in deference to the heat. Wright could hardly keep his eyes off my breasts as we rode, and I have to admit that I did enjoy the way he looked at me.

We pulled up to rest our horses under a large, twisted oak festooned with moss. He tried to kiss me when he helped me down from my horse, but I pushed him away and laughed at him, calling him a flirt.

"Flirt?" he said. He grinned, but I could see no humor behind his smile. "Why, I believe you are the flirt, Mary."

"That, sir, is a woman's prerogative," I answered. I took a small handkerchief from my sleeve and blotted my upper lip and brow.

"And a man's?" he asked.

"Why, to wait upon a woman's!" I exclaimed. "Surely, you are aware of that, sir!" I added teasingly.

"Mary," he said, clearing his throat. "There is something that I have been meaning to say to you. Or ask you, rather," he said disarmingly.

"Yes?"

"I have enjoyed our rides together and, well, will you marry me?"

The proposal as it came surprised me, and I treated it as a jest before refusing it. His eyes hardened for a moment, then relaxed and he forced a laugh.

"I will take it up with your brothers," he said condescendingly. "They know more of what a woman needs during these times than—"

"I do not choose to be chattel property for any man," I said, coolly interrupting him. "I am not subject to the authority of man, nor will I allow any man to have dominion over me. Certainly no man of the like of Wright. I am free to wed as I please or not to. I do not need a husband, sir, to enjoy the benefits of the marriage bed."

"Those are not the words of a lady," he said thickly, his face turning red with fury.

"No?" I asked. "And why not? They are the words a gentleman might use. And does not a gentleman have the privilege of visiting other ladies? Why should a woman not have the same privileges? I think you are placing too much emphasis upon a maidenhead and not enough emphasis upon the maiden. If a man has a choice in such matters in this world, then a woman has the same choices."

He rode away, whipping his mount in fury after my refusal. I remember seeing flecks of foam stream back from that frightened horse's mouth and I knew I had made the right choice, although I had made a powerful enemy for not only myself, but my brothers as well.

Not long after that exchange, Cecelia died and Jim and I had our brief affair. You know the rest of the story.

I've had many lovers since then, but somehow, in the dark of the night, I always see Jim's face above mine and feel his lips upon mine and his arms holding me tightly.

It hasn't been the same since.

THE VIDALIA AFFAIR

In 1827, Bowie became embroiled in a bitter feud with the sheriff of his parish, Major Norris Wright, who shot Bowie in the streets of Alexandria, Louisiana. The truth of what happened there and what happened later on the Vidalia Sandbar is a hotly argued subject. Margaret Bowie clipped an article out of a paper that reported the event after it happened, but neglected to either date the clipping or write down the name of the paper and author. It does, however, seem to have been written by someone who was an eyewitness to the affair or who had intimate knowledge of what transpired.—A. J. S.

From a Newspaper Article Clipped by Margaret Bowie

Major Norris Wright was a moderate man. Moderate in his dimensions, moderate in his dress, and moderate in his personal code. At least, that was how he always appeared.

I heard many different stories as to where he came from, how he gained his wealth, and even how he came to be called Major. I do not know which was true, though I heard some of these stories in the presence of the Major himself.

You see, in those days, I had let myself be drawn into bad ways. I drank bad liquor and smoked bad cigars, consorted with bad women, [Perhaps this is one reason why the article is lacking an author—Ed.] and had the worst companions. All in all, it was a bad life, though exciting at times.

As for the Major, I understand he originally came from Baltimore in Maryland. At that time, many men from the North who had some skill at arms came South. Even though dueling was and is frowned upon by the law, the men of the South believed in honor above all else. A man who had the appearance of a gentleman, and knew how to shoot or use a sword, could make a large amount of money.

Sheriff Major Norris Wright was attached to a conspiracy. The Murrell Conspiracy, to be exact. You see, Murrell needed people in many different positions of authority in order for his plan to work.

The plan was very complicated, and took years to establish. However, before it could be completed, it was uncovered, and broken. Murrell went to prison, and if he hasn't died is still there; hence, my desire to keep my name secret.

Wright made money through many different channels. He had interests in several taverns, inns, and gaming houses; in these his confederates received and sold stolen goods, mostly for counterfeit money, passed information (for a price) to various and sundry thieves, worked land swindles using documents forged by Bloody Jack Sturdivant, sold bills of sale for stolen livestock, including slaves, and made enough money to be placed on the board of directors at the bank in Alexandria.

He also was both an extraordinary pistol shot and a trained swordsman. When he first came south and he needed money, like his friend Judge Crain, he would simply borrow the money and not pay it back. When it came time for his benefactor to collect his due, Major Wright would challenge him to a duel and kill him. Most of this was in his past by the time he ran for sheriff, but those of us in the clan knew it.

As sheriff and bank director he was in position to pass information and stop individuals who might cause problems to Murrell's plans, the plans of the Clan of the Mystic Confederacy. One of these individuals was James Bowie.

Of course, Major Wright also enjoyed the work, because Bowie had set up opposition to Major Wright's candidacy for the position of sheriff. Wright was a lot better hater than he appeared. I suppose I should also mention that there was a woman involved, but I'll kindly keep her name to myself, it not being fit to mention in this testimony.

Anyway, the entire Bowie clan could have caused problems. All were intelligent, cool under fire and could, if pushed, have fought anyone who tried to take what was theirs, and what would be worse is they would lead a fight to help their neighbors.

The Bowies are an honorable clan. Indeed, that is probably their biggest downfall. They have always played by the dictates of honor, even in business.

James Bowie was a very quiet and unassuming gentleman, but when aroused he was hell on wheels. There are stories which I cannot reveal here about fights on the bayous, on the river, in the gambling halls—well, let us simply say that James Bowie was not a man who could be taken lightly unless you wanted to be crippled or killed.

Major Wright started his campaign by casting aspersions on Bowie's pretension to being a gentleman. He did this by having the gamblers at his dives talk about Bowie. They called him a hard-drinking, carousing womanizer. A brawler who more often than not killed his opponents.

These words, with details invented as the gossip advanced, went straight to Bowie's ears. Bowie tracked some down. It was not exactly pleasant for the man who passed these rumors if Bowie found out. Only a few died, and those are not important.

His defense all but halted the lies.

Next, Wright thought to drive the Bowies out through financial means. The Bowies were always gambling on land. These speculations required much ready cash. Norris had the cash and withheld it at the banks. He stopped them from getting loans, the result being that the Bowies lost several good options that would have established them as very wealthy men.

All the Bowies were angry, but James Bowie was quite willing to kill the Major with his bare hands.

He received his chance one day in Alexandria.

I had just spoken to Major Wright about . . . well, maybe I'll keep that to myself, but needless to say it was something not best talked about in the open.

Let me explain this better. Alex at this time was part frontier town, part city. The town square was bordered by a tavern and an

Miscellaneous Data

The Wells family were the oldest and richest in the area; the Cunys and the Bowies sided with them and were called "the Old Planters." Their politics were listed as Henry Clay Whigs. The Maddox party was made up of Jacksonian Democrats.

In 1823 William Fristoe, the sheriff of Rapides Parish and a friend of James Bowie, died in office. Major Wright (some say through tricky politics) was selected to serve out the term, which ended in 1826. In 1826, Wright won his reelection in a hotly contested race. Some say Sam Wells was the opposing candidate. When Wright was killed, Sam Wells became sheriff. Wells died from yellow fever in New Orleans in 1829. He was delivering prisoners.

Norris Wright came from Baltimore with Robert C. Hyson to clerk in the store of Martin and Bryant. Hyson and Wright took over the business after the death of one of its members. In 1825 the business converted into a bank and Wright became a director. This allowed him to turn down loans from the Planters.

Samuel Wells accused Crain of killing Gen. Sam Cuny in a written statement. Since Crain allegedly pulled the first pistol, Wells called it premeditated murder. The case went to the grand jury, but no trace of it or a decision rendered by the grand jury can be found, the records having disappeared.

inn on the north, a blacksmith and livery shop on the east, a courthouse on the south, and several small shops including a jewelry store on the west. The stable of the inn and the livery were built almost together in the shade of a small stand of oaks. Several of these massive old trees were even used as part of the corral.

It was in the shade of these trees that the Major and I met one afternoon. We were hidden from the gawkers in the square and from most of the people moving in the street. Though there were not many, because we had chosen a time, I believe it was 3:00, where the heat of the day combined with the steamy atmosphere would keep most people from witnessing our secret meeting.

I had just whispered the message when he exclaimed, "D——!"

I prepared to flee, but he halted me with a sudden motion of his hand and a hoarse whispered word, "Stay. It's that b——Bowie."

I was somewhat taken aback. Major Wright seldom showed his emotions. He was a very moderate man. Maybe cold would be a better word.

I have never seen such a fierce expression on a man. It was as if a rough chiseled stone statue had come to life. Bowie was said to be a fine-looking gentleman, but now all emotion had been driven from his countenance. His blue eyes had changed to gray and even his sandy, almost red, hair seemed to have become aflame with his anger.

"Sheriff Wright." Bowie's tone was normally quiet, he usually spoke with authority, but never with command, if that makes sense. He said things with such confidence that you just responded the way he wanted you to, without you ever thinking about doing anything else.

"Mr. Bowie," the Major responded with his glacier-cool tone.

"I am given to understand that you have blocked our loan at the bank." He really said that. I can hear it now even though this was almost ten years ago.

"I did." Major Wright actually sneered at Bowie. I knew why, because I saw the man's hand sneaking around to his coattails. I knew the Major had a pair of pocket pistols hidden in his long-tailed coat.

"I take it the bank is adverse to making money." Bowie was striving to keep control, but he was all fire except for that voice, which belonged somewhere at the top of a cold snow-capped mountain.

"The bank deals with gentlemen, not bravos, not men who black-ball their betters."

Bowie stepped forward, and that's when Wright pulled his pistol. The explosion startled both me and Bowie, who flew backwards onto the green grass. The powder blue jacket he was wearing flared up.

Bowie jerked himself to a sitting position and beat the flames out with his hands. He then rolled to his feet.

Wright was in shock. He had expected to commit murder, not be embroiled in a battle, but a battle was looming.

Bowie growled. It was like a huge wolf was suddenly let loose from a chain. Wright was scared, something I never expected to see.

The Major tried to reach for his second pistol, but Bowie was on top of him. The Major was a man of about 160 pounds, and Bowie lifted him into the air by his neck. He then hurled the Major against the oak tree.

The Major was dazed, but Bowie went right to where he lay and jerked him up as though Wright weighed nothing. Bowie held him up with one hand and slapped him. It sounded louder than the pistol shot. Then he backhanded him. Over and over, the Major was struck.

I rolled around behind Bowie and screamed for assistance. I had and have never seen a man so easily manhandled. Bowie's strength must have been enormous.

Finally the blacksmith and some of his cronies, aided by Bowie's own brothers, pulled him away. There were about ten men involved. Bowie pushed them away, scattered them several times as though these tough frontiersmen were no more than children.

Wright, in the meantime, was unable to do more than crawl. He'd tried to potshoot a deer, and got him a wild longhorn, or a gator, or a razorback, or something like all three.

I was trying to slip away before they started asking me questions that I could not, should not answer on peril of my own life and liberty, but I heard a man ask Wright what happened.

"Bowie . . . went . . . crazy." He couldn't hardly talk. The red and purple marks on his throat gave mute evidence as to why.

"Whose pistol?" someone else asked. Bowie responded.

"Look in Major Wright's coat. I believe you'll find the mate."

They did, and I left. I needed a drink, and so I went into the tavern.

Bowie and his brothers came in just as I finished answering in the negative as to what the commotion was outside. The tavern keeper had poured me a brandy, and I moved aside to let Bowie get a drink. He was again the soft-spoken gentleman.

"Why'd he try to kill you, Jim?" Rezin asked.

"I don't know, Reez." Bowie took a sip of his drink.

John said, "Why'd he stop our loan? The bank lost a lot of money. That's not good banking."

"All right, I just can't stand it. I've got to know. Why aren't you dead, brother Jim?"

"The ball hit something in my pocket." He reached into his coat and removed some dingus that I was too far away to see.

"My Mason symbol. He figured I'd blackballed him from the Lodge. Look, the ball is stuck on the eye. That'll bring bad luck."

Bowie looked at the little doodad for a moment, and then said in a voice I had to strain to hear, "I just picked this up at the jeweler. I slipped it into my pocket when I saw Wright over there by the oak. Luck sure is a strange thing, isn't it, boys?"

Bowie tossed the little amulet into a spittoon. He and his brothers finished their drink and left. I dug the Masonic pin out and kept it as proof that this story that I have related to you is completely true, and I have shown this good luck charm to the editor of this paper as evidence.

The very next year James Bowie killed Norris Wright at the Vidalia Sandbar Massacre. And this year, Big Jim Bowie, the only man who ever truly frightened me, died in Texas at some place called Bexar.

I stated earlier that Murrell scared me. James Bowie scared me even more. Even in his death I hesitate to write this, and only my desire to see history set straight convinced me to sell this article.

I began to withdraw from the Clan from that moment on. I was afraid that Bowie might discover that I was at odds with him and would then attack me. Once Murrell was arrested, I escaped and began a new life. I have lived a life that a preacher would envy ever since, and the charm I mentioned has brought me good luck.

The story I have told is a true one. I swear on Jim Bowie's Masonic amulet, the one that saved him from Major Wright's bullet.

The Maddox Party

Dr. Thomas H. Maddox
Col. Robert A. Crain
Dr. James A. Denny
Maj. Norris Wright
Alfred Blanchard
Carey Blanchard

The Wells Party

Samuel Levi Wells III
Maj. George C. McWhorter
Dr. Richard Cuny
Thomas Jefferson Wells
James Bowie
Gen. Samuel Cuny

Spectators with Dr. Maddox

Dr. Provan
Col. Barnard
Capt. John B. Nevitt
Dr. Cox
David Woods

Date

Wed. Sept. 19, 1827. Temperature at 5 A.M. 80 degrees, at
4:00 P.M. 91 degrees, dry, with a wind from the southwest,
skies clear.

Place

Adams County, Mississippi, Sheriff Henry Tooley, Esq.

It is hard for me to believe that I was the cause of men spilling their blood even unto death. I was quite young in 1827, little more than a girl.

Apparently, Jim and I were discovered down along the willows that one day by either Major Wright or one of his friends. At least, that is what my brothers determined, but I have a sneaky suspicion that Annette Jeanne saw us and told Dr. Thomas Harris Maddox what she had seen. I believe she thought that Dr. Maddox would pass word on to the Major since they were friends and all. Annette Jeanne was always after the Major, but he had eyes, at that time, only for me.

Montfort, my brother, became furious when word finally trickled back to us. He immediately called for a horse to be saddled and rode into town to confront Dr. Maddox. Since he cannot see very well—cataracts, you know—he took along a shotgun. When he asked Dr.

Maddox for the name of the person who had perpetuated such a lie, Dr. Maddox refused to answer. That's when Montfort went back to his horse to get his shotgun. Dr. Maddox took to running down the street and Montfort shot and killed a man standing by the barber shop instead.

Naturally, Dr. Maddox had little choice but to challenge Montfort for his actions, but Montfort refused to fight him, saying that he wouldn't fight anyone on the field of honor who wasn't a gentleman. Well, this was just what Dr. Maddox and that weasel Major Wright needed. They began to spread word about town, questioning Montfort's honor. Montfort was furious, but he knew that to fight Dr. Maddox was a useless thing since he wouldn't be able to see the doctor at twenty paces.

At last, Samuel took his place even though his eyesight was only a little better. Well, Dr. Maddox accepted and their seconds began to set the details. I planned on going to the duel with them, but on the morning of the affair, Montfort locked the door to my room and ordered the servants not to let me out until after ten o'clock, well past the time for the duel.

A Note from Thomas Jefferson Wells

I have little to say about the Vidalia duel. There were animosities present. Alfred Blanchard was there.

We had been at variance for a while. Blanchard was an unsavory man. Though he made pretensions towards being a gentleman, he was simply a scavenger.

He would hang around wealthy men and find ways to get them to spend their money on him. We would always buy the dinner, the drinks. They would often loan him money, and somehow after an evening of drinking, they would have forgotten if he paid them back. I never got so drunk that I forgot who paid me back.

His brother was only slightly better.

My major problem with Alfred, though, came about from a little set-to we had at the Alexandria Mid-Summer's Eve Ball. All the plantation gentry were there and we were having a truly wonderful evening. Alfred, of course, was intoxicated. No, that's too fine a word:

he was drunk. He was making a fool of himself and was so obnoxious that he was past objectionable to disgraceful.

I made some comment to this effect and a little later while I was dancing with the pretty O'Hara girl, I heard Blanchard make an obscene comment to me. As I began to turn, he shoved his fist against me. I felt this burning down my side, and then he stepped back with a small knife in his hand.

Someone screamed and Jim and Rezin looked over and saw what had happened. They grabbed Blanchard and, at first, I wondered if they were going to rip him apart, limb by limb. But they simply threw him down the stairs and out of the ballroom. Blanchard does have friends, and they quickly got him away.

Fortunately, the wound was only slight and I was back on my feet in a day or two, ready to kill him at the first chance I could get. Of course, I could have challenged him, but the situation was not quite right. I had to wait for a long time. Until September 19, 1827.

FROM THE DIARY OF
GENERAL SAMUEL CUNY

18 September 1827

I find I must write down some of my thoughts before meeting foes on the island Vidalia in the Mississippi River.

My Friend & Cousin Sam Wells will be facing Dr. Thomas Maddox in a duel of honor on the morrow. With him will be a party of men whose interests are contrary to ours. My own enemy, Col. Robert Alexander Crain—sometimes Judge Crain—will be there as well. Perhaps we shall get a chance to settle our differences as well.

Col. Crain is a rogue. My father once made the mistake of endorsing a note for Crain despite warnings from several individuals who knew about Crain's habit of borrowing money & not paying it back. When the note came due, Crain refused to pay & my father felt honor-bound to honor his signature despite Crain. Money was scarce at the time & we had to sell some slaves in order to satisfy the obligation. That made us a bit of a laughingstock among the people of Alexandria for a while until the day Crain came out to our place & I shot him in the arm. Perhaps if my aim had been better, this affair tomorrow would never have come to fruition.

Dr. John Rippey, whose nieces are married to my cousins Montfort & Samuel Wells, once rented a plantation to Crain & when he asked Crain for rent, Crain responded that he had been insulted by Dr. Rippey, challenged him to a duel, & killed him. It was, of course, murder. Crain had blazed many times while Dr. Rippey had never been hunting let alone shot a pistol.

Crain still never repaid the money although the court, in settling Dr. Rippey's estate, did force Crain to give up the plantation. He managed a huge profit, however, while the affair dragged through the courts for nearly two years.

Strangely, Crain never could understand how I could be promoted to general over him when I was only a lieutenant of horse & he a colonel, but the answer, of course, is relatively simple: no one would serve under him as a brigadier. In fact, many individuals left his regiment following his duel with Dr. Rippey.

I suppose people in other parts of the country think we are fools with our dueling. They do not understand that given the court system we have, the only recourse left open to us is on the field of honor. That is how justice is meted out.

And that is why I must go to Vidalia tomorrow. Jim Bowie will be there tomorrow. And Major Wright. I am uncertain as to what all this portends, but I am sure that the duel will not be confined to the two principals. I am sure that Crain feels the same way.

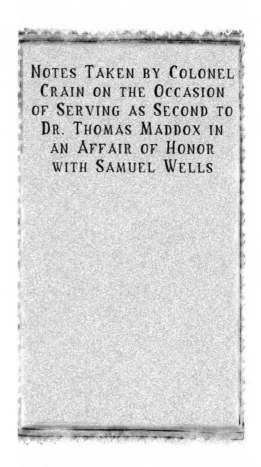

NOTES TAKEN BY COLONEL
CRAIN ON THE OCCASION
OF SERVING AS SECOND TO
DR. THOMAS MADDOX IN
AN AFFAIR OF HONOR
WITH SAMUEL WELLS

A meeting was held between myself, Col. Robert Alexander Crain, originally of Fauquier County, Virginia, & Major George C. McWhorter as seconds to Dr. Maddox & Samuel Wells. Since the challenge was made by my principal, Dr. Maddox, the choice of weapons resided with Mr. Wells, who selected pistols at ten paces.

We agreed upon Vidalia Island to be the site for the affair, about seventy miles northeast of Alexandria on the Mississippi River.

The challenger's party will consist of: Dr. Thomas Harris Maddox, principal. Col. Robert Alexander Crain, second. Dr. James A. Denny, surgeon. Major Norris Wright, Alfred & Edward Carey Blanchard, John B. Nevitt, Dr. William R. Provan, Thomas Hunt, Col. William Barnard, & Dr. William R. Cox, witnesses. My servant, Job, will carry the pistols.

The challenged party is General Montfort Wells, who will be served by his brother as an accepted substitute on account of General

Wells' poor eyesight & pleurisy. His party will consist of Samuel Levi Wells III, principal. Major George McWhorter, second. Dr. Richard Cuny, surgeon. Thomas Jefferson Wells, James Bowie, General Samuel Cuny, witnesses.

The time & date set for the meeting will be September 19, 1827 at noon.

FROM COLONEL CRAIN'S
JOURNAL

Sept. 19, 1827

At last I will have a chance to meet those who have opposed me for so long. I have arranged for a duel between Samuel Wells & Dr. Maddox to be fought at the Vidalia Sandbar, far enough away from the supporters of the Wellses, the Bowies, & the Cunys to ensure our safety should matters come to an expected head & we have the chance to settle all our scores at once.

I do worry about Bowie, though. I have never seen anyone quite as fierce as him &, I must confess, I am a bit cautious about him. Barnard will carry a shotgun & my servant extra pistols, though, so that is some comfort.

WALTER WORTHINGTON BOWIE, FAMILY HISTORIAN

A tendency exists among readers to accept the opinion of family members. In the case of the Bowies, however, that is a dangerous thing to do. Rezin once said that neither he nor his brother ever engaged in a duel of any kind, although several accounts exist of Jim Bowie's triumphs upon the field of honor. The below account, although flawed by time, does provide a quick sketch of the affair.—A. J. S.

The "Sandbar duel," as it was called, which took place on a little island in the Mississippi River opposite Natchez, September 19, 1827, has been more written of, perhaps, than any other of James's numerous fights. The following statement of that celebrated fight is based on a letter written two days after the duel by one of the participants and an article in a Southern paper, published a short time after the occurrence.

For many years a feud existed between two parties in the Parish of Rapides, on Red River. On one side was Col. James Bowie, Gen. Montfort Wells, Samuel Wells, General Cuny, Dr. Cuny, and McWhorter. On the other side Dr. T. H. Maddox of Charles County, Maryland; Maj. Norris Wright, of Baltimore; Col. Robert A. Crain of Fauquier County, Virginia; Alfred and Edward Carey Blanchard, of Norfolk, Virginia; and Dr. Denny composed the leaders of the two parties. Their quarrels finally resulted in arrangements for the fight on the Sandbar, the principals, however, being Dr. Maddox and Samuel L. Wells, the others as witnesses, seconds, and surgeons. After two ineffectual exchanges of shots, Wells and Maddox shook hands, but Cuny stepped forward and said to Colonel Crain, "This is a good time to settle *our* difficulty"; Bowie and Wright also drew, and the firing became general. Crain killed Cuny and shot Bowie through the hip. Bowie drew his knife and rushed upon Colonel Crain. The latter, clubbing his empty pistol, dealt such a terrific blow upon Bowie's head as to bring him to his knees and break the weapon. Before the latter could recover he was seized by Dr. Maddox, who held him down for some moments, but, collecting his strength, he hurled Maddox off just as Major Wright approached and fired at the wounded Bowie, who, steadying himself against a log, half buried in the sand, fired at Wright, the ball passing through the latter's body. Wright then drew a sword-cane, and rushing upon Bowie, exclaimed, "Damn you, you have killed me." Bowie met the attack, and, seizing his assailant, plunged his "bowie-knife" into his body, killing him instantly. At the same moment Edward Blanchard shot Bowie in the body, but had his arm shattered by a ball from Jefferson Wells.

This ended the fight, and Bowie was removed, as it was supposed, in a dying condition. Of the twelve men who took part in the affray, Wright and Cuny were killed, Bowie, Crain, and Blanchard badly wounded; the remaining seven men escaping any serious injury. Colonel Crain, himself wounded, brought water for his adversary, Colonel Bowie. The latter politely thanked him, but remarked that he did not think Crain had acted properly in firing upon him when he was exchanging shots with Maddox. In later years Bowie and Crain became reconciled, and each having great respect for the other, remained friends until death.

A.H.W.
(A Hidden Witness)

The best account of the famous Vidalia Sandbar incident comes not from the participants, who bear a natural prejudice towards the opposing side, but from someone known only as "A Hidden Witness," who happened to be in the right place. From his words, it appears that this individual was afraid for his life and was not among the "gentry" of the day. I believe it was only his addiction to strong drink that drove him to finally break his silence and give the following account of that infamous day, probably long after John A. Murrell had been imprisoned.—A. J. S.

The meeting between Dr. Thomas Harris Maddox and Samuel Levi Wells III was set for high noon, September 19, 1827, at the Vidalia Sandbar, a dueling site of note. The altercation was over a shot taken at Dr. Maddox by Samuel Wells's brother General Montfort Wells after Dr. Maddox allegedly impugned the honor of General Wells's sister by either claiming she had been impregnated by James Bowie or that she had been observed in the field with a buck nigra of rather ponderous possession. Either way, it was an insult to the Wells name and General Wells felt justified in trying to draw satisfaction from a man he deemed beneath his dignity.

It was a hot and steamy day for September. Though it never truly seems to get cold in Louisiana, the sun seemed especially warm as it reflected off the dirty sand of the beach. The six men, the two principals, the two seconds, and the surgeons, Dr. Denny and Dr. Cuny, all commented upon the unseasonable heat as they readied themselves for the medley. Their voices carried to the pile of driftwood collected in a corner of a stand of willows by the spring flood where I was sleeping. At first, I did not recognize the men, but later, after observing what had happened, I discovered their identity.

Colonel Crain and George McWhorter approached each with a nigra carrying a set of dueling pistols. [Ed. Note: These were later to be identified as a matched pair made by T. Mortimer & Sons of London, England, a .36 caliber with a rain-proof pan and roller-bearing on the steel-spring.—A. J. S.] Together, they supervised the loading of the pistols after which Mr. Wells made his choice.

The two men stood back-to-back, pistols held in the ready manner. The umpire asked if any wished to make an apology to avoid the duel, but each having answered in the negative, the count was given, slowly and carefully. At ten paces, the two turned and fired and each missed. The pistols were reloaded and the count given a second time and again each missed.

At this point, they declared that their honor had been satisfied and Wells invited all to share a glass of wine with him and others who were in the edge of the wood as witnesses. I recognized those as Jim Bowie, Tom Wells, and General Cuny who advanced after Wells mentioned them. Suddenly, I heard a noise behind me and turned to see Sheriff Norris Wright and seven or eight men coming out of a stand of sweet-gum on the other side. I knew Wright. Everyone knew Wright, a more crooked man in the area would not be found. Rumors had tied him and Crain to John A. Murrell's Clan of the Mystic Confederacy. I don't know if there's any truth to this or not, but I had heard many talking about this in Mother Surgick's pleasure house Under-the-Hill. With Wright were the two Blanchard brothers, Albert and Edward, and Bill Barnard who carried a double-barreled shotgun.

I scrunched down under those old oak roots and hoped that they wouldn't decide to investigate because it sure would have been hard on me if that faction knew I was there.

Well, Crain allowed as to how he wouldn't drink with Bowie or Cuny, but that didn't stop Wells from trying again. He said he would take them over to Connelly's Tavern at Natchez and buy all a drink there. That's when Crain said, "Be damned before I will drink with you and your blasted friends!"

Unfortunately, Bowie and Cuny were close enough to hear Crain's words and at that, Cuny yelled, "This is a good time to settle our own problems, Crain, here and now!"

The General tried to drag his pistol from his pocket, but the hammer caught in his coat. Crain pulled his pistol free and raised it to shoot at Cuny, but Bowie stepped in front of the General. I suppose he thought that would stop Crain, but it didn't. Crain fired anyway, shooting Bowie in the hip and knocking him down.

He threw his pistol away and tried to draw another, but Cuny had his pistol free by now and shot Crain in the arm. Crain was a cool one and game to the core, I'll give him that—wouldn't expect much else from one of Murrell's cronies—and pulled that second pistol and shot Cuny in the left breast.

Meanwhile, Bowie pulled himself upright and drew a huge knife. Lord, if my blood didn't run cold at the sight of that blade with a brass handle. Light glinted off its edge like diamonds. Bowie started to hobble over to Crain, but Crain threw his pistol in Bowie's face and turned and ran away. I don't blame him for that. I would've run away, too, if I had to look into that face dragging a leg towards me.

The pistol struck Bowie on the forehead, stunning him. He fell to his knees, shook his head for a moment, then started to get up, but Dr. Maddox jumped on his back and tried to hold him. But Bowie was a bull and threw him off.

At that moment, Wright pulled a pistol and fired at Bowie, knocking him down again, but he didn't kill him.

"Goddamn you, Bowie!" he yelled, and unsheathed his sword cane and ran at him. Bowie was flat on his back, dazed from Wright's bullet when Wright stood over and raised that cane like a stake in both hands and drove it into Bowie's chest. Bowie twitched and I thought for sure he was dead. Wright must have, too, 'cause he put a foot on Bowie's chest and tried to pull his cane free, but then Bowie raised his left hand and grabbed Wright by his forearm.

Dr. Cuny's Reaction to Bowie's Wounds

I write this for the layman, although my medical colleagues will undoubtedly find interest as well in the person of Jim Bowie, who withstood all the wounds he received at the Vidalia Sandbar.

Mr. Bowie is a large man a few inches over six feet and weighing close to 220 pounds. He is amazingly well-knit with a hearty constitution.

During the chance encounter, Bowie was shot four times with three balls remaining in his body, two in the left hip and one in the left shoulder. He was grazed by three other balls that drew blood and sustained a large gash upon his left hand. A pistol butt raised a large swelling on his forehead and a sword had been pushed through his sternum into his breast, necessitating its removal with forceps.

I have constantly been amazed at the resiliency of the human body but never more than I was at this time by what Mr. Bowie had suffered. He was abed for several weeks after this, but never despaired, taking the time to read and make plans for when he had thoroughly recuperated to go abroad. He is a testimony to the human spirit.

Wright leaped back, helping to pull Bowie up and that's when Bowie stabbed that huge knife in Wright's belly down low and used both hands, ripping it up to Wright's breastbone.

Wright screamed, then looked down at his guts spilling out onto the ground and said, "My god, the damned rascal has killed me." He fell down, his legs twitched and convulsed, and he died, blood rolling out in a huge pool and sinking into that sand.

Meanwhile, Alfred Blanchard and his brother figured Bowie would be easy pickings, standing there with that sword sticking out of him. He pulled his sword-cane and took to stabbing at Bowie, but

Bowie batted his sword away and slashed Blanchard's arm to the bone. He screamed like a gut-shot horse and Carey Blanchard pulled a pistol and shot Bowie, hitting him in the hip and knocking him down again. He grabbed his brother and ran away with him towards the woods, Alfred's arm streaming blood. That was when George McWhorter winged him with a pistol, but they got away.

Well, I don't know what else happened. It was all over in minutes. I know other shots went off—I remember hearing that double-barreled shotgun—but I don't know where the pellets went or who they wounded. I do know that Bowie and his friends had the field after it was all over.

Dr. Cuny had gone to his brother, but Crain's bullet had killed the General. He worked on Bowie, staunching the flow of blood. He tried to pull that sword out of Bowie's breast with his forceps, but the sword was stuck too deep and the forceps kept slipping away. Finally, he gave up on the sword and took to operating on Bowie right there, digging out the pistol balls and plugging the holes with linen.

I think Crain must have suddenly been overcome with shame for his treachery for he brought Bowie a drink of water, saying, "I thought you could use this."

"Thanks," Bowie said.

"This is a hell of a state of affairs," Crain answered, looking around the field.

"You shouldn't have shot me while I was mixed up with Maddox," Bowie said.

"I figured I had to stop you," Crain said. "You're the toughest son-of-a-bitch I ever saw. Good luck."

And he left.

I stayed hid until they carried Bowie to a boat, then across the river before I came out of my cover. I felt weak and my hands shook like I was coming off a five-day drunk. I can't begin to tell you how frightened I was and took off for the north along the Bloody Trace, working my way over up to the Pinch Gut District in Memphis where I figured to lay over for a while before going down to the Swamp in New Orleans. I waited until someone gave me a picayune before I told this story, but it is true, every gospel word of it.

Bowie was taken to Connelly's Tavern across the river and carried up into a corner room on the second story. There, Dr. Cuny finally managed to remove Wright's sword from Bowie's sternum after obtaining a pair of black-smith tongs. So deeply embedded was the sword in the bone that two people had to hold Bowie steady while Dr. Cuny applied leverage to extract the sword.—**A. J. S.**

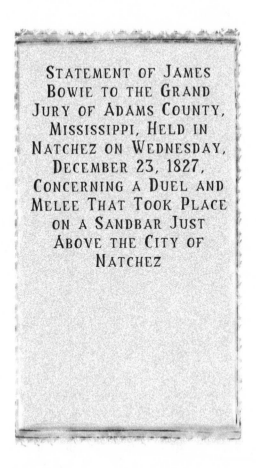

STATEMENT OF JAMES
BOWIE TO THE GRAND
JURY OF ADAMS COUNTY,
MISSISSIPPI, HELD IN
NATCHEZ ON WEDNESDAY,
DECEMBER 23, 1827,
CONCERNING A DUEL AND
MELEE THAT TOOK PLACE
ON A SANDBAR JUST
ABOVE THE CITY OF
NATCHEZ

*I discovered a copy of the statement made by James Bowie after the Vidalia Sandbar fight when I had a little free time on my hands after delivering a prisoner to Natchez for extradition purposes. It was my first time in Natchez and while I was taking in the sights, I suddenly remembered the Vidalia Affair. I visited the newspaper offices and while reading the lurid account of the battle, I discovered the enclosed statement, made on either December 23 or the 24th in 1827, recorded in a reporter's notebook. I tried to verify the contents of the notebook with court records, but those records have been lost.—*A. J. S.

Gentlemen of the Jurie. [sic]

My name is James Bowie. I am a resident of Rapides Parish, Louisiana where I have resided for almost eighteen years since I was a child. The accounts that have been made in regards to the recent occurrences at the Vidalia Sandbar. Most of what has been reported have been lies, even to the place of the battle which was at another sandbar without name just above Natchez.

I wish to remind this jury that I am appearing of my own free will and that this Jury has no right to be investigating what began as an Affair of Honor. The subsequent brawl that took place is most regretable [sic] but happened outside the jurisdiction of this court.

Dr. Thomas Maddox and Samuel Levi Wells III met in an affair of honor. I, and several members of the Wells family, attended as spectators. We stationed ourselves in the woods about two hundred yards from the Field of Honor. Others are more qualified to speak to the issuance of the duel. For the record, I saw the participants after the exchange of two shots each that apparently had no effect on either man. They then approached each other in such a way as to suggest that the affair had been satisfactorily concluded. Seeing them shake hands and taking this to mean that the Affair of Honor had been settled by mutual agreement, I and my friends went forward to congratulate the gentlemen.

Major Wright and Col. Crain and the two Blanchard brothers, Alfred and Carey, also approached the party from the opposite side. As we drew close to the duelists, Col. Crain commenced firing his pistols. Several shots were fired. Each member of the Wright party carried two loaded pistols, and both Wright and Alfred Blanchard carried sword canes as well. I, Gen. Cuny, and Thomas Wells carried a pistol each. I was wounded in the first volley and struck in the forehead with a thrown pistol. Dazed, I drew my pistol after another shot downed Gen. Cuny. Col. Crain ran from the field. I fired at him, but missed as two more bullets struck me, knocking me to the ground. Major Wright took advantage of this and rushed forward, stabbing me in the breast with his sword cane. He placed his foot upon my breast and tried to pull the sword free, but the handle came off in his hand. I drew my knife and reached up, pulling him down on top of me and stabbed him in the stomach, reaching up for his heart. He said, "Damn you, Bowie! You've killed me!" then vomited blood on me and died. I pushed him off and tried to rise whereupon Alfred Blanchard attacked me with his sword cane, slashing me across the arm as I tried to defend myself. I returned the blow with my knife, cutting him deeply, severing, as I later discovered, the leaders [sic] in his arm. He fled the field.

That is what happened. I have here, a brief summation of the affair. I offer it to you now.

From the Personal
Diary of A. J. Sowell
19 Sept. 1872

I do not know exactly how to use the information I received today. I find great confusion twisting and turning within me, troubling me deeply. Today, I arrived in Houston to deliver some depositions to Court and some personal messages from my father to certain members of the Texas State Congress. It was in pursuit of the latter that my steps took me to The Yellow Rose, a discreet tavern where a man might meet a woman of the night a step above the prostitutes of Front Street and the waterfront. The tavern is a large, two-story, frame building. Next door is a saddlery, a bootmaker, and a gunsmith. It is a well-run establishment with an excellent reputation, although it is not an establishment that would cater to the gentry.

I knew the man I was looking for by sight and so did not approach the long, mahogany bar dominating the far end of the room. Instead, I elected to sit at one of the small tables scattered haphazardly around the room. I had an Allen & Wheelock .44 caliber lipfire revolver belted around my waist along with a Bowie knife made by Grand-

father and a Henry rifle I leaned against the wall behind my chair.
The bartender held up a whiskey glass and a beer glass. I motioned
towards the latter and he filled it and handed it to a young lady to
bring to my table. She hesitated long enough to ascertain I wasn't
interested in anything else, then discreetly returned to the bar, giving
a slight shake of her head to the bartender.

The door opened and closed behind a tall, black-haired, black-
eyed man with olive skin. He stood for a second, letting his eyes
adjust to the cool and dark interior. He wore a fine broadcloth suit
and a stiff-brimmed Stetson that he removed and smoothed his hair
with the palm of his hand. A quick smile flashed over his lips as he
called out a name and waved to a man I didn't know, then he moved
easily across the room to the bar, stopping to visit briefly with other
men along the way. I could tell he was popular with the regulars, all
wearing dark suits and ties. Only one other man in the room was
dressed like I in dusty clothes and scuffed boots. He, too, carried a
pistol at his belt while the others, if they were armed, had them
tucked beneath their coats. His eyes glittered like a lizard's as he
watched the olive-skinned man cross the room. I touched my pistol
uneasily, surreptitiously removing the hammer thong and easing the
pistol in its holster.

"A needled beer, please, Dave," the man said. He gave the range
rider a quick look, then dismissed him and leaned an elbow comfortably on the bar

"Barkeep! Since when are niggers served with white folk?" the
range rider asked waspishly. His voice was loud and carried the room.
Heads turned quizzically towards the bar. The olive-skinned man
swiveled his head to stare at the speaker.

"My bar. I choose who drinks and who doesn't," the bartender
said. He slid a glass in front of the olive-skinned man.

"You ain't drinking that here, boy," the range rider said roughly.
He took a small step away from the bar and rested his hand upon
his pistol.

"Mister," the bartender began, then fell silent as the range rider
gave him a hard look. He moved away from the bar and began to
sidle down to the far end away from the conflict.

"What's your name, nigger?" the range rider said.

"Cuny. Norris Wright Cuny," the olive-skinned man replied. He
stared unflinchingly into the range rider's eyes. "And I'm not
armed."

"Just like a nigger to claim that," the other said. "But I'm willing to bet you got a razor or something tucked away somewheres. I reckon that's good enough for me."

I sighed and rose, and crossed over to the pair. "Drink up and leave," I said quietly to the range rider.

His eyes fell down to my chest, saw my Ranger badge, then shook his head and turned slightly, putting his right hand and revolver out of sight.

"Don't think so," he said stoutly. His shoulder moved slightly and I drew my pistol and laid the heavy barrel across his head. He crumbled to the floor without a sound. I bent and took his pistol, a Colt M1860 .44, from his holster and tucked it through my belt. I ran my hand over his body, feeling for other weapons and finding none, straightened and motioned for the bartender.

"Better fetch the sheriff," I said. "We'll lock this boy up till he sobers then set him outside of town."

"Thanks, mister," he said, a bit shaken by the experience. "We don't have much play like that in here. That's usually down towards the docks a ways or over at Galveston. Folks around here live and let live. Especially," he added, flicking a look at the olive-skinned man watching quietly from near my elbow, "since the War, you know."

"I can imagine," I murmured. I nodded at the man and returned to my table.

"What about his pistol?" the bartender called.

I shrugged. "Tell him you don't know what happened to it."

"You gonna keep it?"

"You want him coming back here and shooting up the place when he gets out of jail?" I asked.

"No, no," the bartender said, holding up his hands. "No, you keep it. You earned it. I guess," he amended, frowning slightly. He motioned to a burly young man with a heavy, sloping forehead. "Jimmy, you take this man over to the sheriff's office and tell him to lock him up for being drunk and disorderly."

The young man bent and easily picked up the range rider, slinging him over his shoulder and carrying him from the tavern. I sighed and slipped my hat from my head and ran my fingers through my hair. I hadn't planned on getting involved in local law enforcement, but it's easier to deal with a problem before it becomes a problem than after.

"Thank you," a voice said. I turned my head and looked up at the man called Cuny. "I do believe that man might have killed me."

"Yes, I think he would have," I replied. "He was just drunk enough to be dangerous. Some men are like that. Small men, usually, who need a bit of liquoring to remember that God didn't make them giants."

"May I buy you a drink?" he asked.

I shook my head. "No, one will do me. But you may join me if you wish." He pulled out a chair and sat.

"I'm Norris Wright Cuny," he said, stretching out his hand. I took it, surprised that it was dry and strong despite his recent close call.

"I heard," I said. "I'm also struck by its strangeness."

"Pardon?" He frowned in confusion.

"That you bear the name of two mortal enemies," I said. He laughed easily and sipped his drink.

"You know, you're the first one who made that connection," he said. "Most people know about the Sandbar Incident, but few remember the names of the participants. Yes, I suppose it's strange. Even stranger when you realize that Philip Cuny was my father and Sam my uncle. But how did you know about the Sandbar participants? That was a long time ago. Fifty years or more."

"My father was a friend of Jim Bowie," I said. "Fact is, he rode a bit with Bowie when he was younger. My grandfather even claimed to have made a knife or two for Bowie, but you know old folks and their tales."

"Yes," he said, nodding in agreement. "I'm well aware of that, as you can imagine."

"Pardon my nosiness, but why would your father name you after an enemy such as Major Wright?"

He shook his head, his lips curling in amusement. "Do you know why that incident came about?"

I shook my head. "I was told it was over the honor of Mary Wells."

"That was the excuse," he said. "But the real reason was that the Cunys, the Wellses, and the Bowies were all Whigs. Major Wright and Colonel Crain's group, rabid Jacksonians all, beat them in the election. My father thought at the time that naming me after Norris Wright might settle the bad blood between the two parties. It didn't.

"I never really knew why they used Mary Wells as an excuse," he said, leaning forward over the table and clasping his hands together. "Nobody really said what it was that Maddox said about her. But Maddox had few scruples, according to what others have told me. He thought nothing of dragging reputations through the mud if it got him a point or two at the polls. Colonel Crain was almost as bad." He paused to sip his drink. "You see, Wright wanted Louisiana to grow into statehood—a plan, incidentally, of Jackson as well for that would give the U.S. a strong reason to support expansion. But Wright saw it as a way to increase his fortune. With money, he had power, the type of power that the Masons had."

"I've heard that Bowie was a Mason," I enjoined.

He nodded. "They all were. Men learned quickly that membership in the Lodge would give them the leg up they needed to personal wealth. Now, I'm not certain, but I believe that Bowie and his group managed to keep Wright if not out of the Masons at least out of the offices they needed to consolidate their hold on the power base at the time. There was also a bit of scandal going around at the time that Wright and the Maddoxes had an 'understanding' with John Murrell—you know about him, I suppose?"

I nodded. Everyone knew about John Murrell, one of the bloodiest men who roamed the Natchez Trace and almost succeeded in seizing control of Louisiana.

"I heard stories about Murrell and his Mystic Clan. They almost managed to seize control of the South."

"Yes," he said soberly. "Few people realize how close that was. And, if you remember what I just told you, Major Wright and the Maddoxes wanted Louisiana to grow. Murrell's plan was to seize control of New Orleans and, well, you can see where some people would jump to conclusions about the Maddoxes and Murrell."

"If something wasn't already there, then I can see how that rumor would be effective," I said.

He smiled faintly. "Yes. There is that. But Jim Bowie had applied for a loan through a bank controlled by Major Wright. In reality, there was no reason for the loan to have been disapproved, as Bowie and his brothers had more than enough land for security, but Bowie wanted the loan to buy more land around Rapides Parish. That would have given him control of a very large part of Louisiana. Wright knew that and turned down the loan.

"The Bowies, however, counting on getting that loan, had made sizeable commitments to purchase land. They were stretched pretty thin and had to scramble to meet their obligations. They couldn't meet them all and lost some of the land upon which they had taken options. Wright quickly snapped up those options, isolating Bowie and his people from further expansion in Louisiana."

"That makes sense," I acknowledged. "People have done stranger things in the name of politics."

He hesitated, his eyes flickering towards the door, then back. I could tell he had more that he wanted to tell me, but I also knew better than to push him for it. People have to make their own minds up about certain things before opening up what is really on their minds. At last, he sighed and leaned back in his chair.

"I imagine you can tell that I'm . . . colored," he said, a bitter smile touching his lips. I nodded and sipped my beer, letting him sort out his words in his own time. "For a while, I was involved in the Reconstruction." He shrugged. "That's not so unusual, but it has made me a lot of enemies. I believe that man was hired by some of them to . . . get rid of me. I know this sounds very melodramatic, but I can't think of any other reason for him to be here at this precise time . . ."

"Still a bit of a coincidence, wouldn't you say?" I murmured.

He laughed. "Perhaps I am making too much of the affair. But, if you live the life of a colored man—"

"We all have our prejudices," I said, interrupting him. "That doesn't make prejudice better coming from one man's mouth or another's."

"Yes, but you see, that is part of the answer to your question as well," he said quietly.

I perked up and drained my beer. I signaled to the bartender and held up my glass. Cuny smiled and shook his head.

"I thought you said one was enough," he said.

"I think, under the circumstances, another wouldn't be out of place," I answered.

"Good. Then I'll buy." He held up two fingers and pointed to himself. He finished his drink and sighed and leaned back again in his chair.

"My grandmother on my mother's side was a slave on a neighbor's plantation," he said after our drinks had been brought to our table. "My mother lived her life as a slave even though she gave my father eight children. But," he continued, "I hold nothing against my father for all of that. He freed every one of us and made certain that each of us received an education, even though that was not popular at the time. In fact, it was very dangerous, for some of the Southern states had laws against educating Negroes, you know."

"I see," I said slowly. "At least, I think I do."

"I'm not sure that you do," he answered. "But that is where the problem began. Even though Major Wright blocked the Bowies' loan and kept them from extending their influence beyond Rapides Parish, they were still a force to contend with due to their influence in the Masons. Now, Wright also had his eye upon Mary Wells and when she rebuffed him, Maddox decided to voice it around that she was sleeping with a black man from the plantation. The Wellses had a huge colored man who fought in a few sporting contests which had become more popular than cockfights at the time." A trace of bitterness touched his voice. "That man was my second cousin, Samuel Thomas Cuny. He was very good with his fists. Too good. He killed one of Major Wright's Negroes in a fight. That cost Major Wright a lot of money. He tried to regain it in a horse race against Jim Bowie, but Bowie had a horse that couldn't be beaten. Wright lost even more.

"It was then that Maddox told his lie and two men died because of it."

"And a legend was born," I said.

"Yes," he answered. "And a legend was born."

We sat until twilight, visiting about the ways and means of the day. I returned to my room and took up my pen to make a record of the day's (and night's) occurrences before I forgot them. But as I finish these words with June bugs knocking against the lantern shade, I wonder if Cuny told me the entire truth. His relation of the events seems to be a bit skimpy for the affair at Vindalia [sic] Sandbar. Indeed, I wonder if Maddox told the truth and not a lie. A white woman sleeping with a black man in those times would have been ruined and the black man boiled alive in a large kettle. Even the double standard of today's times that allows a white man to sleep with a black woman does not allow the same privilege for a white woman. This, I am certain, Cuny knows as he must also know that being the son of a male slaveowner is currently politically in vogue. But to be the son of a black man and white woman or even the grandson of such a union would be socially unacceptable.

I believe somewhere in the middle the truth lies. And, I think Jim Bowie, through his love of Mary Wells, made certain that the scandal died that day on Vindalia [sic] Sandbar along with Major Wright.

JAMES BLACK

James Black had a life filled with adversity. He rose to prominence, then fell into virtual obscurity. He had property, but died penniless, living through the charity of the doctor who took care of him.

He was born in Hackensack, New Jersey, in 1800. In 1804, his mother died and his father remarried. In 1808, he ran away from home, was caught in Philadelphia and apprenticed out since he refused to say where he came from.

He learned to work silver, then left Philadelphia and did odd jobs and blacksmith work. He went to work for a blacksmith named Shaw in Washington, Arkansas. Shaw and his sons did actual smithing, Black fixed guns and made knives. Eventually, he became a partner in the business.

Black fell in love with the blacksmith's daughter, Anne, and relations between the partners became strained. Black tried a new business, failed, and went back to work for his father-in-law, started a new business, and eventually failed at that when he went blind.

He spent his last years living with the doctor who tried to cure his blindness. He died in 1872.

James Black charged dearly for his knives, from fifty to one hundred dollars each. Black would sell a knife only if it passed his hickory test. Black would take a new knife and whittle a seasoned piece of hickory for one hour. If at the end of the hour he could still shave the hair off his arm, the knife was sold. Otherwise, it was discarded.—A. J. S.

Dear Mr. Sowell,

You have heard that I was the inventor of the Bowie knife. This is true. In December of 1830, James Bowie came into my shop in Washington, Arkansas. Mr. Bowie rode up to my shop. He was dressed as a gentleman in gray and black and rode a great black horse. I was standing at the front, getting some air, as he rode up.

"Sir," he says, "are you the cutler, Black?"

I assured him that I was, and he introduced himself as Jim Bowie of Louisiana, Arkansas, and Texas. He asked me if I would make a special knife for him.

Mr. Bowie then withdrew a huge knife from the leather sheath at his side. He said he wanted the knife polished, and an ivory silver handle. He also ordered a new sheath also silver-mounted.

"This knife saved my life and I think it needs to be set apart, somehow."

I had heard something about his big duel over Natchez way and thought that this must have been the knife used in that famous fight. I studied it, Mr. Bowie's formidable size, and his hands, since I had heard of him as a noted Bravo and knife fighter I knew what I needed to do.

He then chose another knife so as to have it handy while I fashioned the hilt and polished the blade to a mirror shine. I spent days on this work, but even as I worked I thought and planned, and created. I knew I could improve on the design.

My method of making steel was a secret that I still keep. Before I die, I plan to give that secret to my benefactors.

The work was extremely hard and time consuming, but I made a twin of the knife that Bowie carried. I also made one that was better.

The knife I made was fourteen inches in length and the blade was wedge-shaped in cross-section thus giving it weight for slashing or chopping. It was an inch and one-half wide. I placed a brass backstrap on it for catching the blades of others, and an S-shaped brass crossguard.

The curve of the blade to the point was not symmetrical, but went to a point that was perfectly centered. The ivory hilt was fastened to the crossguard by a brass ferrule. The full tang was weighted so that it balanced for throwing. The blade would make two revolutions in thirty feet.

The knife was a thing of beauty, but in Jim Bowie's hands, it was the greatest weapon of the frontier. When Bowie arrived at my shop, I showed him the first, and he was well satisfied. I had targets available for practice behind my shop and we retired there so that he could throw his new weapon.

He flipped the blade up and threw it. It was such a beautiful motion that there seemed to be no force in it, but the blade went three inches deep into a chunk of pine I had hanging up between uprights.

"I am very satisfied," Bowie said as we walked to remove the knife from the target.

This knife, though, was only a butcher's knife, well balanced with a beautiful hilt, but it was nothing to the ebony-handled knife I showed him next, the one I described earlier in this letter.

I had made a leather sheath from bull's hide and then had the leather polished until it shone.

Bowie was stunned. He took the knife from the sheath and studied it. His eyes glowed. I pointed at the hilt.

"Look at the initials, JB, cast in the hilt. I thought you might like this one a bit better," I said.

He turned and threw the knife at a target. The knife buried half its length through the pine and I couldn't help shuddering as I thought what would have happened had that been a man.

I charged him one hundred dollars for the two knives. Bowie showed his knife to his friends and many of them came to my shop for one like his. Many others tried to make similar knives, but none could. Not even the Sheffield Company in England.

Respectively yours,
James R. Black [RUBRIC]

GOVERNOR DAN W. JONES

The Jones family cared for Black after his blindness. Black was absolutely destitute, had no way of providing a living for himself and had no family to fall back upon for his care. He kept the secret of his process to himself, fearing that if he let that out, then he would have nothing with which to bargain for his room and board. The day finally came when he decided to release his wonderful process of making metal. Arkansas governor Jones remembers that day.—A. J. S.

Dear Mr. Sowell:

Yes, I do indeed remember James Black, a smith from Washington, Arkansas, and am quite aware of the wonderful story in regards to Mr. Black having made the first Bowie knife.

About 1831, James Bowie came to Washington, Arkansas (to visit his brother John), and gave James Black, a smith, an

order for a knife, furnishing a pattern, and desiring it to be
made in sixty or ninety days, at the end of which time he would
call for it. Black made the knife according to Bowie's pattern,
but since he had never made one that suited his own taste in
point of shape, he concluded this would be a good opportunity
to do so. Consequently, after completing the knife ordered by
Bowie, he made another; and when Bowie returned he showed
both knives to him, giving him his choice at the same price.
Bowie promptly selected Black's pattern.

Shortly after this, Bowie became involved in a difficulty
with three desperadoes who assaulted him with knives. He
killed them all with the weapon Black had made; and after this
when anyone ordered a knife from Black, he ordered it made
"like Bowie's"; and still later, "Make me a Bowie knife." Thus,
the famous weapon acquired its name. Other men made knives
in those days, but no one has ever made *the* Bowie except
James Black. Its chiefest value was in its temper, for Black
undoubtedly possessed the Damascus secret. It came to him
mysteriously and it died with him the same way.

Time and again when I was a boy, he said to me that notwithstanding his great misfortune, God had blessed him in a
rare manner by giving him such a good home, and that he
would repay it all by disclosing to me his secret of tempering
steel when I should arrive at maturity and be able to utilize it
to my advantage.

On the first day of May, 1870, his seventieth birthday, he
said to me that he was getting old and could not in the ordinary course of nature expect to live a great while longer; that
I was now thirty years old with a wife and growing family, and
sufficiently acquainted with affairs of the world to utilize properly the secret which he had so often promised to give me;
and that, if I would get pen, ink and paper, he would communicate it to me and I could write it down.

I brought the writing material and told him I was ready.
He said, "In the first place"—and then stopped suddenly and
commenced rubbing his brow with the fingers of his right
hand. He continued this for some minutes, and then said, "Go
away and come back again in an hour."

I went out of the room, but remained where I could see
him, and not for one moment did he take his fingers from his

brow or change his position. At the expiration of the hour I went into the room and spoke to him. Without changing his position he said, "Go out again and come back in another hour." I went out and watched for another hour, his conduct remaining the same.

When I came in again and spoke to him at the expiration of the third hour, he burst into a flood of tears and said:

"My God, my God, it has all gone from me! All these years I have accepted the kindness of these good people in the belief that I could repay it all with this legacy, and now when I attempt to do it, I cannot. Daniel, there were ten or twelve processes through which I put the knives, but I cannot remember one of them. When I told you to get pen, ink, and paper, they were all fresh in my mind, but they are all gone now. I have put it off too long!"

For a little more than two years he lived on, but he was ever an imbecile after that.

I hope that this does help you in trying to discover a profile of James Bowie. I never met the man, but feel that I have through the story told above by Mr. Black so many times during the years that he spent with us. I regret that I cannot give you a more complete look at Mr. Bowie. Far too often we are forced to draw conclusions about a man and his character from stories that we learn from those who claim they did know him. Unfortunately, such a claim cannot be made by me.
Respectfully,
Daniel W. Jones [RUBRIC]

NOAH SMITHWICK

Noah Smithwick left Kentucky for Texas in 1827. Over the next thirty-three years, he worked to make the state a better place. He was a blacksmith and armorer, soldier, Indian fighter, and Texas Ranger. One of the many things he did was to make a large number of Bowie knives at his forge.—A. J. S.

In answer to your question, Jack, I did make some original Bowie knives. I made them every time I set up a forge, but the way this came about was this:

I had known Jim Bowie since around 1828, not long after we first came to Texas. In 1890, I had a forge set up in San Antonio de Bexar, which most of us called Bear, at the time.

In 1830, Jim Bowie brought me a fine blade to copy. The blade was about ten inches and maybe two inches thick. It was the one he used in the famous fight on the Sandbar. He had it refitted with ivory handles and the blade highly polished. There was even a new sheath made for it that was silver-mounted.

He asked me to duplicate his knife. It was plain that he wanted a good camp knife, and this blade would have a variety of heavy uses around the camp, and of course, as a weapon it had proved itself well in Bowie's hands.

I made the knife and gave it to him. Since people knew that I had made an original Bowie knife for Jim Bowie, using his as the model, they flocked to my forge. Depending on finish, I was able to sell them for five to twenty dollars each.

I met Bowie many times before his death at the Alamo. Though I never met his wife, I heard much about her, and after her death, I saw him reduced to tears.

I have heard much, over the years, about Jim Bowie, both good and bad, but one thing I will say is that Jim Bowie was a faithful friend. Whatever faults Jim Bowie had, abandoning a friend was not one of them.

A story made its rounds in San Antonio that Bowie got into a fight. A friend of his watched the whole thing. When the fight was over, Bowie asked his friend why he didn't help him. The friend said, "Jim, you were in the wrong."

"I know it," Jim said. "If I'd been right, I wouldn't have needed you."

When he died, we lost a wonderful man.

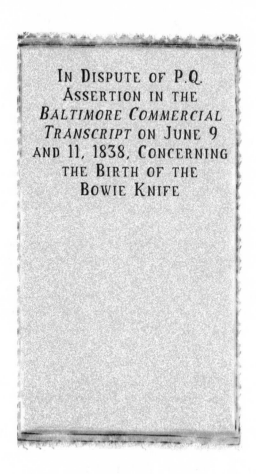

IN DISPUTE OF P.Q.
ASSERTION IN THE
*BALTIMORE COMMERCIAL
TRANSCRIPT* ON JUNE 9
AND 11, 1838, CONCERNING
THE BIRTH OF THE
BOWIE KNIFE

The Planters' Advocate, *August 24, 1838*

The first Bowie knife was made by myself in the parish of Avoyelles, in this state, as a hunting knife, for which purpose, exclusively, it was used for many years. The length of the knife was nine and one-quarter inches, its width one and a half inches, single edge and blade not curved; so the "Correspondent" is as incorrect in his description as in his account of the original of the "Bowie-Knife." The Baltimore correspondent must have been greatly misinformed respecting the manner in which Col. James Bowie first became possessed of this knife, or he must possess a very fertile imagination. The whole of his statement on this point is false.

The following are the facts:

Col. James Bowie had been shot by an individual with

Lucy Leigh Bowie

One day while Rezin was thrusting his knife into a ferocious bull, the animal lunged in such a way as to draw the blade through his hand, making a very severe wound. It was after he had his hand dressed that Rezin called for his plantation blacksmith, Jesse Clift. With a pencil, he traced on paper a blade some ten inches long and two inches broad at its widest part, the handle to be strong and well protected from the blade by guards. He then gave Clift a large file of the best quality steel and instructed him to make a knife out of it. The knife was very serviceable in hunting, and Rezin prized it so highly he kept it locked in his desk when he was not wearing it.

whom he was at variance; and as I presumed that a second attempt would be made by the same person to take his life, I gave him the knife to be used as occasion might require, as a defensive weapon. Some time afterwards (and the only time the knife was ever used for any purpose other than that for which it was intended, or originally destined) it was resorted to by Col. James Bowie in a chance medley, or rough fight, between himself and certain other individuals with whom he was then inimical, and the knife was then used only as a defensive weapon—and not till he had been shot down; it was then the means of saving his life. The improvement in its fabrication, and the state of perfection which it has since acquired from experienced cutlers, was not brought about through my agency. I would here assert also, that neither Col. James Bowie nor myself at any period in our lives, ever had a duel with any person soever.

Rezin Bowie

Iberville, Louisiana

JOHN LATTIMORE

John Lattimore was the son of Dr. William Lattimore, a respected planter who lived below Natchez. He had a large plantation with hundreds of slaves and represented his district as a territorial delegate in Congress from Mississippi.—**A. J. S.**

Know Mr. Bowie? I should smile! He saved my hide when Bloody Jack Sturdivant fleeced me down in Natchez back in '29. My, my. I haven't thought of that in years. Not in years. I kept it from Daddy for years, thinking that he never knew how stupid his boy had been when he sent me to Natchez to sell our cotton crop that year. 'Twas the year he died that Daddy told me he had heard all about it from Sam Wells. He never brought it up to me because he figured I'd learned my lesson and I did return with the money from the crop and all and that was all that counted. He did send Mr. Bowie an emerald stickpin as a way of saying thanks when Mr. Bowie was recovering from wounds in one of our cabins along the Trace, following his canebrake fight. But I'm getting ahead of myself. Things like that happen to old men and it's been nigh on seventy years or so since that happened and my memory's like a rusted bucket full of tiny holes: little things slip away now and then.

But I do remember that day. Yessir. August 13, it was. I remember everything about it. Hot. Hotter than usual for that time of year and so muggy that sweat just puddled around your trouser line and the niggers took to holding up in the shade of the warehouses down on the wharf every chance they got and no overseer said much to them about it. That kind of heat where you just gasp for every breath, thick and heavy.

I got a good price for our cotton—a little over ten thousand dollars: we had a *good* crop that year; lost none to weevils—and was heading back up the bluff after tucking the money into a money belt I had on beneath my shirt. Josiah, my slave, stayed close by my left shoulder. Those were bad days, then, bad days. Natchez-Under-the-Hill—we called it "Natchez-Under"—stood on a kind of shelf out from this bluff. Above it, the respectable people lived, although I wonder just how respectable those folks were: most of them owned a tavern or brothel on the flats under the hill.

Yet, Natchez-Under had an appeal for a reckless youth and I was no different from others who visited that place. My, my. I remember some good times down there what with Madame Aivoges and her emerald green eyes and red hair as bright as a flame that made a man feel all warm and weak inside. And Annie Christmas—stood six-foot in her lace net stocking feet. A big woman, full of love for the keelboaters who came down the river and boys like me in off the plantation, cocky as hell with spurs aching to be sharpened.

A lot of medleys were played down there between keelboaters and planters' sons. Those keelboaters were tough ones, quick with a knife. And there wasn't any quicker than Bloody Jack Sturdivant. Or meaner, for that fact. Rumor had it that he did a little counterfeiting upriver around Illinois someplace in a place called Cave-in-Rock. It wasn't so much a cave as caves go, but it was enough. A lot of men are buried up there in the woods and limestone pits around that cave. John A. Murrell and Sturdivant stayed there a time or two. Some say Murrell, one of Sturdivant's confederates who passed that bogus money around, was the bad one and he was bad enough, but that

Bloody Jack, well, he'd just as life carve on you like a Christmas goose as give you the time of day. And of course, that was what drew the young people to him, willing sheep for fleecing. He got away with a lot, too, as he was good friends with Col. Robert Crain, Judge Crain, he was then: crooked as a cheap cigar.

One of Sturdivant's runners saw that cash change hands in the Cotton House. I didn't know he was a runner at the time—just thought he was a friendly sort who was out for a good time, like me, before heading back up the Trace before dark. Nobody rode that Trace after dark unless they were trouble or looking for it. We called it the Devil's Backbone. It ran from Natchez upriver clear to Nashville. An evil road, thick laced with wild grapevines and trees festooned with Spanish moss. Where it cut through the canebrakes the cane stood ten, maybe twelve foot high and so thick you couldn't see nothing but the trail in front of you. Worst place was at the Devil's Punchbowl: a depression four or five hundred feet wide and so thickly grown that you could barely see your hand before your face. Something strange about that place, too. A compass never worked in it. Just sort of spun around in circles. A lot of people disappear there. Swallowed up.

I felt a tap on my shoulder about a block after leaving the wharf and heard Josiah tell someone to back away. I looked around and saw this thin, sallow-faced man about my age dressed in a bottle-green coat glaring up at Josiah's shiny black face.

"You givin' me orders, nigger?" he said, kind of arrogant like. Black-haired and black-eyed he was. "I don't care whose nigger you are, you try those uppity ways with me and I'll have you arrested."

"Not gettin' uppity, suh," Josiah said. But he stood his ground. "Yo' just keeps yo' distance from young Massuh less'n he says diffrnt."

"That's all right, Josiah," I said, stepping between them. "I apologize, sir. Josiah was just doing what he was told."

"No offense, then," he said, smiling. Like a shark, I know, now. But then, he seemed friendly enough. "I was just wondering if you could direct me to a place called the Christmas House? It comes highly recommended."

"Of course," I said, laughing. "But it's only noon. It won't open until five or six."

His face fell at that and he shook his head, sighing. "Well, I guess I'll just have to give it a miss. I sort of thought that it would be a

way to kill a little time before I head back home. I'm Phillipe Cabanal, by the way."

"John Lattimore," I answered, taking his hand, clammy and limp
like an old dishtowel. "Perhaps I can buy you a drink?"

And that was the mistake I made. Good runners like the kind
Sturdivant used had a way about them that made you take charge of
the evening affairs. Handy trait it was, too, for if you went to the
sheriff after getting fleeced, why they could always say it was your
fault.

Josiah tried to keep me from going, but I told him to wait outside
for me while I went into Sturdivant's place. We started drinking
Sugar Tits—dark, Barbadoes rum steeped in raw cane sugar. I don't
know how many drinks we had together or even who suggested a
game of cards, but suddenly I was sitting at a table in that smoke-
filled, evilly-run place and across from me was Bloody Jack himself.
He didn't look like the villain I had heard so many stories about.
Broad-shouldered, he was, with thick, black hair carefully oiled and
combed down, and eyes as black as an abyss. He dressed neatly, with
an old-fashioned, long linen scarf around his neck in place of a tie
or cravat and a long, black Bolivar coat. Oh, he was fancy, make no
mistake about that. Just the sort of man who would appeal to a young
rooster.

It didn't take long before I had run through all the money I had
with me. The next thing I remember, someone threw me out the
door of the tavern. Josiah helped me up from the mud and brushed
me clean while I leaned drunkenly against the building.

"Keep your mouth shut and go home!" someone ordered—I
think it was Cabanal, but I can't be sure anymore. "Else you'll be
floating down the river to that fancy plantation of yours!"

Well, I started to sober up from all those Sugar Tits real quick
when I realized what had happened. Josiah didn't say anything to
me, but I could see the disappointment in his eyes and the way his
lips sort of turned down at the corners.

He helped me stagger up the bluff. Fog had settled in pretty thick,
so I jumped out of my skin when someone gripped my elbow and
said, "John Lattimore! Doctor Will Lattimore's boy! You've shot up
some since I saw you, and I guess you can't blame me for not knowing you with all that mud on your face! What happened to you?"

I tried to jerk away, but he had a grip that made me yelp. Then,
I heard Josiah call him "Mastuh Bowie" and I knew him. I suppose

I should have known him anyway, had it not been so foggy. Not many men were as tall as him—well over six foot—and he had this red-gold hair that seemed to shine in the dark.

I told him what had happened. I'm afraid I got a lump in my throat and had to turn away to keep from crying when I realized that I had betrayed Daddy's trust. Jim stood silent for a long minute, then sighed and gave a queer sort of laugh.

"Come on," he said. "Show me where this happened." His voice was soft and, well, musical, I guess. He always seemed to sing his words more than say them. Until he got mad, that is, then his voice sort of tightened up. You remember when you were a kid and dragged your fingernails over a slate board in school? Like that. Made your flesh goosepimple.

I didn't want to take him back to Sturdivant's place—I guess he had three of them, now that I think about it—but Josiah spoke pretty sharply to me: "Mastuh John, yo' better do like Mistuh Jim tells yo'. Yo' made 'nough fool outta yo'self an' now yo' taks what 'elp yo' kin git."

I really didn't like a nigger talking to me like that, but Josiah had been with me a long time. Daddy had kind of assigned him to me when I was young and he had wiped my nose and dragged me out of more than one scrape while I was making a fool out of myself growing up. I knew if I sassed him and Daddy heard about it, well, I would have a tongue-lashing from Daddy that would make a horsewhip feel comfortable.

"All right," I said, kind of surly like. "Come on. I don't relish this one damn bit, though."

We stumbled back down that bluff. Leastways, I stumbled while Josiah and Mr. Bowie kept me from falling on my face in the mud and making a bigger fool of myself. At last, we came to the tavern—I think it was called Grady's Tavern although Sturdivant owned it—and I hesitated before the door.

"What's wrong?" Mr. Bowie asked.

"They said they would kill me if I came back," I said.

"Do you want to walk away from this?" Mr. Bowie asked. "Your choice. We can leave, now. Or, we can go back in and try to recover your money."

"How?" I said hotly. "I don't have a damn penny left."

"I'll stake you," he said, and grinned, his smile reckless. "What do you say? You were game enough to enter once before tonight.

You stick with me, boy, and we'll get your money back. I know any game in Sturdivant's dens is crooked, and I've handled his kind before. Come on! Want to try it again?"

"Why not?" I said, suddenly remembering how I was manhandled out of the tavern.

"Good lad," he laughed, and threw open the door and walked in. He had to bow his head a bit beneath the low doorframe. The room was as thick with cigar smoke as the fog outside. Voices trailed off at our entrance. I noticed Mother Slappert's girls, who had been hanging about, trying to pick up tricks, were gone.

"I told you not to come back, boy," a tough said. He straightened from where he lounged against the wall and swaggered over to us. "Now, you gonna leave, or do I feed your guts to the catfish?"

"He's with me," Mr. Bowie said.

"And who might you be?" the tough said. "His mammy?"

A low laugh tittered around from those near us. One man, however, rose, leaving his drink on the table, and started for the door.

"Where you going?" someone called.

"Out of here," he said. He nodded at us. "Good night, Mr. Bowie," he said.

Mr. Bowie nodded, and the man left, closing the door behind him. The tough straightened, but he still had to look up at Mr. Bowie.

"Jim Bowie?" he asked. Mr. Bowie nodded. "I've heard about you."

"That puts you up on me," Mr. Bowie said. "I've never heard about you."

Laughter sprung up around us and someone grabbed the tough by the arm and pulled him away. "Come on, Bojee," someone said. "Sit down and shut up before you get yourself in real trouble."

"Which table were you at?" Mr. Bowie asked me. I pointed and he nodded and crossed over to it. I followed along beside him, conscious of the eyes upon us and promising the good Lord that if he'd only help me get out of there alive I'd never go under the bluff again.

We stopped in front of the table and Sturdivant looked up at me, smiling. "Back so soon?" he asked. Then, his eyes flickered over to Mr. Bowie and the smile sort of froze on his face. "Evening, Jim. Been a while since you've been down here."

"Don't have much call to do so, Jack," Mr. Bowie said.

"You after another horse?" Sturdivant said. Mr. Bowie had

bought this racehorse from him—Steel Duke, or something like that—and raced it against Major Norris Wright's Kerry Dancer . . . no, I lie: Kerry Isle. A lot of problems came out of that.

"No," Mr. Bowie said calmly. "I'm just seeing how the other half lives."

"And what might that other half be, Jim?" Sturdivant said.

Mr. Bowie shrugged. "People like you, Jack," he said.

Sturdivant didn't like it, but decided not to push it any further. He looked back at me. "Well? You going to sit in? Table stakes, you remember."

My face began to burn from embarrassment. I started to tell him that I didn't have any money and he damn well knew it when Mr. Bowie quietly pressed a wallet on me.

"Go ahead," he said. "Maybe your luck has changed."

I sat down and played for about twenty minutes or so. My luck hadn't changed; the stack of money slowly dwindled in front of me. At last, Mr. Bowie clasped me on the shoulder, saying: "Lattimore, why don't you let me sit in a while for you. Maybe I can shift Lady Luck in your favor."

Sturdivant leaned back in his chair, staring coolly at him. "I don't believe you were invited, Bowie."

I stood up and Mr. Bowie slid into my chair, smiling across the table at Sturdivant. "Sure I was, Jack. Remember what you said when I bought Steel Duke? You told me to step around any time."

"This isn't that time," Sturdivant said.

"It's any time," Mr. Bowie answered. "Your deal, I believe?" He glanced around at me. "Why don't you get us each a drink? Monongahela and not that black rum. Make sure the bottle's unopened, too."

A low murmur rose at the insinuation. Sturdivant wanted to say more, but changed his mind and riffled the deck, slipping the cards from one hand to the other. He dealt and Mr. Bowie won, and the game continued for about an hour with Mr. Bowie breaking about even at the table. They were playing bluff with jacks and nines wild. Suddenly Mr. Bowie laughed.

"Come on, Jack! Surely you can do better than that!" he said.

"What?" Sturdivant said.

Bowie reached out and pushed some cards away with a forefinger, not turning them up. "Those are the wilds ones: jacks and nines. Or I'm a liar."

It got awfully quiet in the taproom. Sturdivant went pale like swamp mist and leaned away from the table. His hand slipped under his jacket. "You better explain yourself, Bowie," he said.

Bowie flipped over the cards; jacks and nines. "I just did, Jack." He rose and scooped the money up, dropping it into his hat.

"Here, now!" Sturdivant protested. "You can't do that, Bowie. You must be drunk! Put that money back on the table."

"Sturdivant," Bowie said, and his voice sounded like those fingernails coming across a slateboard. "One of your runners brought this boy in a few hours ago to be robbed. Now, Dr. Lattimore is a personal friend of mine, and I won't see his boy robbed. I took enough from the table to repay what he's lost. That's all."

Sturdivant shook his head. Dozens of eyes watched him, glowing redly in that smoke-filled room like rat's eyes. He couldn't let that challenge go and still be Bloody Jack. He'd already killed half-a-dozen men, five with a pistol and one with a dagger, and burned down a couple of homes that belonged to a couple of unlucky ones who ran against Major Wright for sheriff. His reputation was worth more than the money Mr. Bowie had taken. At least, to him it was.

"You can't accuse me of cheating and walk out of here, Bowie," he said. "I can't allow that. I must demand satisfaction."

A small smile lifted Mr. Bowie's lips, but it took a brave man to look into his eyes, which had become dark-gray. "Anything you say, Jack. How?"

Sturdivant took a knife from beneath his Bolivar coat and dropped it onto the table. Mr. Bowie nodded and slipped out of his coat, handing it to me. He took a pistol from a pocket and gave it to me with instructions to shoot anyone who interfered. Then, he drew that knife.

I had heard about that knife and what Mr. Bowie had done with it and maybe it was the stories that made me sick to my stomach. Maybe it was the knife. I turned away, taking deep breaths to calm my lurching gorge. Then, I looked back: it glinted like death. The blade looked discolored, graceful watermarks running its length. The crossguard was of brass with tiny balls at each end and a brass back ran the length of the blade to where it suddenly curved to a point that rose to the middle of the blade. A musky smell like dried blood seemed to rise from it.

"Grady," Sturdivant called. "Draw a circle on the floor. Ten foot?" He looked at Mr. Bowie.

"With left wrists strapped together?" Mr. Bowie said, agreeing.

A shudder ran around the room. Everyone there knew that Bowie had thrown another glove in Sturdivant's face. The gambler nodded and took the linen scarf from his neck and handed it to a dealer who bound their arms together.

"Your call, Jack," Mr. Bowie said. Sturdivant nodded at one of the dealers, who slowly counted to three.

When he cried out the last number, Sturdivant dropped down nearly to the floor on one knee and swept his dagger at Mr. Bowie's belly, but Mr. Bowie jumped back, pulling hard on Sturdivant's arm.

Sturdivant tried to gain his balance, and Mr. Bowie swept in and under his guard, stabbing deeply into Sturdivant's arm. I saw that blade sink into Sturdivant's arm. The flesh turned blue, then I heard the knife grate on bone and the hackles rose on my neck. Sturdivant's dagger fell to the floor as Mr. Bowie pulled the knife out. Blood ran like water. Mr. Bowie cut himself free and took the scarf, wiping the blood from his knife. I still got a piece of that scarf somewheres around here.

"I won't kill you, Jack," Mr. Bowie said quietly. "But remember this: leave my friends alone."

We left after that. Sturdivant sent three toughs after Mr. Bowie a little later along the Trace after he found out that his arm and hand would be worthless for the rest of his life, but Mr. Bowie killed all three.

He accompanied me back up the hill to his lodgings and arranged a room for me and Josiah, telling us that he didn't want us out on the road until morning. He sent my clothes out to be cleaned and ordered a fine meal for us.

When I left the next morning, he gave me all the money I had lost from Daddy's cotton crop along with a note explaining that he had asked me to take dinner with him and time got away from us.

"I suggest that you stay away from Natchez-Under for a while," he said. "That's not a place for gentlemen. Even those looking to have a good time."

I thanked him and rode away. I know Daddy saw through the note, now, but he didn't say anything then except to tell me how lucky I was to have made a friend in Mr. Bowie.

I had a chance to visit with Mr. Bowie off and on again over the next year or two. He was always polite and never mentioned that night again. He didn't have to; I still haven't forgotten the lesson he taught me about trust.

JOHN STURDIVANT

John "Bloody Jack" Sturdivant was a counterfeiter and one of the worst rogues on the Mississippi River. He was a member of the Cave-in-Rock gang, among whom was numbered John Murrell, one of the most murderous bandits along the Natchez Trace. Sturdivant killed two men in pistol duels and one with a knife. In addition, he burnt down four houses for political favors. At the time of his famous duel with Bowie, Sturdivant was the most dangerous man on the river and commanded a gang of about thirty cutthroats who ambushed and killed many men along the Trace, smuggled slaves, and stole cotton shipments, whatever would turn a dime.—A. J. S.

Yes, I remember Bowie. How could I forget that sonofabitch? See this arm? Useless! Useless! He cut the leaders with that damn knife of his! Damn near bled to death until Mother Slappert managed to get it stopped. That damn drunken doctor did a half-ass job sewing it up, too.

Damn him!

Spiteful? Hell, yes! What do you expect? I can't even pick up a coffee cup. And when I walk, the damn thing flaps like a goose wing. You want to try and make love with a goose wing? Or a living? I'm seventy years old now, and I tell you that if Bowie could come back I'd cut his throat for him. I'd wait until he was drunk and asleep, then cut his throat.

I've outlived my time. For a man like me to live past fifty is vulgar, immoral. Those venerable old men, those silver-haired and reverend seniors, have lived a full life, a life of their own choosing. Bowie robbed me of that! Of life! What is life with only mere existence? No thrill, no chase?

I make no apology for the life I led; it was the life I chose. But Bowie . . .

It began with a race horse I won in a card game—not a very good wager, I admit, for a horse like that is of little use to me. I was not born to the purple, nor could I gain it. That was a closed door to me. It was the winter of my discontent and I had been rudely stamped by the circumstances of my birth. Oh, I could strut before a wanton ambling nymph, but only a nymph; other women would wipe their shoes upon me if I chose to stoop and I chose never to stoop.

Oh, I had pretensions—who does not in such circumstances?— but little good they did me. I was the one the gentlemen (and their ladies) came to when they lusted after the shadows of life, the secret life of their dark side. At night, they would come to me, slinking down the bluff to the flat, disguising their actions under their veils of self-indulgence.

You know about the dark side, don't you? It is the mark of an adventurer, of people like Bowie who could move at will in both worlds, hiding their darkness beneath the glimmer of fine dress and manners.

But manners and fine dress did nothing for me.

An accident of birth kept me from their light.

Bowie bought the horse and raced him against Wright. Wright's horse wasn't good enough and that heated the bad blood already between them. Most people think that horse race caused all the problems, but there was more to it than that; Wright had bought mortgages Bowie and his friends had on land grants and was threatening to foreclose on them. But it wasn't business; oh no, not business.

Bowie was having an affair with a woman Wright wanted. And you want to know the funny part about it all? She was the wife of one of his friends. Wright's friend, I mean. I don't remember her name. Judalon somebody. It really doesn't matter. Bowie was the dog in her kennel and Wright was furious about that.

Yes, the Lattimore boy was cheated in my place. But those people who came there knew they were going to be cheated. They expected it and I made sure that they got their money's worth and something to talk about at their *soirées*. Made them look dangerous, you know. It was part of the thrill of coming down the bluff. My man just picked the wrong one to stiff. But who knew that Lattimore was Bowie's friend? I didn't. And when he made that grandiloquent play in my place, why I had no choice but to challenge him. I had to, you see. Otherwise, Bloody Jack Sturdivant would have been ruined on the river. And there were plenty waiting for me to fall.

I gave him warning. "Jim," I said. "You must be drunk. You know that I can't allow something like that to happen. Put that money back on the table."

I had heard about Bowie's eyes—changing from blue to gray like the river surface before a storm—and when he turned those eyes on me, I felt a coldness clear to the soles of my feet. You've never seen the fires of hell, but once you have, why, you never forget them.

"Sturdivant," he said. "One of your blacklegs brought young Lattimore here and your professional thieves robbed him. Now, I know a young lad needs to be taught lessons, but you weren't even subtle!" He pointed at the table. "You didn't even cleanly shave the cards. Now, his father is a personal friend of mine, and I won't see him robbed. I took enough from the table to pay what you owe him."

I could feel the eyes of the crowd upon me. Rat's eyes, waiting to see me fall so they could gnaw at my guts. I shook my head. "No, Jim. That don't make it. You'll have to fight me before I can let you leave with that money."

"Are you sure you want to do that?" he asked softly, so softly that I don't think any of the others heard him. My mouth dried up so suddenly that I didn't trust myself to speak. I just nodded. The rest you know. I hate him for what he left me. No, I hate him for more than that: we were alike, the two of us. Yet, he could move about at will above the bluff while I had to be content with living under the bluff.

And he had friends.

ANNIE CHRISTMAS

Annie Christmas, a prostitute, witnessed the fight with Bloody Jack Sturdivant from the small balcony above the main floor. Here, the girls hired "cribs" or small rooms from Mother Slappert to entertain their customers and the vantage point gave them the opportunity to look over the gambling crowd for the "high-roller" who might be willing to part with a dollar or two for fleshly entertainment. Annie was one of the most popular prostitutes in Natchez-Under during that time. A big woman, nearly six foot in height, she was large-hipped with a wasp waist and what many claimed to be the biggest breasts in the town — a major factor in the advertising of her charms that made her a wealthy woman and eventually madam at her own place. A lot of people thought she always had her own place because wherever she was, men called it the Christmas House. Men flocked to her room of business, intrigued at the thought of making love to the Amazon who could drink most men under the table, and many madams vied for her, offering her inducements to come to their houses in hopes that the spillover from the

demand for Annie's services would help business with other girls they em-
ployed. At the time of Bowie's fight with Bloody Jack Sturdivant, Annie was
almost self-employed, giving a token of her wages only to Mother Slappert,
who was managing that end of Sturdivant's business.—A. J. S.

I had just finished entertaining a couple of "gents" at a "tea party."
The men used to sneak down the bluff when their wives were off at
their tea parties and we'd have ourselves a little ménage à trois, you
know, two gentlemen and a lady. My, how I remember those times!
A lot of the girls didn't like tea parties, but, well, I damn sure didn't
avoid them! That was one time when my blood got to singing and
my juices would pour out of me. Most people thought the tea parties
were for the men who got to craving something different, but I tell
you that a working girl needs something different, too. I remember
Tom and Sid Albert coming to town and making a game out of it,
both of them humping away, trying to outlast the other. Sometimes,
we would get to going so strong that the bed would give way and
we'd be rolling all over that floor, lights glistening off our naked
flesh, sweat rolling, wet nakedness wherever you looked.

Oh. Where was I?

Yes, now I remember. The Alberts were in town, then, and we
had just finished a tea party when I heard loud yells and an unholy
commotion down below in the tavern. I rose and quickly pulled on
a shift to see what was going on. Only other thing I wore was my
stockings that I tied with red ribbons, the knots held by little rosettes.
When men get their juices stirred by a fight, they become very horny
and take to looking to dunk their rod in any quim available. It's a
working girl's dream and if she's quick enough and experienced
enough, she can bring off half-a-dozen cockchafers at double or even
triple price before their blood cools with liberal applications of Monongahela. The cotton and tobacco aristocrats who used to slip down
the hill at night to mingle with the mudsill weren't long on holding
their liquor, and if a girl didn't catch them early in their cups, she'd
spend half the night trying to bring a rod to standing attention. Too
much liquor leaves a man cold as a wagon tire. But a fight, well, that
just served to make men plumb ramstugonous.

I elbowed my way through the other girls lining up by the balcony
railing and plopped my elbows on it and leaned over my forearms,
pushing my titties up as high as they would go, knowing that some

below would be feeling Johnny move already. I spread my legs so they could get a good look at the possibles and looked down with interest at where someone had drawn a large circle in chalk on the tavern floor. Jack Sturdivant stood on one side of the circle while Jim Bowie stood on the other. My interest peaked and I perched right there, slapping a hand away some horny bastard kept trying to slide up my leg above my stockings.

"Ain't no free feeling here!" I snapped absently.

"Bowie called out Bloody Jack!" someone said hoarsely from behind me.

"Like hell!" another answered. "He caught him with trimmed cards and Jack challenged him."

"Big mistake, that," a third chimed in. "I've seen Bowie in action. Over in New Orleans. Killed a man square there."

"About a million people claimed to see that fight," the second answered. "Wisht I had a dollar for each one."

"You calling me a liar?" the third demanded.

"Shut up," I said, without turning around. "I want to see this." They fell quiet.

Grady (I think that was his name—Jack's flunky bartender) tied their arms together with a silk scarf. My interest began to climb. I'd seen a lot of men hacking away at each other, but this was a new twist. A strange excitement began to build in my stomach. Something about men playing their medleys always made my blood hum and my skin jump around with goose pimples. I leaned further over the balcony to catch every moment of the fight.

Actually, it wasn't much of a fight. Jack took a swipe at Jim who just sorta leaned back on his heels away from it. He jerked Jack off balance, then took a little half-step forward and plunged that knife of his deep into Jack's arm and the fight was over. When Jim stuck him with that knife, why, I came twice right there on the balcony. My legs trembled like I had St. Vitus's Dance or something. Oh, my, I remember that. I remember everything about that night.

I saw him leave with that boy he had rescued and I slipped back to my room and threw a cloak on over my shoulders. I stepped into a pair of slippers and hustled down the back stairs and followed them to the trail that led up the bluff back to the respectable people. I watched Jim say his goodbyes and heard him warn that boy to stay away from Sturdivant's places.

The boy left and I stepped out from the shadows to face Jim. I pulled that cloak back so he could see that I had little on beneath. He smiled, his lips sorta curling up at the corners, and this real mischievous light sparkled from his eyes.

"Hello, Annie," he said. "I didn't expect to see you down here."

"Been a while, Jim," I said. We had been together quite often after Cecelia Wells died just a couple of weeks before she and Jim were to be married. He'd come my way one night after he'd had too much to drink up on the bluff and one thing led to the other. For a while, we ran the danger of becoming pretty steady, but that could be only temporary and both of us knew it. Tonight, though, was something different. Maybe it was because I saw him fighting Bloody Jack at a time when I needed someone like Jim.

"How've you been keeping yourself?" he asked.

I tried to draw a deep breath, but my chest ached and I shuddered and gasped. The grin slipped from his face and he stepped forward, putting his arm around my shoulder to steady me. I came again, my cunny running slick and wet. I grabbed hold of the lapels of his coat and hung on like a drowning person to a stick of wood while I shuddered with the waves of desire washing over me, wetting me.

"Damn," I groaned.

"Annie, what's the matter?" he asked anxiously.

I told him and he laughed and held me close. "Well," he whispered, "maybe we should do something about that."

"Hell, yes," I mumbled. I grabbed his hand and ran, half-dragging him behind me, back to my own rooms. I lived as far back away from the water as I could get. A delusion of respectability, I suppose, but I held my business down at a couple of places on the front and kept my private life back under the shadow of the bluff.

I left Jim by the door while I entered and struck a match and lit a lamp on a small table. Suddenly, I felt nervous. I had never had a man back in my private rooms before Jim. I turned to look at him, half-fearful of what I would see. Would he laugh at my pretensions? I wondered.

He stepped into the room and took a long look around. The room felt shabby. He looked at the wallpaper with tiny rose garlands on it, the lamps with the painted shades, the Hepplewhite tables and newer Hitchcock chairs with heart-shaped chair backs stenciled with tiny rose buds—seemed pretentious to me, now. His eyes paused at the Boston rocker, a spindle-backed chair with cyma-curved arms also stenciled with tiny rose buds, I had placed near a window to get light, and on the small marble-topped table stacked with copies of *Niles' Weekly Register* and *Port Folio*. He walked over to it and picked up the book I was reading at the time, looking at the title. His eyebrows rose, and he turned to me in surprise.

"*The Sketch Book of Henry Crayon, Gent.* You surprise me, Annie," he said. He opened the book at where I had placed a lace ribbon for a marker and read aloud:

" 'The nation,' continued he, 'is altered; we have almost lost our simple true-hearted peasantry. They have broken asunder from the higher classes, and seem to think their interests are separate. . . .' "

Waves of red crept slowly up my neck. I felt my cheeks growing hot. "Well?" I demanded defensively.

His blue eyes crinkled and he smiled. "I like that."

"Just because a girl . . ." I fumbled for words, embarrassed that he now knew my secret.

"Nice," he said. A gentle smile spread over his face as he looked at me.

I fell in love.

"It ain't much," I started to say, but he stepped close and put his fingers on my lips, shushing me.

"It's all it needs to be," he said softly.

And he leaned down and kissed me. Gentle, at first, then I found myself tearing his clothes off and he picked me up and carried me into my bedroom and we tumbled onto the bed, hugging and kissing. My skin felt like fire.

Big, he was. Bigger than most men. And patient. Teasing. He wasn't a man looking for a woman; he was a lover.

I don't know how many times we fucked that night. I didn't think I would ever get enough of him. Every way possible. We even invented a few ways or, if we didn't, we sure enough improvised a few that neither of us had tried before. At least, I hadn't. And that was my business.

Except tonight, I pleasured myself.

And he let me.

I remember riding him . . .

Ah! Even now, I feel his arms, the rough, red, curly hair on his chest, his hands caressing my buttocks, my legs above my black net stockings, my nipples getting hard and . . . I've had a lot of wild times with a lot of wild men before but nothing like that last night with Jim.

I still make love to him for in my memory, he is always there. I can feel him, taste him, smell him. Always.

I suppose it is because he was always a gentleman. Even when we met on the street, he would treat me like a lady, tipping his hat and saying, "Good afternoon, Miss Annie." Just like I was somebody.

He gave women what they want: the right to men without the demand of a wedding bed. That is a propriety that is an invention of men to separate their lust from their sense of social standing. A wife makes their lust lawful and others are needed, for that lust must have an outlet to keep the wife as near a virgin as possible, thus keeping her name from being impugned as a dishonorable woman.

What woman wants that?

Believe me when I say that women, too, feel the same lust as men and feel the frailty of the flesh as often as do men. Why, then, are they denied this by a man's sense of what is right and wrong?

Jim never did.

With Jim, a woman felt no shame for desiring him. Rather, it became a religion, a communion, if you will, not only of desire, but the flesh as an altar upon which that desire is sacrificed as many times as one feels the need to be holy.

Jim was my deepest religious experience.

DR. WILLIAM LATTIMORE

Dr. William Lattimore was one of the most respected planters from the country below Natchez. At the time of the Sturdivant incident, he had been a territorial representative in the United States Congress from 1803 to 1807 and again from 1813 to 1817. He had a large country seat. He owned hundreds of slaves and was widely in demand not only for his crops, which seemed to be consistently of the highest quality, but also as a gracious guest in palatial antebellum homes. —A. J. S.

For man's everyday needs, it usually is enough to have the ordinary human consciousness, but when that is in a young man who has responsibility for the first time, sometimes common sense has to stand aside for spirit.

That is what happened in '29 when I sent my son to Natchez with our cotton crop to sell. Normally, I would have gone along, but

politics held me up. I decided to trust young John to deliver the crop
to the Cotton House on the Natchez wharf. I cautioned him about
coming straight back with the money and to watch himself carefully.
Perhaps I overdid my warning for such things are often tantalizing
to young people. When a father tries to protect his son there is a
natural resentment and rebellion, for the son feels that the father is
treating him as a child and not an equal. Foolhardy, perhaps, but a
natural trait.

I knew James Bowie. Knew him well and valued his friendship
greatly for he was an honorable man. We did not move in the same
social circles, and that is as much my fault as his—we simply did not
have the same interests. I did exchange drinks with him on occasion
and ate with him many times when our paths crossed. He came to
my house on several occasions, but there was still a social strain
between us. My friends were not his friends although he could and
did visit with all of them at one time or another. Being in land
speculation as he was, political friends are good to have.

I heard about John's involvement with Sturdivant the day after it
happened when an acquaintance of mine came for lunch. He had
been "sporting" with Annie Christmas in Grady's place when Bowie
walked in with young John. He was a bit surprised when they went
over to the table where Sturdivant and one of his runners were fleecing some keelboaters and began to play. He didn't pay much attention to what happened for a while because he became, ah, somewhat
engrossed with Miss Christmas and they had retired to one of the
rooms upstairs for somewhat of a nocturnal pursuit. Suddenly, he
heard some people shouting angrily and came out to see what was
going on. Bowie and Sturdivant were facing each other in a chalked
circle. The fight didn't take long, but he remembers Bowie refusing
to kill Bloody Jack when he could have, telling the man to leave his
friends alone. Then, he left with young John.

I invited him out to our place for dinner, but he sent his man out
with an apology. That was just before the sandbar incident. He was
sorely wounded there and killed two, maybe three men including
Major Wright. No loss for that one!

Wright was one of the most arrogant and underhanded individuals I have ever known! He was not above trying to use his money
to influence votes or, well, let us just say he was an entirely unscru-
pulous individual.

I remember once in '27, I believe it was, when I was a Congressman, Wright tried to compromise me with a couple of young ladies from Madame Shipley's establishment. He wanted some land that we had set aside for the Creeks to be put into public domain. But I found out that he and his friends had already filed on the land and were holding the titles *in situ*, ready to file as soon as the land was declared open. I told him that under no circumstances would I bring that up for debate on the floor and not only would I not sponsor any bill for stealing that land from the Indians, I would fight any attempt to do so.

He laughed and said that he would be willing to contribute a substantial amount of money to my campaign if I would change my mind. I threw him off my place and told him I would have him horsewhipped if he came anywhere upon my land.

After Bowie killed him, I sent a couple of my men in to watch Bowie discreetly while he recuperated from his wounds. When three of Sturdivant's men ambushed him down along the Trace, I arranged for him to recover in a hunting cabin we had down there and put a guard around the cabin along with a couple of niggers to watch over him until he recovered.

I saw him once again on a riverboat while he was going back to Texas after settling a land claim. He fought a duel there on behalf of a woman. It seems that is really the true story of Bowie: he was always helping someone even to risking his life. Friendship and honor meant a lot to him. We need more men like him. Especially now.

DR. JAMES LONG

Dr. James Long was born in Virginia, but moved at an early age to Tennessee. There he obtained a medical degree and became acquainted with Andrew Jackson. In June 1820, he took a band of seventy-five followers to Nacogdoches and on June 23, 1820, named himself President of the Supreme Council of Texas. Upon his return to Texas, he was captured, taken to Mexico, and never returned, leaving behind a twenty-two-year-old widow and two young children. This is an account of his dealings gathered in a journal he wrote before he left.—A. J. S.

I write this to be left behind as a testimonial in the event I do not return from my journey back into Texas for the purpose of informing those who follow me of my work.

I first met James Bowie in 1817 or '18. I saw him at a fashionable tavern in New Orleans where I had been trying to meet someone who knew Jean Lafitte, the notorious leader of a band of privateers and freebooters who lived near Galves Town in the Republic of Texas.

Bowie was pointed out to me. Little did I know how important he would become to me over these last three years. I remember being struck by his appearance. He seemed to be about my age, in his mid-twenties (although I later discovered that he was only twenty), large, a strongly built man with almost red hair and deeply set gray eyes. He was tanned like an outdoorsman and moved with an economy of motion that bespoke tremendous natural coordination. When I questioned my companion about him, he told me that Bowie was a gentleman with a reputation for having been in some chance medleys. At the time, he was smuggling slaves into the United States from Texas. I became immediately interested in him since slavery was unlawful in Texas, but perfectly legal in Louisiana, though the slaves could not be imported. Mr. Bowie was taking illegal goods from one country and illegally crossing a border with these illegal goods. Sort of thumbing his nose at the law, so to speak. Once in Louisiana, however, the goods again became legal and the people flocked to buy them.

At my suggestion, my companion invited Mr. Bowie to our table. I had thought I would be meeting a crude ruffian, but I became very pleasantly surprised to discover that Mr. Bowie was a complete gentleman of the old school.

I remember a snippet of conversation from that night.

"So, you know Texas, Mr. Bowie," I said.

"No one knows Texas, sir. It is a huge expanse of land. There are swamps, grass, and tree-covered hill country, vast plains and desert. Much of this land is claimed by Indians," he answered.

"What kinds of Indians?" I asked curiously.

"Karankawa cannibals, Tonkawas, Caddos, Kiowa, Comanche, Lipans, and Apache. Mostly, though, there are Wichita, Creeks, and Cherokees who are moving out of their ancient tribal lands. That's a few of the tribes. There are more." He became quite animated during his explanation. "The Comanche and Apache are the strongest. The Karankawas are the most to be feared, however, since they eat the dead. I've had some little set-tos with the Kronks. They claim the land west of Galveston Bay to Corpus Christi Bay. If you go by land, you have to sneak through their country. They're big Indians. Around six-foot, mostly."

He paused to sip at his brandy for a moment or two, then continued with his narrative.

"The Kronks usually go naked. They wear tattoos around their breasts and lower lips. The lip is sometimes pierced by pieces of cane. If this is not enough, they cover themselves in alligator grease and the dirt and smoke from the fire gets into that grease and forms a kind of mud. Sometimes, they paint their faces, half-red, half-black. It makes them as ugly a sight as you would ever want to see.

"The only time you are sure of them is when they are wearing a breechcloth. They wear those when they go to war where they carry a long bow almost as large as themselves.

"When the hunting has been good, they're a peaceful and happy group of cousins. When they are hungry, they'll eat anything. Including humans."

He tapped his fingers nervously on the table in front of him, reflecting moodily, lost in the vision of the past.

"Once I was taking a group through their territory when I was surprised by a small band of three or four. Before I knew it, they had shot a man. Their arrows are made of cane and are about three feet long. It went clean through the man and buried itself in a bank."

Mr. Bowie stopped. The scene swam before my eyes: marsh country with stunted trees, darkness, an arrow whirring though a man—probably a slave, though Bowie had the tact to keep that information to himself. I decided then and there that I needed him for my venture.

"What kind of Indians live near Nacogdoches?" I asked casually around a sip of brandy.

"Caddos live mostly in the eastern part of Texas," he replied.

"Could you get supplies from the United States past those Indians and into Nacogdoches?"

He smiled. "Easily."

I leaned over the table and spoke low, telling him everything. I told him about the political climate in Washington and about how Texas had already been settled by Americans and how we had the duty and the God-given right to unite those Americans with the rest of the country. His eyebrows rose in surprise.

"You want to invade Mexico?" he asked.

"Only Texas," I replied.

"Texas is a part of Mexico," he said patiently.

"But it may secede into the United States," I confided.

"Wouldn't the states have to be consulted? It seems to me that this could bring about a war between the United States and Mexico. Is that something anyone wants?"

A tiny smile played around his lips. A lot of profit could be made from such a war. For a moment, I wondered if there was anything to that, then dismissed my thoughts.

"There are many who would welcome such a war, but Mexico would not fight," I said confidently. "They don't settle Texas because they are too thinly spread and too dissatisfied with their own government."

Bowie reflected upon my words for a moment. "You know, a man will have an old plow sitting in his field unused because he's using a new one. But the minute someone tries to walk off with that old plow, that's the very same minute the man grabs his rifle and protects his property."

My companion and I laughed, treating his response as a joke, but many times I have had occasion to reflect back upon that bit of homespun wisdom. Perhaps I should have heeded it more. A little more preparation and maybe some of my troubles with Texas would have been lessened. Maybe I wouldn't have had to flee. However, that night I knew I had to have Mr. Bowie at my side. I knew that this was a man upon whom I could depend and a man who could help Texas grow.

"Mr. Bowie," I said soothingly, "I want you to be a part of my country. I want you to be involved in the future of Texas."

"Well," he laughed. "I confess that country suits me. And there's plenty of land there for the taking."

"You shall have a million acres," I said impetuously. "I'll start by making you a colonel and after I'm elected President of the Council, I shall make you a member of Congress."

"A pretty picture, General," he said. "I think I might be willing to work with you."

And as quickly as that, Jim Bowie became one of the bulwarks of my new country along with Ben Milam and my brother David.

Mr. Bowie became the purchaser and transport chief. By 1820, I had over three hundred men who needed to be furnished with food, clothes, guns and ammunition.

"Jim," I asked him later after we became more familiar with each other. "What do you think would be our best way of dividing duties?"

"I think I'd be best working outside," he answered. "I've never been one to stay cooped up inside. The support you have in New Orleans won't mean anything unless we can turn it into men and supplies we can get in Nacogdoches."

And that is exactly what we did. Mr. Bowie smuggled in arms, trade goods for my brother to use to placate the Indians, and to establish trade, making us less a threat and more a partner with them. This policy helped make us safe, yet there was always the chance that Mexicans would be coming to take back their state.

Mr. Bowie never lost a cargo and got the best prices in New Orleans. Usually he would start off with his cargo of goods for Nacogdoches, then he would take my order for more arms, powder, shot, or whatever, and travel to Galves Town where he would buy Negro slaves from Jean Lafitte and take them overland to Louisiana.

I had planned to make Lafitte the admiral of the navy, but he betrayed me to the Mexicans. That, however, is a story for later. Right now, I need to finish this about Mr. Bowie.

In the years I knew Mr. Bowie, I never met a braver, more even-tempered man. His intelligence and high principles were an inspiration to us all. And yet, I have never been able to understand his need to roam through the wilderness.

Mr. Bowie was cultured with a sound foundation in literature, painting, and music. He could and did discuss philosophy and knew the fine principles of logic that allowed him to circumvent argument. And although he would drink a glass of brandy and smoke a fine cigar with his friends, the cigar and brandy meant little to him. His natural exuberance worked to make him friends and although he did drink with them, I have never seen him drunk or accept more than one cigar.

He was a gallant man who never spoke about his affairs with numerous ladies, not even those of a somewhat tarnished reputation, as is the habit among most gentlemen when sharing cigars and brandy after dinner.

Yet he still preferred the wilderness to the drawing rooms of polite society. He worked with his brothers to bring technological advancement to Louisiana, yet he would also disappear at times to smuggle slaves into the country.

He was an extremely complex man, yet never have I known a more compassionate one. He treated his slaves as friends and trusted them almost like family. He seemed to be indifferent to money.

Once, I thought to bring him up on that and mentioned that he seemed to be drawing a reputation as a "blackbirder," one who smuggled Negroes into the United States.

"Yes?" he asked and waited. I felt my face growing red, but plunged on ahead with my probing.

"You are a gentleman, a respected member of our new country . . . and the old," I added.

A bemused smile crossed his face. "That's good to hear," he said casually.

"You are invited to the best homes—which happens to no other slaver—and do not seem touched by this . . . notoriety. How is this?"

He shook his head. "I don't know about all of that. I'm just doing my best to help the family. I like the challenge of doing something better. I like solving problems and doing it the easiest way I can. When you ask yourself what's over the rise or behind a group of trees, the simplest thing to do is to ride over and look." He paused for a moment, then continued. "And while you're riding, you have time to reflect. Think. Plan."

"But what about the hardships?" I asked.

"Another of man's oldest problems. Survival."

He smiled that smile I knew that signified the subject was closed. But I determined that when I returned to Texas, I would take Mr. Bowie with me as my second-in-command. He is a natural leader, but this I didn't discover until the time we were attacked by wild Indians and Mr. Bowie directed the defense and inspired the men.

Once, a fire broke out in a log fort we had erected for defense. A small town sprouted outside the fort's walls and one night, one of the cabins caught fire and the small settlement was in danger of being burnt to the ground.

I remember looking out over the stumps to the shantytown of small cabins and lean-tos. The air was heavy and the clean smell of the freshly turned earth was lost in the smoke. Black storm clouds changed the colors of the countryside, lending a dark and malevolent vision to it.

A flash of lightning came out of the sky and burst upon the cabin belonging to Merridew East, a newcomer and malcontent who constantly bred sedition among everyone. The flash momentarily blinded me and when my vision cleared, I ran towards the cabin, yelling instructions at my men. East had a woman and her child living with him and already the flames blocked the door, preventing their escape.

Mr. Bowie arrived first, sized up the situation, then seized a log about six feet long and two feet in diameter and rammed it hard against the side of the cabin, driving a hole through it. He danced into the flames, grabbed up the baby in his left arm and the woman with his right, and leaped out of the shanty just as the roof collapsed.

Bowie's heroism was lauded by all. The next morning, he left Nacogdoches. Constant praise of his actions made him extremely uncomfortable.

But I cannot forget the picture I had of him, standing there, a young giant in his buckskins black from smoke and gray from ash, his face reddened from the heat. He looked like a god.

There is no one who would be better for Texas than James Bowie and I intend, upon my return from establishing a republic, to make him my second-in-command.

REVEREND C. W. SMITH

The Reverend C. W. Smith was the first Methodist minister to preach in Texas. Indeed, he little knew how much danger surrounded him when he went to Texas, where it was against the law to have any faith but Catholicism. It was a serious offense against the laws of the country to visit, trade, or own land without first signing a document that proved you were a Roman Catholic.

James Bowie converted to the faith prior to his marriage with Ursula de Veramendi, though he had probably been raised somewhat in the teachings of the Church since his early years in Louisiana were under Spanish rule.—**A. J. S.**

I have written in my own journal about my meeting with the famous James Bowie. I always think of this fortuitous circumstance with awe and wonderment and then I thank God for the blessings He has bestowed upon me.

I was sent to minister to the spiritual needs of the men and women of the United States who had departed for Texas.

I am not sure how much information is needed by the average reader of today to understand the conditions of those days. Everything seemed to be in movement. People felt the lure of the West. I felt it myself. In the West, a person could grow as big as his dreams, and I had dreams based on my calling. I felt I could help my fellow man be better through speaking the word of God to him.

It was with great pleasure and excitement that I accepted this post in Texas, even though I hardly knew the hardships of camp life or the dangers of the trail. I felt as though I would be able to speak to the multitudes and help them know the wonders of the Lord. Yes, I was young, but my faith was, as it is, sincere.

I crossed the Mississippi by riverboat. That huge expanse of water had been all that separated me from the wilderness. On the far bank there was a little shanty town erected to help outfit people who were leaving civilization. I later discovered that many of these people were bandits, outlaws, or pirates of the worst sort.

HORS FOR SALE CHEAP read the sign. I smiled to myself as I thought about the wrongly spelled word, and that good feeling prompted me to go in to purchase a mount for the ride into Texas.

A tall, red-haired man dressed in buckskins was talking to a shorter, massively built man wearing a blacksmith's apron. The frontiersman carried a huge rifle, a .50 caliber, I believe, a brace of pistols stuck under his belt, and a huge knife hung from the belt in a polished leather sheath, along with pouches for carrying balls, patches, traveler's rations, and other necessities. The man dressed for the wilderness was arguing with the blacksmith.

I say arguing, but that might give the impression of anger. It was anything but a strong exchange. "Jim," the smithy said in a hurt tone, "don't I get to make some money? I got to make a profit, don't I?"

The backwoodsman replied, "Pete, you trim the newcomers from every boat, and there's a new boat every day and sometimes twice a day." He slapped him lightly on the stomach. "I don't see you losing any inches. I am for Texas and I need good stock at a good price."

"Okay, Jim, your price, but I wouldn't do it for anyone else."

"Not even for this poor parson who you are planning to rob in broad daylight?"

The two men both looked at me, and I must have looked perplexed, because the blacksmith hurried to placate my trepidations. "This here rooster's a friend of mine, and we was haggling over price. It's just a friendly little squabble, you know, among friends."

"Well," I said, "suppose I take the same price and maybe my new friend here will ensure I get good stock." I almost laughed at the man's horrified expression. "If you would be so kind, sir. I also am for Texas."

The big man smiled and then we both laughed out loud, for the blacksmith was grumbling as he slowly walked to the back of his shop, and through the large door to the corral where he kept riding animals.

"Actually, sir, I do know livestock fairly well, but I could not help but join in the banter."

"The name's Jim. I'd be happy to ride to Texas with you."

And with such simplicity, we became friends. He helped me to purchase supplies at a decent price and made sure that I only bought what I needed.

After leaving the little road town, we traveled for several days. My friend Jim was a wonderfully knowledgeable man. He seemed to know everything about the country. He hunted so we were able to conserve supplies, and he also knew what plants were edible and where the good water lay. Even so, he never introduced himself as more than Jim.

The first large town we reached was called Nacogdoches. This town had a history of being American from the time when James Long tried to make Texas a separate country.

The town was a collection of ramshackle buildings amongst stronger, more solidly constructed log cabins, as well as the mud houses of the Mexicans. It had many saloons and *cantinas*, and along with the substantial farmers and landowners were border ruffians.

I begged some space on the porch of a local general store and proceeded to tell all who would listen that I would hold a Methodist service on Sunday.

Sunday came and the crowd was large, men, women and children filled the street in front of the general store. While many were obviously hardworking citizenry, there were many genuine hardcases enmeshed in the congregation.

It was the first time I ever delivered a service to a crowd of arms-toting outlaws. Indeed, many of the men wore several pistols, knives, and carried long rifles.

Even so, it was my first service in this new land and so I endeavored to do the best I could.

We started with singing, and the songs of praise were beautiful, albeit off-key and containing some flat and sour voices. It was still praise to our Lord.

After the singing it was time for me to give the sermon. I began to speak. From experience, I can say it was not the best choice, but then I was new to the area and I was willing to try and speak about taming the wilderness and God's message.

Unfortunately, I was badgered from the audience. One man in particular—big, burly, black-bearded, bristling with weapons and dressed in grease-stained leather—seemed to know the passage of "be fruitful and multiply," and he tried to shock the women in the audience with his use of God's word.

My companion, Jim, came onto the front platform of the store. He was no longer in hunting clothes, but stood in fine gentleman's raiment and addressed the crowd.

"Please, ladies and gentlemen, and those who don't fit in either category." Jim had a fine speaking voice and while usually it was low and clear, when he needed volume, he had it. "You know who you are."

"Yeah," said the burly rascal. "We know who we are, but who are you?"

Jim acted like he hadn't heard but kept addressing the crowd. "I just rode from Mississippi with this man, and I think he's a good man worth listening to. I plan to see he gets a fair hearing."

A series of catcalls and hooraws arose at this. The sheer volume made me fear for his safety, but the burly man spoke up again.

With his hands on the butts of pistols stuck in a sash at his waist he repeated his question. "I said, who are you, Mister?"

"That's immaterial, but my name's Jim Bowie."

A hush fell over the congregation. The black-bearded man pulled his hands from his pistols as though they were suddenly as hot as hellfire.

"Speak now, Reverend. They'll give you a fair hearing."

And they did. My first sermon in Texas was to the best behaved group of cutthroats I have ever seen, and all because of my friend, the bravo, James Bowie.

I said as I started this tale that I was always awestruck when I thought about it. The Lord sent Jim Bowie to me. I would have never been able to have cowed that crowd, and would have probably lost all credibility as a man of God if Bowie had not verified me. And yet James Bowie—Jim—was known to have gambled, and taken lives in duels.

It made me think, once I started hearing about my friend, about how a reputation can be either a compliment or a detriment to one's life. Jim was a fine gentleman, but his reputation established him as a cold-blooded killer, or at least, an adventurer looking for excitement, and yet I never heard him brag about himself, or his adventures. Always a gentleman, never a braggart. Not too bad an epitaph for Jim Bowie.

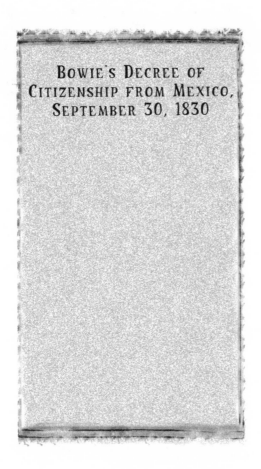

BOWIE'S DECREE OF
CITIZENSHIP FROM MEXICO,
SEPTEMBER 30, 1830

His excellency, the Governor of the State, has been pleased to forward the following decree:

The Governor of the State of Coahuila and Texas to all its inhabitants, Know Ye: That the congress of the said state has decreed the following:

Decree No. 159. The Constitutional Congress of the free, independent and sovereign State of Coahuila and Texas decrees the following:

A letter of citizenship is hereby granted to the foreigner, James Bowie, providing he establishes the wool and cotton mills which he offers to establish in the state.

The Governor of the State will be guided by this decree, and for its compliance therewith he shall have it printed, published, and distributed. Issued in the City of Leona Vicario on September 30, 1830. Ramón García Rojas, Congressional Chairman; Mariano García, Congressional Secretary; Vicente Valdez, Congressional Secretary, pro-tem.

Wherefore, I command this decree to be printed, published and circulated, and command proper obedience thereto.
Leona Vicario,
October 5, 1830

Rafael Eca y Múzquis [RUBRIC]
Santiago del Valle, Secretary [RUBRIC]

In the City of San Fernando de Béxar on the 25th day of April, 1821, I, the priest Don Refugio de la Garza, pastor of this city, having performed the investigation prescribed by the Canon Law, published the banns on three consecutive feast days—*"Inter Missarund"*—during the high mass to wit, on the 10th, 17th, and 24th of said month, and having found no canonical impediment even after the lapse of twenty-four hours from the last publication of the banns, I married and blessed at the nuptial mass—*"In Facie Ecclesiae"*—publicly in the Church Don Santiago Bowie, a native of Louisiana of North America, legitimate son of Raymond Bowie and Albina Yons, and Miss Ursula de Veramendi, legitimate daughter of Don Juan Martín Veramendi and Doña Josefa Navarro. Their parents stood as sponsors, and Don José Angel Navarro and Don Juan Francisco as witnesses. In witness whereof I have hereunto affixed my signature.
Refugio de la Garza [RUBRIC]

CAIAPHAS K. HAM

Caiaphas K. Ham fought with Bowie during Texas's War for Independence. But more than that, he was one of Bowie's few friends who stuck with him through thick and thin when he went into a deep, dark depression following the death of his wife, Ursula, and his two children and tried to drink the world dry. Ham and Bowie were familiar figures on the frontier, sharing hunting adventures, speculations, and the friendly camaraderie that confident men share on the frontier. Ham defended Bowie's reputation more than once when the torn warrior lay defenseless and his enemies licked their lips and moved in for the kill. He was with Bowie at the famous San Saba fight and others.—A. J. S.

More and more people seem to be becoming attracted to Jim. Can't say as how I can blame them. He was sorta like a candle who burned so brightly that he just naturally attracted the moths who wanted to be butterflies. I remember when I first ran across Jim. I was immediately attracted to him, too. Shucks, I guess I'm no different than the others.

About 1828 or sos, I began to notice men and estimate their character. At that time, Col. Bowie was a gentleman of prominence. He already had a reputation for great courage, always ready to defend himself and friends, but never the aggressor. No sir, never.

He was a clever, polite gentleman always attentive to the ladies on all occasions and seemed to entertain a devotion for them which we called chivalrous in those days. Seems to be mostly missing nowadays what with the young men running around so's they almost trample any lady what gets in their path. They could use a few lessons like those Jim taught.

He was a true, constant and generous friend, but you get on his wrong side and he became an open and bitter enemy who didn't go around your back talking about how bad you were. No sir. He'd most likely come right up into your face and tell you very quietly what he thought about you. This habit made him quite a few enemies, but he took his enemies as well as he took his friends. And believe me when I say that one look at him made you understand why he was a foe no one dared to undervalue and many feared.

At times, when unexcited, he had a calm seriousness about him that shadowed his countenance, giving him an assurance of great willpower, unbending firmness of purpose, and unflinching courage. But . . .

Well, when anger stoked him, his face bore the semblance of an enraged lion and a man felt fear deep down in his craw. More than one man puddled his breeches when he saw that look blazing from Jim's face.

It was silver that was Jim's downfall, but, hell, ain't it everybody's? We all got these dreams of getting rich quick instead of laboring for it. I ain't no different. But with Jim, why, it was more like an obsession than anything else.

In Bexar, the Lipan Indians came in from the West to do their trading and paid for their plunder with chunks of silver ore, rich and unsmelted. Damn, but that was a sight! Many had tried to follow them back to their village, but not many returned and if they did, they'd only mumble strange stories about what had happened to set them off their feed.

Jim, though, was different. He didn't try to sneak off behind them.

No sir. He came right on up to them, squatting on his heels in the sun on the plaza and talkin' with them like they was the people next door. That's when I met him.

I'd been off with the Lipans and made friends with Fat Rabbit, one of the Lipans. One day, we were off hunting and Fat Rabbit points to a big hill and says that that hill was plumb filled with silver and we'd go there some day, but we had to be careful 'cause if the others found out what we were up to, they'd cut our throats lickety-split! But, hell, they moved the camp the next day and we never got back down that way as long as I stayed with them.

When I told that story to Jim, tiny lights danced in his eyes. I don't think it was the silver as much as what he'd have to go through to get it. The adventure, you know. That's what it really was that drove Jim to wanting that Lipan silver.

He went to talk with the lieutenant-governor of Bexar, Don Juan Martín de Veramendi, telling him what he wanted to do 'cause Jim was figuring on marrying the don's daughter, Ursula. They all tried to dissuade him from his idea, but Jim had the bit in his teeth and the next spring, he met Xolic, a Lipan chief, in the plaza and made close friends with him. Jim gave Xolic a silver-inlaid rifle and got an invite to go hunting with the tribe.

When he came back, he was all excited 'cause Xolic had taken him to the hill of silver—*lomas plato*—and Jim planned on putting together an expedition and going after it. But Xolic died before he could get us all together and this here Indian whose face always looked like he'd swallowed a green persimmon—*Tres Manos*, Three Hands, they called him 'cause he wore this mummified hand of one of his enemies on a string around his neck—finds Jim and tells him to keep out of Lipan lands or he'd stretch Jim's guts from tree to tree.

Jim damn near settled that man's hash right then and there, but we pulled him out of the plaza and calmed him down. That just made Jim even more determined than ever, and a couple of weeks later, fall of '31 it was, Jim had his expedition: his brother Rezin, Jim Coryell, Dave Buchanan, Bob Armstrong, Jesse Wallace, Matt Doyle, Tom McCaslin, me, Jim's man Black Sam, a Mex called Gonzales and a mulatto boy we all called Charles, and off we went, looking for Jim's hill of silver that had once belonged to a mission of friars the Indians had killed.

We was down by the San Saba River, searching for that silver mine, when we got ourselves surrounded by somewheres up to a

couple hundred Injuns, riding like the wind and screaming like a
bunch of demons. I never heard a human voice make that sound
before and it right made my hair crawl up my neck and disappear
under my hat.

"What do you make of them?" Jim asks me.

"Wacos," I replied. "Lot of them, anyways. I can tell by the cut
of their scalplock. Most look like Tehuacanas, though that batch over
there are your friends the Lipans and that gent in front on the pinto
ain't none other but old Tres Manos himself. Reckon we're in for
it, gentlemen."

Well, Rezin thought it'd be mighty smart of us if we tried to
make some peace with them and he and Buchanan sallied right on
out to have a little talk with them. Buchanan said something to them,
then one of them Wacos waved a bloody scalp and shouted "How
do? How do?" and the next thing I knew bullets were buzzing around
us like angry hornets.

Buchanan went down, one ball breaking his leg, and Rezin heft
him over his shoulders and took off running back towards us in the
trees. About eight Indians came riding out to gut him with their
lances, but Jim and me and Coryell and McCaslin came out from
the trees and ran out to meet them.

"Don't miss, boys!" Jim yelled. But hell, we had no intention of
missing any of them and left four saddles running empty in short
notice. That sent the rest of the Indians scampering back to their
friends on the ridge.

Well, we got back to the woods and here came Tres Manos on
that pinto of his, riding back and forth in front of the Indians, in-
sulting them, trying to work them up to charge us. Jim gets real
quiet, and says, "Who's loaded?"

"I am," I says.

"Then shoot that *valiente* on that painted pony and do a fine job
of it while you're about it."

Now, that was a pretty piece off, but I stood and rested my rifle
in the fork of a black oak, and pulled down on that Indian. At first,
I thought I'd missed him, but then he threw his arms up in the air
like he was calling on the Almighty, and tumbled off the rump of
that paint.

The Indians began to taunt us, but Jim ignored them and directed
us into a patch of trees a little thicker'n the ones we were in. He left
three of the younger ones with the animals and scattered the rest of

us around. We had planned well for that trip. Plenty of lead and powder and I tell you we salted many an Indian there. Five days, we fought them, arrows and bullets flying thicker than hail around us.

I don't know how many times they charged us, but we routed their hides every time. At last, they tried to burn us out, and a couple managed to get in close—three, I think, if I remember right—and my bladder swells to near bursting 'cause I figger there's others around. But Jim yells at us to watch the front and he pulls that terrible blade of his and proceeds to carve all three of them up quick-ern you can spit and say "some punkins."

I thought to come and give him a hand, but he swore an oath that would make the Lord back off. Black-faced from the smoke, eyes red like fire, blood wet on his breast from where he gutted one of them Indians, he looked like Satan himself had stepped outta the fires of hell. I quick decided the Indians were safer than to cross him and went right back to shooting through the smoke.

Well, we got outta that scrape, thanks be to Jim.

The knife?

Well, I can tell you about that. We had been hunting over along the border and Jim killed a deer. I helped him dress it out and after gutting it, he lay it aside and helped me lift it up to tie it over the withers of a mule we'd brought along for that purpose.

I reckon we got maybe five, six mile away from there when he suddenly remembered that he forgot to pick it back up. That was the knife his brother Rezin had made for him at his plantation near Avoyelles in Louisiana. Well, we rode back to get it, but it was gone. Never knew what happened to it.

About six months later, Jim rode back to Rapides Parish to settle a little land dispute and went on into Washington, Arkansas, to see this blacksmith he'd heard about named James Black. He'd carved a knife from a piece of soft pine as a model and when he went back through a month later, Black had made him that knife. Gave you chills to look at it. Smelled like dried blood. Heavy blade, like a hatchet. Brass along the back and crossguard to catch another edge. That was a knife meant for killing and nothin else, believe me!

I remember once along the Bravo when a ragged gent asked to share our campfire. We had been hunting and Ol' Jim had stepped into the river in an attempt to get a shot at a fine buck. His foot slipped and he fell in, baptizing himself from head to toe. Well, we decided that the day was near finished anyway and besides, Jim was mighty cold. This was November around '29, I reckon, or thereabouts. Time doesn't matter much once it's passed and it's the story that's important anyway.

Where was I?

Oh, yes.

So, we built a fire in a small oak grove and Jim stripped naked and hung his clothes on branches near it to dry. He wrapped himself in a blanket and was hunkered over the fire, trying to get warm, pouring hot coffee down his gullet to take the chill out of his innards, when this seedy devil and his two boys rode up to the fire and asked to share it. They looked as poor as Job's turkey. The old man wore a tattered wolfskin coat pulled around him and tied with a piece of twine and a pair of duck breeches worn shiny from riding. The brim of his hat looked like a termite had been at it and his face had been a stranger to a razor for about a year. His boys had cold eyes, fish eyes, though neither of them had spent time with a razor. Fuzz curled along their chins and cheeks. I had an all-overish feeling about the sight of them and made a point of sliding two pistols closer to my middle and loosening my knife in its sheath.

"Howdy," the man said gruffly. "I'm Seth Jenkins and these're my boys, Jacob and Esau. Looks like yer alone out here. Wondered if'n you mind we share yer fire?"

Now, Jim was never one to deny a man hospitality. He nodded and gave this pleasant grin at the man and said, "Light and sit a spell. Coffee's on and mores where that came from. I'm Jim and that fellow over there is Caiaphas."

I said my howdy as the man climbed down and tossed the reins of his horse to the youngest of his boys and walked stiffly to the fire. He took a dirty cup from a sack he had slung over his shoulder, ran a grimy finger around the inside of the cup and squatted and poured himself a cup of coffee. I watched the boys, 'cause I knew Jim had that man with him, and I didn't like what I seen. Them two boys tied off their horses, then walked to the fire, splitting so's they could come around us from two directions.

"You fellers look like you's come a long ways," Jenkins said. He blew across his coffee and sipped noisily, ignoring me. I could tell he had placed Jim as being the big toad in the puddle.

"Hunting," Jim said and grinned wryly, gesturing at his wet clothes, acknowledging the corn of his clumsiness. "But fell into the water like a damn fool."

"Happens you don't watch where yuh put yer feet," Jenkins said. "Boys been out here long?"

I knew then that he had placed us as a pair of no-account corn-crackers and had decided to kill us and absquatulate with our plunder. I watched Jim carefully, but he didn't rise to him.

"Nope," he said. "Fact is, we just got here less than a week."

Now, that may not have been the exact truth, but it was close enough. Jenkins took that to mean we had just been out West a short time, but Jim was talkin' about our hunting trip from Bexar. But that Jenkins and his two boys were just too eager for our belongings to give much thought to what Jim was saying. He cast a look over in my direction, sort of measuring me, then gave a little nod of his head, more of a twist, I s'pose, at Jacob and turned back to Jim.

Jacob turned those fish eyes on me and grinned a black-toothed smile. "Pa and usns ain't been but wanderin' round tryin' to find a place to settle," he said.

"That right?" I answered. That younger boy began to sidle off to my blind side like a fierce dog. I kinda turned my shoulder to keep him in sight and he shakes his head and grins at me. I'm thinking that both of them are shy a dipper or two to make a jug when that Jacob tries to bring his rifle down on me. I jerked my pistols from my belt and put a ball through his forehead, but that Esau was a tricky one and ducked down when I turned and fired.

I drew my knife, but he grinned and raised his gun, then I heard something whizz by my ear and a *chunk!* like an axe splitting a log, and Jim's knife split that boy's head like a melon. I turned and looked at him and Jenkins. Jenkins had his knife in his hand and was trying to bring it around to gut Jim, but Jim held it away from him, then curled one of those big arms of his around the man's head, seized his greasy beard, and jerked his arm around like he was flipping a tree outta his way. That man's neck made a dry *pop!* and he went all glassy-eyed and just dropped down at Jim's feet.

Ain't many men strong enough to do that. Or quick enough. Or, for that matter, willin' to look out for their friends 'fore they look out for themselves. But that was Jim's style. He never seemed to put much value upon his life. I remember mentioning something along that line to him once while we was sharing a fire up on the plains and he just gave that deep laugh of his and said:

"Caiaphas, a man can live his life afraid for it or he can live it."

I reckon that's as good a way to follow as any.

Now, I don't mean to be saying that Jim was serious all the time. Nope. Not at all. But there was a bit of seriousness to his funnin' as well.

I remember a time down in San Felipe when me and Jim and Joe Powell were sitting in Peyton's Tavern having a tot when this man rode in with a real comely young woman from over West a spell. Now, the man said he was a minister of the gospel and that he and the young woman wanted to get hitched and were looking for a priest.

That sounds funny, I know, but Mex law was such that no marriage in Coahuila was legal unless it'd been performed by the Catholic Church. If that man and the young woman wanted to get married, why, they just had to find a priest to firm up things for them despite what religion they wanted to follow on their own.

Well, Jim he took a look at that man and frowned and stared down in his cup, muttering as to how he was sure that he had seen that man somewhere before and he didn't have "reverend" affixed before his name at the time. Blamed, though, if he could recall just where it was.

About that time, the man just gave up looking for the priest and allowed as to how he guessed they would have to settle for a "constitutional marriage" instead of a church marriage. I could see right away that that didn't settle well with the young woman. A marriage like that was a weak one, mainly to keep a couple respectable until they could find a priest. All it involved was the two of them standing in front of the *alcalde* and saying that they did what he told them to do and then go off and live like man and wife until a priest could be found. That was pretty hard in those days because most priests like their comfort and not many wanted to live north of Mexico City in the frontier away from the fine wine and parties.

The young woman had just about given in to the man's sweet talking, her eyes shining with what she thought was love and all—most young people are that way, you know; all of them seem to think they know all there's to know about love when they ain't got a Philadelphia lawyer's clue as to what it's all about; they're just all honey-fuggled—when Jim suddenly rears back and says: "Whoa. I remember now where I seen him; over in Arkansas way where he escaped from jail after the sheriff caught him stealing a horse. He left a wife and child behind as I recollect."

"Why, that man's got nothin' but shecoonery on his mind!" I exclaimed, and started to rise when Jim clamped that big hand on my forearm and pinned me to the table, knocking over my draught. I hastily resettled that cup.

"This is how we're gonna play it," he says, leaning across the table and motioning for Joe to join us. He talked real quickly, then stood up and went off to fetch the *alcalde* while I put on my straight face and got up and walked over to their table.

"Beg pardon, ma'am, sir," I says with my hat in my hand. "I couldn't but help hearing . . ."

"What do you want?" the man says, giving me the cold eye.

Well, I almost settled his hash for him right then and there, his manners being such as they were, but I held on to my temper and just gave him this grin that was all teeth.

"Ain't nothing to me, mister," I says. "But if'n it's the priest you want, why he'll be back in a couple of hours. He's just downriver a bit at some Mex's place what got bit by a rattler and is takin' some time to shuffle off this mortal coil, so to speak," I finished grandly. His eyebrow twitched a bit and I knew that I had scored with that one.

"Really? Oh, John! Isn't that the most wonderful news?" the woman says, her eyes shining like mirrors.

"Why, yes. I guess so," he says, and I can tell that he ain't a bit happy about what I've just told him and he looks at me again and if I had just stepped into a nest of rattlers he wouldn't use a ball to put me out of my misery.

About that time, Jim comes into the tavern with the *alcalde* and the man's eyes light up. "But," he says to the woman, "we could get the hitchin' done right now instead of waiting." And he gets up and goes over to where Jim and the *alcalde* are leaning on the bar having a talk.

"I'm sorry, *señor*," he says. "But I have just received word that the good Father will soon be back. There is no reason now to enter into constitutional bonds."

I could see the tiny muscles working along the man's jaw and I think it's about time I paste him one on the mouth when I catch that warning look from Jim and hold my piece. I turn back to my table to get my cup of brandy when the door opens and who walks in but the priest with the hood pulled far over his head, shuffling like he was carrying the weight of the world upon his shoulders.

"But, see here, *señor*," the *alcalde* continues. "Here is the good Father, now."

Well, the good Father don't speak any English, which perplexes the man, so Jim, he leaps in and offers to do some translating for the couple. The man has this here doubtful look on his face, but the young woman smiles and thanks Jim greatly for his help and the die is set. The man ain't got a choice if he wants to play a flute over that woman.

Jim has this real lengthy talk with the Father, then tells the man that the *padre* is willing to hear the man's premarital confession which they can do if both step into the room next door. 'Course, Jim has to go, too, but the *padre* swears him to the seal of the confessional to make all things legal.

Now, the man seems real doubtful about all this, but he knows he's been rookered, and he follows them into the next room. Jim pretends to close the door behind them, but leaves it open just enough for us in the tap-room to hear everything going on.

There's another long exchange of Mex-talk and then Jim speaks up loudly and begins to ask some highly embarrassing questions of the man about horse dealing over in Arkansas and his wife and child, and the man, thinking that the door is closed like an oyster shell, gets to sputtering and stammering and finally spills the oats about himself with the *padre* going "ah!" every once in a while and clicking his tongue whenever Jim pauses to do a bit of translating.

I steal a look at the young woman while all this is going on and the blood just leaves them red cheeks, leaving her looking as waxen white and cold as death. Pretty soon, the tears begin flowing and I naturally get up and ask if there's anything I can do to help her.

"Yes," she says, sniffling and wiping her nose on a dainty hanky she takes from her sleeve. "You can take me back to my daddy's place, if you will, sir."

I didn't need a howdy to send me on my way. I gathered that young woman's belongings and took her out of Peyton's place and back home.

When I returned a few hours later, there's Jim and Joe having a tot and toasting themselves. Joe looks up at me and pulls that hood over his face.

"Well, how'd I do?" he asks. "I make a good *padre*?"

We all had a good laugh over that one and for months after, whenever someone did something wrong, Joe would make a cross over them and say, "Bless you, my child!" and send us off laughing again!

ST. LOUIS
GLOBE-DEMOCRAT,
NOVEMBER 1898

The following article appeared in the St. Louis Globe-Democrat *in November 1898. I quote only a part of it to show one individual's idea of how Bowie came to go on his famous San Saba expedition. I question the reliability of the article since it is allegedly signed by someone who calls himself "Brazos" but I did find a shaft and a rough circle of rocks that appeared to have been deliberately erected as a means of fortification between the Dry Frio and the Frio rivers. I remember my Father saying that he heard Bowie give just such a description in Gonzales about 1831. I had no chance to explore further as my men and I were expecting an attack by some Indians we had been trailing and we fortified our camp at that very same spot about a hundred yards from water.—*A. J. S.

. . . By some means James Bowie got possession of a lot of old maps of Western Texas, and upon many of these were marked places that had been abandoned for a hundred years. Nobody knows where he obtained his map, but possibly through relatives of his wife who had been trading for a long time with various Indian tribes of the area, including the Lipan Apaches. We do know, however, that it was not long after his marriage before he began to talk of recruiting an expedition in search for St. Denis's silver mine, and the old house, which, at that period, was in the very heart of the country of the terrible Comanches. At that time, the house was only a little more than a hundred years old, and there was not a white man in Texas who had ever seen it. Colonel Bowie knew that there was such a place on his old map, and he had heard many stories of the wonderful wealth that St. Denis had gathered in the mountains near the old house and he did not allow many days to pass before he found himself at the head of some twenty-five or thirty adventurers prowling about in the mountains of the Guadalupe, southwest of San Antonio. After searching for more than a week, Bowie himself discovered St. Denis's old log house with St. Denis's name and the date, 1714, carved on a rock beside the foundation.

REZIN BOWIE'S ACCOUNT OF THE BATTLE OF CALF CREEK NEAR SAN SABA

The reader will notice a few discrepancies between the account given by Cai-aphas Ham and the report written by James Bowie for Veramendi and Rezin's writing below. This, I suggest, is due to the time lapse between them, James Bowie's being rendered first, Ham's second but a product that came after many tellings in several saloons, and Rezin's as an afterthought in an attempt to set the record straight but only confusing it further by the failing of memory. —**A. J. S.**

Their [the Indians'] number being so far greater than ours, one hundred sixty-four to eleven, it was agreed that I should be sent out to talk with them, and endeavor to compromise rather than attempt to fight. I accordingly started with David Buchanan in company and walked up to within forty yards of where they had halted, and requested them in their own tongue to send forward their chief, as I wanted to talk with him. Their answer was "How do you do! How do you do!" in English and a discharge of twelve shots at us, one of which broke Buchanan's leg. I returned their salutation with the contents of a double-barreled gun and a pistol. I then took Buchanan upon my shoulder and started back to the encampment. The Indians then opened a heavy fire upon us which wounded Buchanan in two more places slightly, and piercing my hunting shirt in several places without doing me any injury. When the Indians found their shots failed to bring me down, eight Indians, on foot, took after me, with tomahawks, and when close upon me, were discovered by the party who rushed out with rifles, and brought down four of them, the other four retreating back to the main body. We then returned to our position, and all was still for about five minutes.

We then discovered a hill to the northwest, at the distance of sixty yards, red with Indians, who opened a heavy fire upon us, with loud yells, their chief on horseback urging them in a loud audible voice to the charge, walking his horse, perfectly composed. When we first discovered him, our guns were all empty, with the exception of Mr. Ham's. James Bowie cried out, "Who is loaded?" Mr. Ham answered, "I am." He was then told to shoot that Indian on horseback. He did so and broke his leg and killed his horse. We now discovered him hopping around his horse on one leg with his shield on his arm to keep off the balls. By this time four of our party being reloaded, fired at the same instant, and all the balls took effect through his shield. He fell and was immediately surrounded by six or eight of his tribe who picked him up and bore him off. Several of these were shot by our party. The whole body then retreated back of the hill out of sight with the exception of a few Indians who were running about from tree to tree out of gun shot. They now covered the hill the second time, bringing up their bowmen, who had not been in action before, and commenced a heavy fire with balls and arrows, which we returned with a well-directed aim with our rifles. At this instant another chief appeared on horseback near the spot where the other one fell. The same question of "Who is loaded?" was asked. The answer was "nobody," when little Charlie, the mulatto servant, came running up with Buchanan's rifle which had not been discharged since he was wounded, and handed it to James Bowie, who instantly fired and brought him down from his horse. He was surrounded by six or eight of his tribe, as was the last, and was borne off under our fire.

During the time we were defending ourselves from the Indians
on the hill, some fifteen or twenty of the Caddo tribe had succeeded
in getting under the bank of the creek, in our rear, at about forty
yards distant, and opened a heavy fire upon us, which wounded Mat-
thew Doyle, the ball entering the left breast and coming out at the
back. As soon as he cried out that he was wounded, Thomas Mc-
Caslin hastened to the spot, when he fell, and observed, "Where is
the Indian that shot Doyle?" He was told by a more experienced
hand not to venture there, as from the reports of their guns, they
must be riflemen. At that instant, he discovered an Indian, and while
in the act of raising his piece, was shot through the center of the
body and expired. Robt. Armstrong exclaimed, "Damn the Indian
that shot McCaslin; where is he?" He was told not to venture there
as they must be riflemen, but on discovering an Indian and while
bringing his gun up, was fired at, and part of the stock of his gun
cut off, the ball lodging against the barrel. During this time our
enemies had formed a complete circle around us, occupying the
points of rocks, scattering trees and bushes. The firing then became
general from all quarters. Finding our situation too much exposed
among the trees, we were obliged to leave them and take to the
thickets. The first thing necessary was to dislodge the riflemen from
under the bank of the creek, who were within pointblank shot. This
we soon succeeded in doing by shooting most of them in the head,
as soon as we had the advantage of seeing them, when they could
not see us. The road we had cut around the thicket the night previous, gave us now an advantageous situation over that of our enemy,
as we had a fair view of them in the prairie, while we were completely
hid. We baffled their shots by moving six or eight feet the moment
we had fired, as their only mark was the smoke of our guns. They
would put twenty balls within the size of a pocket handkerchief when
they had seen the smoke. In this manner we fought them two hours,
and had one man wounded, James Coryell who was shot through the
arm, the ball lodging in the side, first cutting away a small bush which
prevented it from penetrating deeper than the size of it. They now
discovered that we were not to be dislodged from the thicket, and
the uncertainty of killing us at random, they suffering very much
from the fire of our rifles, which brought half a dozen down at every
round, they determined to resort to stratagem, by putting fire to the
dry grass in the prairie for the double purpose of routing us from
our position, and under cover of the smoke, to carry away their dead

and wounded which lay near us. The wind was now blowing from the west and they placed the fire in that quarter, where it burned down all the grass to the creek, and then bore off to the right and left, leaving around our position a space of about five acres untouched by the fire. Under cover of their smoke they succeeded in carrying off a portion of their dead and wounded. In the meantime our party was engaged in scraping away the dry grass and leaves from our wounded men and baggage to prevent the fire from passing over them; and likewise in piling up rocks and bushes to answer the place of breastworks. They now discovered that they had failed in routing us, as they had anticipated. They then reoccupied the points of rocks and trees in the prairie, and commenced another attack. The firing continued for some time, when the wind suddenly changed to the north and blew very hard. We now discovered our dangerous situation, should the Indians succeed in putting fire to the small spot which we occupied, and kept a strict watch all around. The two servant boys were employed in scraping away dry grass and leaves from around the wounded men. The point from which the wind blew being favorable to fire our position one of the Indians succeeded in crawling down the creek and putting fire to the grass that had not been burned, but before he could retreat back to his party, was killed by Robt. Armstrong.

At this time we saw no hope of escape, as the fire was coming down rapidly before the wind, flaming ten feet high, and directly for the spot we occupied. What must be done? We must either be burned up alive or be driven into the prairie among the savages. This encouraged the Indians and made it more awful; their shots and yells rent the air—they, at the same time, firing about twenty shots. As soon as the smoke hid us from their view we collected together and held a consultation as to what was best to be done. Our first impression was that they might charge us under cover of the smoke, as we could make but one effectual fire. The sparks were flying about so quickly that no man could open his powder horn without running the risk of being blown up. However, we finally came to a determination: had they charged us, to give them fire, place our backs together, draw our knives and fight them as long as any of us were alive. The next question was should they charge on us and we retain our position, we must be burned up. It was then decided that each man should take care of himself as well as he could until the fire arrived at the ring around our baggage and wounded men and there it should be smothered with buffalo robes, bear skins, deer skins, and blankets, which after a great deal of exertion, we succeeded in doing. Our thicket being so much burned and scorched that it afforded little or no shelter, we all got into the ring that was made around our wounded men and baggage, and commenced building our breast-works higher, with loose rocks from the inside and dirt dug up with our knives and sticks. During the last fire the Indians had succeeded in removing all their killed and wounded which lay near us. It was now sundown and we had been warmly engaged with the Indians since sunrise, and they seeing us still alive and ready for fight drew off at a distance of a hundred yards and encamped for the night.

The Indians made no further attack but quietly withdrew. During the day's conflict, we had killed some eighty Indians including the Lipan Chief Tresmanos who gave James such a hard time with threats upon his life. When our two wounded men had recovered sufficiently to travel, we abandoned our rude fortification, destroyed our remaining stores, buried our tools, and took up a line of march afoot for Bexar whereupon we arrived in due time.

Rezin Pleasant Bowie [RUBRIC]

Although called the Battle at San Saba River, the fight James Bowie had with the Comanche Indians while leading a small party in search of the lost silver mines is believed to have taken place on Calf Creek, in Mc-Culloch County. Some, however, believe that the fight took place at Bowie Spring on Celery Creek, a few miles north of Menard. Rezin Bowie also penned an account of the fight that can be found in Yoakum's History of Texas [1885]. *The following is Bowie's personal report to Don Juan Martín Veramendi, his father-in-law and vice-governor of the state of Coahuila.*—A. J. S.

To the Political Chief of Bexar:

    Agreeable to your Lordship's request, I have the honor to report to you the result of my expedition from San Antonio to San Saba. Information received through different channels in relation to that section of country, formerly occupied by Mexican citizens, and now in the hands of several hostile Indians, induced me to get up that expedition, expecting that some benefit might result therefrom, both to the community and to myself. But, as my intentions were known to and approved by your Lordship, I deem it useless to enter into these particulars. I left this city on the second of November last, in company with my brother Rezin Bowie, eight men and a boy. Wishing, with due care, to examine the nature of the country, my progress was quite slow. On the 19th we met two Comanches and one Mexican captive, the last acting as interpreter, at above seven miles northwest of Llano river on the road known as "de la Bandera." The Indians, after having asked several questions in regard to the feelings of the Mexicans toward the Comanches, and receiving an assurance on my part that they were kindly disposed toward all peaceable Indians, told me that their friends were driving to San Antonio several horses that had been stolen at Goliad. I promised them that they would be protected, and they continued on their way to the city to deliver the said horses to their proper owners or to the civil authority. On the following day at sunrise we were overtaken by the captive, who informed us that 124 Tahuacanoes were on our trail, and at the same time showing us the medal this year by his captain from the authority of this city, which was sent us to prove that the messenger was reliable. We were then apprised that the Tahuacanoes had the day before visited the campaign ground of the Comanches, and told them that they were following us to kill us at any cost. Ysayune (such was the name of the Comanche captain) having become informed of the determination of the savages respecting us, tried first to induce them to desist from the prosecution of their intention, insisting that they should not take our lives, and telling them he would "be mad" with them if they went to attack us, but they separated, dissatisfied with each other. Ysayune sent us word that if we would come back he would do all he could to protect us, but that he had only sixteen men under his command, and thought we could defend ourselves from the enemy by taking position on a hill covered with underbrush, which the captive was ordered to show us, adding that the houses on the San Saba were close by. (The houses alluded to were the remains of those belonging to the San Saba Mission that had long been abandoned.) We did not follow the Comanche's advice, thinking that we could reach our destination, as we did, before the enemy could overtake us. But once arrived, we could not find the houses, and the ground upon the San Saba offering no position for protection, we went about three miles north of the river, and there selected a grove wherein to encamp for the night. There was a smaller grove about fifty yards from the one chosen for our encampment, and I caused it to be occupied for the night by three men, so as to prevent the enemy from taking possession of it, and thereby have an advantage over us. However, we passed the night without being disturbed.

On the 21st, at 8 o'clock A.M., we were about to leave our camping ground when we saw a large body of Indians close upon us, and at a distance of about two hundred yards. Several of them shouted in English: "How do you do? How are you, How are you?" We soon knew by their skins that they had among them some Caddoes, and we made signs to them to send a man to inform us of their intentions. Just then we saw that the Indian who was ahead on horseback was holding up a scalp, and forthwith a volley of some ten or twelve gun shots was discharged into our camp, but without effect. At the arrival of the Indians, my brother repaired with two men to the smaller grove which was between us and the Indians, but when I saw that most of them were withdrawing and sheltering themselves behind a hill about one hundred varas northeast of our position, expecting that they would attack us in a body in that direction, I went to tell my brother to come back, and on our return, Mr. Buchanan was shot and had his leg broken. We had scarcely joined our camp when, as I expected, the Indians came from behind the hill to dislodge us, but as the foremost men and among them one who seemed to be their leader, fell, they busied themselves in removing their dead; and to do this they had to come closer and fight sharply, but it was at the cost of more lives on their part. This contest lasted about fifteen minutes; but when they perceived they could not enter our camp, they withdrew, screening themselves behind the hill and surrounding timber, and thence commenced firing on us from every direction. While we were thus engaged fifteen Indians, who from the report of their firing, seemed to be armed with rifles, concealed themselves behind some oaks in a valley about sixty varas to the northwest. These were the severest of our foemen, and they wounded two more of our men and some horses. At about 11 o'clock A.M., seeing they could not dislodge us with their firearms, they set fire to the prairie, hoping thus to burn us or compel us to abandon our camp. So soon as the prairie was on fire they loudly shouted, and expecting their stratagem would be successful, they advanced under protection of the smoke to the position they had first been obliged to abandon; but when the fire reached the valley it died out.

Thinking the siege would be protracted, we employed Gonzales and the boy Charles, in making a breastwork of whatever they could lay their hands upon, such as boughs and our property. From that moment until 4 o'clock the firing slackened gradually and the Indians withdrew to a considerable distance. But the wind having shifted from the southwest to the northwest, the Indians again fired the prairie, and the conflagration reached our camp, but by dint of hard work in the way of tearing the grass, and by means of our bear skins and blankets, made use of to smother the flames, we succeeded in saving the greater part of our animals and other property. We expected a furious attack of the enemy under cover of the smoke, in order to penetrate our camp, but the greater part of them withdrew to a pond, distance about a half a mile from the battle field, to procure water; and those of them that remained kept up firing and removing their dead. This work on their part went on until about 6:30 P.M. when the battle closed, only one shot being fired by them after 7 o'clock, which was aimed at one of our men who went out to obtain water.

We had agreed to attack the enemy while they were asleep, but when we reflected that we had only six men able to use their arms, and that the wounded would have to remain unprotected, we thought it more advisable to remain in our camp, which we had fortified with stones and timber so as to make it secure against further assault. On the 22nd, at about 5 o'clock A.M., we heard the Indians moving to the northeast, and at daybreak none were to be seen. However, at about 11 o'clock we observed thirteen of them, who, upon seeing us, withdrew suddenly. Subsequently, in order to intimidate them and impress them with the idea that we were still ready for a fight, we hoisted a flag on a long pole as a sign of war; and for eight days we kept a fire constantly burning, hoping thereby to attract the attention of any friendly Comanches that might be in the neighborhood and procure some animals for the transportation of our wounded and camp property.

On the evening of the 29th, the wounded being somewhat relieved, we began our march for Bexar, and on striking the Perdanales river we observed a large Tahuacanoe trail, and noticed several others between that stream and the Guadalupe river, all seeming to tend in the direction of a smoke that curled upward from some point down the Perdanales. Upon seeing these trails we took a more westerly course, and after having crossed the Guadalupe we saw no more signs of Indians, and arrived here on the 6th inst. My only loss among my men during the battle was by the fall and death of the foreman of my mechanics, Mr. Thomas McCaslin, from a bullet that entered below the breast and passed through the loin. He was one of the most efficient of my comrades in the fight. I had also three wounded, five animals killed and several hurt. We could make no estimate of the loss of the enemy, but we kept up a continual firing during the day and always had enemies to aim at, and there were no intervening obstacles to prevent our shot from having their full effect. We saw twenty-one men fall dead, and among them, seven on horseback who seemed to act as chiefs, one of whom was very conspicuous by reason of the buffalo horns and other finery about his head. To his death, I attribute the discouragement of his followers.

I cannot do less than commend to your Lordship, for their alacrity in obeying and executing my orders with spirit and firmness, all those who accompanied me. Their names are: Robert Armstrong, Thomas McCaslin (killed), Daniel Buchanan (wounded), James Coryell, Mateo Dias, Cephas K. Ham, Jesse Wallace, Sr. Gonzales, Charles the boy. God and liberty, James Bowie [RUBRIC]
Bexar, December 10th, 1831

COL. JOHN S. FORD

Word got back to San Antonio about the fight Bowie's party had with the Indians along the San Saba before they did. Somehow, in the telling, the outcome became twisted and word had arrived that the party had been slaughtered to a man with Bowie's scalp, along with the others, hanging from the tent pole of a savage in the wilderness. The entire city went into mourning with the doorway and windows of the Veramendi Palace being draped in black crepe. Col. John S. Ford summed it up best in his diary when he lamented the loss. Unfortunately, Colonel Ford's diary is not available for public scrutiny, the family refusing to let it out for publication.—A. J. S.

The shades of night had fallen on the city. Sad hearts were bewailing the fate of the adventurous Americans. A party of men, mostly on foot, weary and soiled by travel, entered the streets of the Queen City of the West. Some of the men were recognized. A shout went up; it was repeated; it spread from street to street, from house to house. Stout men quivered with excitement, tears of joy dimmed bright eyes. Fearless men rushed forward to grasp in friendship and admiration, the hands of citizens who had proved themselves heroes in a contest demanding courage, prudence, endurance, and all the noble qualities adorning the soldier and the patriot. "Bowie's party have returned! They have won a glorious victory!" was the cry. Lights blazed from house to house as word traveled from neighbor to neighbor. The people in their heart of hearts decreed them a triumph. And well they deserved it. The pages of history record but few achievements.

Tom Owl

More than one person has a story about Bowie's San Saba fight. Indeed, if everyone who claimed to have been there with Bowie and Ham and the others had indeed been with them, there wouldn't have been a Lipan Apache left anywhere in the entire world. As it was, given the Homestead Act, the Civil War, and the firm belief in Manifest Destiny that permeated the nation, I'm surprised that any Indians survived at all. Some of the Lipans, the wild bulls of the tribe, joined with their cousins, the Mescalero and the Chiricahua, riding with Nana, Loco, even Geronimo. But for the most part, the Lipans tried to avoid war with the white man. They had learned early that as an isolated tribe, the Lipans had little chance against men who "numbered among the stars their numbers." The Lipans were moved from reservation to reservation as the Bureau of Indian Affairs tried to find a home for them. At last, they were settled up around Fort Sill in the Nations. Shortly after that, they appeared to have disappeared, but the truth of the matter was that they realized what had happened to the Cheyenne and Sioux could easily *happen to them. They disappeared into the outback, sacrificing their unity within a tribal structure for survival. They became farmers and ranchers, scattering themselves among the other tribes, merging their identity with the wilderness and the land. They became silent, holding meetings more in the manner of family reunions than tribal councils, doing business with the white man casually and quietly. Their tribal honor became sacrificed for survival, for the Lipans, unlike other Indians of the stamp of Rousseau's "noble sauvage," believed the survival of the body was necessary for the survival of the soul. It took a while, but at last I found one: Tom Owl, a boy who had been sent to the Carlisle Indian Barracks in Pennsylvania by the Indian Bureau after diphtheria killed his parents. He replied to my query about the San Saba fight in 1892.—*A. J. S.

I supposed it would eventually come down to this. I'm just surprised that it has taken so long for someone to get around to me. There's quite a movement going on now among a few college professors to get the facts right. Or, at least right to their way of thinking. Maybe, however, people are just beginning to rethink their heroes. Maybe people are seeing their heroes now in a tragic sense with feet of clay. Then, of course, there are those who simply cannot understand heroism and want to cut everyone down to their own mediocre size.

Frankly, I've had to give some thought as to whether I was going to write and explain what happened at the fight or not. A literate Indian isn't a healthy thing to be in this day and age, you know. People take great comfort in thinking that we are all pagans, savages, and barbarians. As long as they have something or someone they believe is more miserable than they are, why then they can find some reason to be happy. There's comfort in knowing that you aren't at the bottom of the ladder, you know. And there is something romantic about Indians to some who constantly think we all roam around still hunting buffalo, wearing beads and little else, riding naked across the prairies with feathers dangling from our hair. We can thank James Fenimore Cooper and Ned Buntline for that image. People do not realize that the noble savage really did not exist. He was a myth made up in people's minds to satisfy their own romantic whimsies.

You understand, though, that what I know about San Saba I have from my relatives. My uncle fought in it. Tres Manos, they called him because he had a mummified hand hanging on a cord around his neck. He was the crazy one of the family, according to my father.

From the stories they told about him up in the Choctaw hills, I can understand why everyone pretty much left him alone.

Once one of the Council refused to let Tres Manos go walking with his daughter. That night, my uncle caught one of the man's horses, tied a tumbleweed to its tail, lit the tumbleweed on fire, and sent the horse into the village. Most of the village caught fire from the mad horse and three men were trampled to death when they tried to catch the horse. Another time he took flint chippings from the toolmaker's work place and put them into someone's meal. Cruel, he was. And a bit mad.

So when Bowie, El Cuchillo, they called him, came to our village to hunt with Esteban, the chief, Tres Manos treated him with scorn. One day, according to Father, Tres Manos tried to take El Cuchillo's knife. But Bowie picked him up and threw him among the cooking pots in a fire. Tres Manos's clothes caught on fire and he frantically pulled them off to keep from getting burned. The laughter of the tribe shamed him as he was forced to run naked through the entire village, dogs snapping at his bare heels, hands covering his private parts to keep them from being bitten. The women of the village called him Manoslito thereafter, but only behind his back for as is such with people like him, he could not stand ridicule and men such as this are indeed dangerous men.

But I think the worst day for Tres Manos happened when he and his hunting party cornered a group of Comanches on an oxbow by the river. The way across to the land was a thin sand spit only and the Comanches defended it well against Tres Manos and his men.

Bowie went upstream, stripped, and swam underwater to the back of the Comanches. When he emerged, dripping from the river, his long hair pasted against his neck, his big knife clutched in one hand, the lone lookout shrieked in terror. Bowie fell upon the Comanches, his knife flashing. Tres Manos took advantage of the confusion and sent his men over the spit and onto the island. Later, they found the marks of Bowie's big knife on seven of the ten Comanches.

That night, the Lipans held a dance to celebrate their victory. But it was Bowie who was singled out for praise by the dancers, not Tres Manos. My father remembered how his eyes smoldered and burned, hot coals of hatred, across the fire at Bowie. Whenever he spoke of this, my father shuddered and said he had seen terrible things, but never the dark fire that he saw that night in the eyes of Tres Manos.

I suppose that is why many men were killed in the Fight of the

Broken Trees when Bowie and his men were trapped by Tres Manos and his men near San Saba. Tres Manos had his chance to kill Bowie and would not come away from the fight. He no longer thought with reason, but with passion, and passion never mated well with reason. Time after time, Tres Manos sent men into the trees after Bowie and his men and time after time they were killed or beaten back.

At last, Tres Manos tried to burn them out, but the wind turned and our people were almost destroyed by the fire they set themselves. They were hard-pressed to put it out before it swept the plains, destroying the winter grass. After this, my people began to turn away from Tres Manos and his demands to send them again into the trees. At last, Tres Manos led a party into the trees by himself, and that was his death.

What I know, I know from my father, who did not wish to take part in the fight for El Cuchillo was a friend of the Lipans. But he was afraid for by this time, Tres Manos had made many friends and gained much power. At the time, though he had lost many of those who claimed to be his friends, Tres Manos was still a dangerous man. A madness seemed to have descended upon him. Spittle formed in the corners of his mouth and his eyes rolled in their sockets until the white shone brightly in the daylight. From what my father says, I have little doubt that Tres Manos had been driven mad by his desire to kill Bowie.

My father was there when Tres Manos went into the trees and tried to kill Bowie. El Cuchillo gutted him like a deer. My father forced the others to leave after he saw Tres Manos die.

The fight was a mistake, for the Lipans became laughing horses for their enemies. The Comanches and the People from the West became bolder and bolder, raiding our villages, stealing our horses. My father said that the Fight of the Broken Trees marked the end of our life for from that time on, we could no longer command respect among the other tribes. It did not matter that Comanches and others were with the Lipans that day; the Lipans had been the leaders, thanks to Tres Manos, and so had the responsibility for success or failure. No shame could be placed on those who were not Lipan.

But Bowie must also take a part of the blame for the loss of our respect among the tribes, for we had welcomed him into our village only to be betrayed by him when he searched for the Spanish silver. It was the secret of my people and our strength for with the silver, we could buy respect from the Spaniards and Mexicans. Bowie wronged our people and broke his word to us that he would keep our secret as if he were a Lipan, too. But that, I have learned since being here at Carlisle, is common practice among the white people. They have no truthtellers in their tribe, no honor.

JUAN NEPOMUCENO SEGUÍN

Juan Nepomuceno Seguín deserves much more from history, from Texas, than he receives. He was one of the largest ranchers in Texas, a member of the young lions, a political leader in Bexar, a Texas senator, mayor of San Antonio, a captain of a troop of cavalry he raised himself, commander of a regiment at San Jacinto, and a major influence with the Texas-born Mexicans.

A man of strong convictions, he fought for what he considered right, which is why he fought Santa Anna, but when his political opinions differed from those of newcomers to Texas, mostly from the States, some trumped-up charges were laid against him and he was forced to flee to Mexico. There, Santa Anna imprisoned him.

After the Mexican-American War, Juan Seguín was able to live in Texas, but he was never able to be the political force he had been before the war. He was also a good friend of Jim Bowie.—A. J. S.

I knew Don Jaime well. He was my very good friend. He was one American who did not assume he was better than you simply because of where he was born, and yet he was of good blood himself, *de verdad*.

I do not remember exactly what year it was when first I meet Jaime. It was in Texas, and at an inn. He was traveling across Texas, looking at the land. We struck up a conversation and we were friends from that moment on.

I rode with him when we first became *Los Leoncitos*, "the young lions."

It was in Bexar around 1830, and I was only twenty-four years old. It was a good time for me, but we were having some trouble with one particular band of Comanche. I was in my office at the Rancho Seguín when my foreman ran in against all etiquette.

"*Patrón! El Comanche!*"

"*Dónde?*"

"*El Rancho sur.*"

"Rouse the *vaqueros*! *Andale!*"

Just then my *mozo* came to the door. "Don Jaime Bowie and several riders are here, *señor*."

"Good! Show him in."

My rifle and best pistols were on the wall. I removed them and began to check their loads when Don Jaime and Caiaphas Ham entered.

"*Con permiso*, Don Juan. I have brought my friend with me."

Jaime always spoke very curiously. His voice was very powerful, very deep, but as he spoke, one could hear gentleness in his voice. You would always listen to Jaime for he spoke only when what he had to say he felt was important.

"I am sorry that I do not have time to be a gracious host," I replied. "My *rancho* has been raided by Comanche."

"I had hoped the loaded guns weren't for me or Cap here," he joked, but I could tell by the way he touched the knife at his side that he was interested.

"They attacked my little village on the south ranch. I must ride."

"Besides, Caiaphas, Ben McCulloch, and five other men are riding with me. We've had a few raids all over Texas, and we thought to raise a company of rangers. We were hoping you might have a few *vaqueros* who would ride with us."

"And not me?"

"I did not want to assume to take you away from your important work at the ranch. And the politics in Bexar," he added.

"My *segundo* will provide supplies, fresh horses, what you need. I will change and then we will ride," I said.

We rode as fast as we could to my village where we had taken horses to be broken. The wails of the women greeted us as we rode into the village. The Comanche had ridden through the village, robbing the storehouse, killing four *vaqueros*, three women, a child, and taking two other children with them when they left, both boys, one having six, the other five years.

Petra came out to tell me about the Comanches. I had attended her wedding to Fermin, who now lay with the dead inside the church next to the little rock grotto of the Virgen de Guadalupe.

"Juan," Jaime said, coming up to me. "I sent out the Lipan Apache who works for you. If we follow quickly, we might catch up to them, but I'm not sure that is a good idea. They might kill the boys."

"What do you suggest?" I asked.

"Leave the trail to the Apache and ride directly north. We might reach the hills above the Rio Frio before they if we do this," he said.

I shook my head, objecting. "But, we might lose their trail. You are only guessing about what they are planning."

"True," he said. "But I think that is our best way. To surprise them. They will be expecting us to come from behind, not ahead."

And that is what we did. We left the trail the Comanache had taken and rode north to find the trail to the Llano Estacado. We rode hard and late that night, we reached the rocky hills and set up a hidden camp and placed our watchers.

"You think they'll come this way, Jim?" asked Ben McCulloch.

"I expect them sometime early tomorrow afternoon," Jaime answered. "They'll be making a big detour south and west, then swing north to cut across the river. This is the best crossing for miles. They'll be here."

He settled down to the fire and began to sharpen his big knife. I remember that knife. Every time I saw it, I remembered the stories that people whispered about what he had done with it. They were just stories, but in stories there is always some truth and it is the truth that may be there that is frightening.

The next day, we filled our waterskins and hid in the rocks. Jaime was right. The noon sun had just passed when we tasted the dust of the horse herd on the wind coming from the south. I looked to my arms. We were all well armed, Jaime more than the rest of us.

"They'll stop by the river to water the horses," Jaime said softly. "Wait until you hear me fire."

I nodded and he slipped away to tell the others. Sweat stung my eyes and my hands grew slippery upon the rifle, but my mouth became dry. Strange. One would think the hands would become dry, but such is not the way.

I settled the sights of my rifle upon one brave, squat like a toad. I followed him, waiting, waiting for Jaime to give the signal. At first, I thought that they would ride across the river, but the horses stopped and began to mill around, each trying eagerly to get to the water.

Suddenly, Jaime fired. Startled, I pulled the trigger of my rifle. The Comanche I had been aiming at threw up his arms and tumbled backwards off his pony. More shots rang out. I reloaded as fast as I could. I fired again, then stopped as Jaime appeared on the rocks over the Indians. His knife flashed in his hand as he dropped down upon them like a cat.

He slipped among the Indians like a shadow, his knife flickering, the blade now red with blood. One Comanche screamed and ran away, trying to hold himself inside, but he fell before going very far.

The rest of Jaime's men fell upon the Indians. Fearing that I would be missed, I rose and ran down into the cloud of dust. A Comanche suddenly appeared in front of me, his mouth stretched wide, his eyes blazing with fear and hate. He swung a club at me. I ducked and shot him with one of my pistols. A blow upon my back sent me sprawling into the dust. Someone leaped upon me. I smelled grease and sweat and a hand pulled back my hair. Then, I heard a *chunk!* and a groan, and the Indian sprawled over the top of me.

I heaved him off and sat up, trying to peer through the dust. I looked at the Indian: his legs jerked and twitched, his hand trying to hold the blood inside his throat. A lance narrowly missed me. I seized it and rose, looking for the enemy. But then, it was over and the dust settled.

"Are you all right?"

I turned to face Jaime. His shirt had been ripped by a knife and a long scratch ran down his cheek. His eyes shined with excitement.

"*Sí*," I croaked. I swallowed and tried again. "*Seguro que sí.* And you?"

"Oh yes," he said. He looked around and pointed. I turned to look at Caiaphas Ham, who had pulled the children away into a nest of rocks. "I think we got your horses back, too."

That was the first of the Young Lions, the Rangers.

UNCLE BEN HIGHSMITH

Uncle Ben Highsmith was one of the original settlers of Texas. Born in 1817 in Mississippi, he came with his father to Texas in 1823. During his many years, he served with Jim Bowie at the Grass Fight, and with Sam Houston at San Jacinto. As a Texas Ranger, he fought Comanche and Cherokee, and he was with the Rangers during the Mexican War. Few men have shed as much blood for Texas as Uncle Ben—A. J. S.

Jack Sowell asked me to have written down all I know about Jim Bowie. I cant hardly see no more so I have to have somebody else put my story on paper. First, let me say that I knew Jim Bowie from the time I was only a young one.

My first trip with him was in 1830. It was then the first Texas Rangers company was formed. Bowie was known as the Young Lion, and all his rangers kinda went under the same name.

Texas was a state of Mexico at the time and under the official
protection of the Mexican government. So their soldiers were supposed to keep Indians and bandits away from the settlements.

It never worked that way, though. Most of them Mexican soldiers
werent worth a pig in a poke. They would hole up in a town and
nothing short of a general would get them out. Unless they could
smell a profit, and then they still had to be sure they outnumbered
the enemy by three or five to one.

Maybe I shouldnt blame them too much. They was mostly men
out of jail from down south sent up North to get rid of a problem.
The government seldom paid them and except for the really good
officers, never trained them. So, we had a bunch of sorry convicts
dressed up fine and given a bit of authority. The upshot of it all was
that we Texians were at the mercy of the heathen hordes. Mostly
Comanche, but Kronks and Cherokee, Tonks and Kiowa, even
sometimes the Apache attacked us whenever they felt frisky or run
low on supplies.

I stop to think here a minute and want to say that there were
some good Mexican soldiers. I know, cause I fought them, but most
of the soldiers sent to Texas were sent to take advantage of the settlers from the states, and not to fight Indians.

Indians raided as a way of life. If they didnt have enough, they
went and took it from somebody else. I guess thats mankinds way,
so I wont worry about the right and wrong of it, but I will sure say
that mankinds way also provides for defense. Us Texians felt we
needed to protect ourselves.

My family first settled on the Colorado River about two miles
from the town now called La Grange. It was there in 1829 that I
saw firsthand what I was just talking about. The Comanche had always gotten along with the settlement in our neck of the woods, but
that year they told the men that when the Comanche moon came
theyd be down to raid and if they were still living in the settlement,
the Comanche would kill them.

Zaddock Wood and Stephan Cottle packed up their families and
moved to Rabbs Mill. Six families stayed close to mine and food got
mighty scarce cause nobody wanted to be out farming too long. We
were staying with Elliot C. Buckner.

There werent much to it; we could weather it out, but we needed
supplies and come spring of 1830, Jim Bowie rode in.

Now Jack says hes been gettin stories from others, so I wont go into long descriptions of Bowie. I will just say he rode in on a fine big horse, not a thoroughbred, but a Morgan, one who could travel the wilderness and keep going. Hed conserve his strength so his rider could always have something when the need rose for fast moving. Jim was wearing buckskins that had a reddish tinge to them so they looked like a sunset. I guess thats foolishness, but its somehow right.

You see, when Bowie came into sight it always seemed like all eyes would turn towards him. It wasnt cause he was a dandy. He took care with his clothes and he always was dressed right for the place he was at, but he werent fussy about them. If they got dirty, hed clean up as well as he was able, and finish the job when he got to someplace he could.

There were several things about Jim. He never bragged. He never swore. He only got angry when someone needed killing and seemed always to fit his surroundings even with these peculiarities. He dint drink much, at least when I first knew him. That changed a little later on, though I think people may have let that part of the story grow so as to knock Jims memory down a peg or two.

Like I said, Jim was always the center of attention, without him ever making a conscious effort to be the center of attention. It was just that something about him always made you strive to be his friend, at least that was the way with the good people. There were some who would see Jim stride into a room and would automatically decide that he was something they could never be and then theyd have to try to make him a little less.

The trouble with that line of thought is that hed show how well he could fight. The man was a holy terror, no doubt of that. Hed fight fist or knife or pistol or rifle but hed match any man and best him.

Well, Jim came riding into our yard that day and he says, "Ben, will you take care of my horse while I see your father?"

He slid down off his horse keeping that big rifle—the one Big Foot Wallace ended up with—and keeping it pointing up friendly like. He looked at me but made no effort to force me to take his reins. You see Jim didnt force anyone. He asked a favor and you just wanted to help him out.

"Sure, Mr. Bowie. Pas inside," I said.

"Now, Ben, cant you call me Jim? Youre full grown or near enough."

I remember feeling like I was a king or something right after he said that. Well, Jim went inside and I stabled his horse and brought his pack into the house. He was talking with Pa about the Indian troubles we were having.

It was a long discussion, but it was decided that the only solution was to go into San Antonio on a trading expedition. Over the next couple of days we gathered up anything worth trading, chose the best horse for riding, and those best for packing goods. We also figured out who would go.

The party was Jim Bowie, W. B. Travis, Ben McCulloch, Winslow Turner, George Kimble, Sam Highsmith and me. This was the birth of the Texas Rangers.

It might not seem to be much to you now, but back then it was a real adventure. Since it was spring, it was raiding time. There were Comanche, those whod run us to our neighbors and kept us hungry, then there was Caddoes and sometime Kronks who were cannibals. The civilized tribes of Cherokee and Creek werent so civilized that sometimes they werent above getting their own from the white man.

On the first night out, I asked, "Jim, can I see your knife?"

"Sure," he replied and pulled it from his side and flipped it through the air to catch it by the point, and then tossed it into the cottonwood tree next to where I was standing. I swear it takes longer to tell than it took to happen.

I pulled that big knife out of the tree and stared at it. I was twelve years old and so couldnt be too anxious, but I still needed to look at this mankiller. It was about a foot long and curved at the front. The blade was heavy and if you looked at it from the point, you could see how the whole blade was formed. Kind of like a wedge or an axe blade, with the thick top covered with brass. It had a big brass guard to protect the hand and the soft brass backstrap could easily catch the steel of someone who he was fighting. The handle was ebony.

I handed it back to him and told him that was some knife. I saw he had another that was about nine inches long which he used for cutting meat and such. The pattern was similar but Jim was always thinking and inventing things.

On the third day we saw faint smoke rising from behind a clump of live oak. "Looks like someones cooking," Sam said. Jim looked a little concerned and said, "Lets ride."

It was a craftsmans cabin. The timber was well dressed and fit well. A little green, which is why it didnt burn completely.

Jim walked his horse around the cabin as I stared at the rich black earth that had been prepared for the crop. Hed not wasted. He cut his trees for the cabin and pulled the stumps so that he could plow the land. The rest of the forest could slowly be cut back as he was able to grow more crops, in the meantime he would have some forest for hunting.

Jim rode to the front door, climbed off his horse with his big rifle ready to fire. One pound of lead only made sixteen bullets for it. It had the kick of a mule and whatever he hit went down and he seldom missed. He had that rifle pointed at the door when he told Ben McCulloch to get down and side him.

Ben did as he was asked. He stood next to the door with his own long rifle cocked and ready to fire. The rest of us checked our loads and kept checking the countryside for hidden Indians.

Jim hit the door with his shoulder and went right on inside. There was no shot so McCulloch went in behind him.

They came out shaking their heads. I had to look, and what I saw has lived with me to this day. The man and his wife had been scalped and mutilated. I wont tell you all they did but it was enough to send me out into the fields to pour my breakfast onto the earth. The first and last time that ever happened.

We buried the couple and Jim said a prayer over them. It didnt take us but an hour to get into the saddle again. We fed and watered the horses and grabbed a bite ourselves. There wasnt any doubt that we wanted to find the raiders and wreak vengeance on them.

"How many you think there are, Jim?" I asked, knowing that hed just become colonel of our regiment of seven riders.

"Tracks were too confusing to say for sure, but it was a small party of ten to fifteen. Nothing we cant handle."

It was just past noon when we decided to take a chance and ride up to the top of a hill. It wasnt as reckless as it sounds cause the hill was covered with timber so careful riding still kept us hid from the Indians.

We could see them at the bottom of the hill. It was a little valley with a creek, meadow, and a stand of trees butting up against another hill. There were thirteen Comanche, two of them young enough to be considered boys, the rest young warriors, say around twenty or just past. They were letting their horses drink in the stream. They werent in any hurry.

Jim pondered the sight for a second. "If none of us miss, we could cut the force in half but the rest would make that stand of trees before we could reload. From those trees, theyd make the hill and be gone before we could finish them. So, we will trap them. Now, heres how we do it."

He grinned at us and said, "Sam, you and Ben get to play hero. Think youre up to it?"

Who wouldnt be. They said sure and Jim said, "If you ride down this game trail you will hit the far side of that meadow before the Comanche get too far into the trees. Theyll want to take your horses and rifles so theyll chase you if they think they can get them. Now, if you were to ride on this side of the creek and straight down from where were sitting those Indians will sneak up on you."

"And I suppose you fellers will amble on down to the edge of the trees and have some loaded rifles and pistols ready to lend a hand," Sam said. He laughed and him and Ben climbed up on their horses. Well, that was just a bit too much for me.

"What about me?" I asked. "Im part of this group too."

"I need you to mind these horses," Jim said. "Just like those Indians have someone minding theirs. See what I mean?"

"Yes sir," I said, but I was mighty disappointed that I wasnt going along with Sam and Ben as they went on down to act as bait for the trap.

They rode along, joking like they was the only ones in the world until they came to a big lightning struck tree that they could use as a bit of cover. Ben walked his horse over to the log and tied on to it with Sam right behind him. They laid out their pistols and rifles and I would have swore they was getting ready for a little nap if I didnt know different.

Those Indians took a long time to creep up on them, but Ben and Sam got up to walk a little ways away from their guns to make water and those Indians snapped right up that bait like rising trout.

A war whoop made me jump near out of my skin although I was waiting for it. Sam and Ben took off back to their guns and jumped behind the tree. Sam shot a buck carrying a lance in one hand and a buffalo shield in the other. Ben hit another and then they pulled up on their pistols and let go with all four bullets.

Now, them Indians had been counting their shots and after that the Indians decided to come right after them. Thats when our boys opened up on them. Those Indians were so surprised that someone was behind them that they stopped long enough for Ben and Sam to finish reloading their rifles. They fired again and that must have confused them Indians cause some took off one way and some took off another.

None made it to the creek, though, or the trees. Jim and me gathered up the horses while the others hunted down the stray Indians that had gone the other way.

We took them horses to San Antonio and sold them and split the money between us. That was the first time I was in town alone without my Pa and I took advantage of it. Everybody wanted to hear the story and bought us a drink every time we told it. I had it down pretty pat by midnight, I tell you, but my head was swimming from all that whiskey and I found a stable and passed out in the straw there. I had me a fine time.

Well, thats how the Rangers got their start. It became sort of official when a group of the men decided they needed to have some sort of militia and they all elected Jim their colonel.

I was given what they called garrison duty and though I didnt like it, I did it.

On their first outing, Jim and his men ran into some Kiowa. Jim had to wade into them with his big knife flashing and those who saw him said it was like watching a lion. And so people took to call us the Young Lions.

I was fifteen when I ran away from home and fought in the Battle of Velasco. That was where some Texians were unlawfully detained by a man named Bradburn. I was in Mr. Elliot C. Buckners company. Strap Buckner, the giant, was killed leading us in the foray along with several of the company. I fought in many a campaign since then. I was even with Bowie at the Grass Fight.

Oh, I joined the Rangers that were sanctioned by the State and can say I was one of the first then too, but nothing was like those early years riding with Jim Bowie and the Young Lions.

MAJOR BEN C. TRUMAN

Many tales exist about Bowie's duels. So many, in fact, that one is hard-pressed in order to separate the truth from legend. Major Truman interviewed an old steamboatman who allegedly was upon the paddlewheeler Rob Roy *when Bowie came to the aid of a young woman whose husband had become the victim of a fleecing by a pair of riverboat gamblers.*

According to the man Major Truman interviewed, in the summer of 1833 this young gentleman and his new bride made a trip up North in the course of which he apparently gathered a large sum of money for investment back in Natchez. The gamblers managed to entice him into a friendly game of "twenty-card poker," a game played with only the tens through the aces and limited to four players, an advantage for crooked gamblers who can control the timbre of the game by limiting the players.

The young man lost everything and was in the process of trying to hurl himself overboard to spare himself and his bride the shame he would encounter when he reached Natchez, when Jim Bowie stepped in and pulled the young man back from the rail. When the bride tearfully made Bowie aware of the situation, Bowie made them promise to wait in their cabin until he had a chance to set things right.

*Bowie entered the gaming room and used an old trick to get himself invited into the game by buying a drink and trying to pay for it with a hundred-dollar bill. The gamblers bit and immediately invited Bowie to their table for a friendly turn of the cards. Bowie played carefully, conserving his money. When the riverboat was near Rodney where it would take on wood, the gamblers made their move. The pot quickly built to $100,000. The following tells the end of the tale.—*A. J. S.

Well, I was lucky to be in the saloon at the time and saw what happened. Whilst the betting was going on the stranger (we didn't find out later that it was Jim Bowie and I wonder what would have happened if the others knew his name) had kept his eye on the dealer and had prevented any changing of cards. Toward the last he saw a card slipped by the dealer to the man who had made the blind, when, seizing him by the wrist with one hand, he drew a murderous looking knife with the other and forced the gambler to lay his cards on the table face down. All sprang to their feet and the stranger quietly said that when that hand was raised and it should be found to contain six cards, he would kill the owner; telling the other to show his cards, he threw down his own hand, which consisted of four kings and a ten spot. The baffled gambler, livid with rage and disappointment, swore that the stranger should fight him, demanding, with an oath, to know who he was anyway. Quietly, and as if in the presence of ladies, the stranger answered, "James Bowie." At the sound of that name two of the gamblers quailed, for they knew that the man who bore that name was a terror to even the bravest; but the third, who had never heard of "James Bowie," demanded a duel at once. This was acceded to at once by Bowie, with a smile; pistols—derringers—were the weapons selected, the hurricane-roof the place, and the time at once. Sweeping the whole of the money into his hat, Bowie went to the room where the unhappy wife sat guarding her husband's uneasy slumbers, and rapping on the door, he handed her, when she had opened it, the hat and its contents, telling her that if he did not come back, two thirds of the money was her husband's and the balance his own. Ascending to the hurricane-roof the principals were placed one upon the top of each wheel-house. This brought them about twelve yards apart, and each was exposed to the other from the knee up. The pistols were handed to them and the gambler's second gave the word, "one, two, three, fire, stop," uttered at intervals of one second each, and they were allowed to fire at any time between the utterance of the words one and stop. As "one" rang out in the clear morning air both raised their weapons, as "three" was heard the gambler's pistol rang out and before the sound had ceased and whilst the word "fire" was being uttered, Bowie's pistol sounded, and simultaneous with this sound the gambler fell, and giving a convulsive struggle rolled off the wheel-house into the river. Bowie coolly blew the smoke out of his pistol, shut down the pan, and going down into the ladies' cabin obtained his hat and divided the money which it contained into three portions. Two of these he gave to the young wife and the other he kept, as it was his own money. Having awakened her husband, the fond wife showed him the money, and told him all she knew about the affair, not having heard of the duel. When the husband became acquainted with all the facts, his gratitude to his benefactor was deep and lasting. Not desiring to be made a hero of, Bowie, when the boat reached Rodney, went ashore.

JUDALON DE BORNAY

*Jim Bowie met Judalon de Bornay on his first trip to New Orleans when he traveled there to find a buyer for the Bowie lumber cut at their sawmill in the bayous. It was quite by accident that Bowie met her brother in a coffeehouse and became fast friends with him, their friendship resulting in an invitation to the de Bornay home. There, Bowie met the petite Judalon, whose flawless ivory skin and large, black eyes entranced him. Had this meeting occurred after Bowie acquired the manners and "polish" by which he charmed business associates and Ursula de Veramendi years later, his future would have undergone a drastic alteration. But Bowie was a back-woodsman and although possessed of charming ways, they were not the so-cial manners of an extremely mannered period. Judalon scorned his advances, putting Bowie in a black, brooding melancholy that resulted in a certain recklessness surfacing that caused the death of a dueling master, a M. Contrecourt, whom Bowie killed in a duel, sword against knife, in a darkened room at St. Sylvan's. That was the birth of Bowie as an adven-turer.—*A. J. S.

M. James Bowie was a buffoon, an ass who had pretensions that we could not tolerate in Orleans society. I remember well when my brother brought him home, awkward, his feet clumsy, hands callused, and trying to appear a gentleman although he did not know how to wear the lace and Spencer coat that my brother had introduced him to. I smothered my laugh and flirted with him, amusing myself with how far I could tease him.

I overestimated once and remember how M. Bowie seized me, bruising my poor arms with his crude fingers, and held me close.

"Judalon," he breathed. "When shall we marry?"

"Release me!" I commanded him sternly.

His eyes widened in surprise, then he smiled. The oaf thought that I, a de Bornay, was teasing with him. He tried to kiss me. Perhaps he did. Well, he did. Yes. For a moment, I almost weakened in spite of myself, then I remember my station in society and his place and I remember his story about broom-jumping and so I did not wish to jump a broom with him, I pushed him away and struck him across his cheek with my fan.

"Brute!" I said, summoning up the most scorn I could to put in my voice. "Did you think that you would be allowed in this house if it were not for my brother? How dare you take such liberties with me? *Sacre!* I shall have you horse-whipped for this!"

And I stormed out of the sitting room, leaving him standing there with the egg upon his face.

I see M. Bowie only once more and it is then I realize my mistake. I have married with Phillipe Cabanal, a weak man whose gambling ruined us in society, forcing us to move to Natchez. I saw M. Bowie there, true, but he did not, or at least pretended not, to see me. Phillipe and I had moved into a small house at the edge of the bluff in not the most respectable part of town. I could not entertain as Phillipe lost our money at the gaming tables. Then, he went into business with M. John A. Murrell and our fortunes rose dramatically. No longer was I *elle est toujours à court d'argent.*

Soon, we were able to move to a more respectable part of town. Phillipe stayed away from the gaming tables and went into business with M. Murrell, selling cotton and speculating in various cargoes for shipment downriver. I do not pretend to know this business, but I was shocked when suddenly the authorities appear at our door and arrest Phillipe. He was, how you say, *il fut pris la main dans le sac.*

Fortunately, our money had been placed in a bank in New Orleans and it was there that I promptly moved before the scandal of Phillipe coming to trial. I pretended that we had been divorced and as such, I was spared ruination within our society. *Je m'en lave les mains.*

I also became the object of several younger men who saw in me a *relever un défi* and in *moment de défaillance* I allowed them their *conquête.* The theater, the ballet, the music. Ah, it was gay times!

It was at the theater that I saw M. Bowie in the company of M. Forrest. I arranged for my escort to approach them.

"Ah, M. Bowie. It is a pleasure to see you," I said, smiling. I knew how I looked. I had spent hours arranging my hair, my gown, cut low to show my breasts, selecting my jewels.

His eyes grew cold. "Is it, Mme. Cabanal?"

"Ah, but I am now again Mlle. de Bornay," I said roguishly, flirting again with him. "I have left Phillipe."

"He is a fortunate man, indeed, then," M. Bowie said.

My escort stepped forward and impulsively slapped M. Bowie's face. "That is not something one says to a lady!"

"You are right," M. Bowie said. "And I would apologize if it had been a lady I addressed!"

My cheeks burned at his words for I knew that others around me had heard his words. My escort then challenged M. Bowie and M. Bowie arranged for his second to meet Dominique You, a pretender to society, one of Jean Lafitte's men.

They met two days later at The Oaks at the Allard Plantation. I heard about it from the young man's second. My poor darling! He tried to play the gentleman to the end, but I should have told him that M. Bowie was no gentleman. When the referee counted the paces and reached "ten," my darling executed the most appropriate turn-face, but M. Bowie simply leaned around and casually shot him between the eyes.

"A magnificent shot!" exclaimed the second. "But a barbarian made it!"

That afternoon, M. Bowie appeared at my gate. I received him, dressing myself hurriedly in my most becoming gown. He scarce noticed it as he said, "Judalon, I have now killed at least four men on your account. I have no intention of killing a fifth. Henceforth, keep your distance."

"M. Bowie!" I exclaimed indignantly, but the boor turned and left, leaving me alone in my house on Chartis Street.

I believe my servants told of this encounter for visitors to my *salon* became fewer and fewer and when the tiny wrinkles became more apparent, so did the young men.

I am alone. . . .

JOSÉ ANTONIO NAVARRO

In 1833, an epidemic of Asiatic cholera swept over the land, killing many. In Victoria, many, including the great empresario *Don Martín de León and John Austin, the* alcalde *of San Felipe, fell victim to the Pale Horseman. Whole families were being wiped out. Bowie decided that his family should visit Monclova, where the Veramendis had a summer home away from the heat of San Antonio. Ursula pleaded with her husband to come along with them, but Bowie had business to take care of before traveling to Monclova. In July, the Veramendis left, Ursula and their two children, her parents, and certain members of the household. What they did not know was that the plague had reached also into Coahuila, into Monclova. In September, Bowie learned about the death of his family from a friend of her uncle, José Antonio Navarro, who had received a letter from the Coahuilan city.* —A. J. S.

Please, my good friend, do a favor for us in this, our hour of grief. Poor Bowie is now a widower, and I wish you would in some way advise him of the sad news.

Strange, is it not, that in wanting to save his family, Bowie sent them away to their certain death for the plague has, so far, apparently missed Bexar, if what I read from your letters is true. Sometimes, I wonder if Bowie sent Ursula and his children away for selfish reasons or if he truly was concerned with their health. I suppose it does not matter anymore. The Pale Horseman has ridden hard over our family. All are gone. All.

I suppose you had better tell Bowie to stay away from here. He can do no good except find his own death and that will serve no purpose except to make him a martyr that no one will remember.

I do not know if I will see you again, my friend. That is now in the hands of God.

José Navarro [RUBRIC]

FROM THE JOURNAL OF
A. J. SOWELL

Why? I have been asked this question many times. Why do I have this obsession about James Bowie? I can't quite answer the question, even when I ask it of myself. Admiration? Perhaps. Any person can be subject to the pride that comes with being friends with someone who has made his mark on history, but I think Sam Houston made me wonder about the man who became a hero. Houston told me stories that firmly established the legend in my malleable mind.

When I first met Sam Houston, in 1860, he was sixty-seven and near the end of his life. I was twelve. Houston was desperately trying to stem the tide approaching as the War Between the States, which would result in our secession from the country we had worked so hard to join.

Father and I were in the Capital on Ranger business and we chanced to enter the plaza near Ranger headquarters. Houston sat whittling under a tree, holding court while he talked to various and sundry individuals who happened to pass. He recognized Father and called him over.

Houston was immense, standing over six feet tall and as massive as a granite cliff. He was loud and exuberant, and spoke of himself in the royal person. "Houston says the Union must remain a union. Our differences must be settled in honest debate in the Congress of the United States, not in the individual state legislatures. You never hear me talk of the rights of Southern states because all states have equal rights." That is one of my favorites.

He looked down at me, his eyes twinkling in his tired and seamed face. "Sowell, who's this little ragtag following you?"

Father smiled. "This is my son, Andrew Jackson." I wondered why he didn't just say "Jack" like usual. But then, Houston pushed that thought from my mind.

"Houston is pleased to meet you, Andrew Jackson Sowell." He stood and gave a little bow. I stammered something about my name being my uncle's name as well, and Houston laughed, the sound booming around the courtyard.

He threw out a huge paw that swallowed up my young hand. "That's a proud name. Houston is pleased to be your servant."

Of course, I knew the name Sam Houston. Who didn't? What I didn't know at that time was just how close he was to the former president whose Hermitage was only a few miles from my father's Tennessee home and whose name I was carrying in honor of him.

Houston asked about Indian depredations in our neck of the woods, and though Father gave him information, it seemed to me that Houston already knew most of it. Gradually, however, the talk turned away from Indians, scoundrels, and politics, and then Houston talked to me. Almost no one knew more tales of frontier Texas than Houston, and he was having a fine time telling these to me when he noticed I was carrying a Bowie knife my grandfather Asa Sowell had made. He asked to see it, admired it, then started telling me about the man the knife was named after: James Bowie.

Well, I knew Jim Bowie's story, or at least I thought I did. My own kinfolk told me about him, but when Houston spoke about his friend, I could almost see him: a tall man with reddish hair, gray eyes, with shoulders like a young Hercules, a soft-spoken Southern gentleman who became a demon when aroused. But as Houston continued his story, a different Bowie began to emerge. I began to see the man who had strong plans for Texas. I watched Father nodding and smiling as Houston spoke, and those little motions and twitches, smiles and grimaces, made me realize that the same man could be seen differently by different people.

As Houston continued with his stories, I became more and more intrigued by the differences between what he remembered and what I had learned from my own family and others who had offered a tale or two to my boyish demands.

That night as Father and I retired to our room, I sat at the little oaken desk and made some notes in a cheap, ruled notebook that Mother had made me take along on the trip, demanding that I write something on what had happened every day in lieu of spending the same time in school. I remember taking the notebook from her thin hands with a deep sigh about how she was spoiling what was supposed to be a fun trip by turning it into a school trip. But now, as I wrote, trying to imitate the rhythm of Houston's speech and laboriously trying to spell what fell so easily from his lips, I decided that I would try to find out more about Bowie.

The next day when I found Houston sitting comfortably under the tulip tree in the middle of the plaza, fragrant whiskey fumes bubbling gently from his lips, I asked him if he would tell me where I could find out more about Jim Bowie. He grinned, rumpled my hair, then said, "Why don't you write Bowie's people? Some of them are still alive, and they'd probably be more than willing to tell you what you want to know. Houston can get you started. He still has the address of Bowie's mother back on Bayou Teche. Now, Houston reckons she's most likely dead, but there'll be someone there related to old Jim, more than likely."

Mother helped. Even then, it took me nearly two weeks to get those letters written. And while they were gone, I fidgeted and squirmed with each mail delivery, fuming about how long it took the mail to get out of Texas and back.

One day, though, I got a surprise: Bowie's mother was still alive! There was the proof, a package from Elvie Bowie filled with letters and documents from both her husband Rezin and her son Rezin. The family portraits that she drew gave me a picture of the young Jim Bowie riding alligators in the swamp, fighting, running slaves, finding adventure wherever he could.

I wrote her another letter, thanking her for the package. She answered again, giving me a little more information. That was the start of a long exchange of letters between us that continued until she died. By then, I had a string of letters going out on a regular basis to people all over Texas and places beyond. But the picture I wanted of the man remained opaque.

It still is.

I was fifteen the year Sam Houston died. Before he died, he helped me see history in a different light. Now, as I try to write about Jim Bowie and the Texas War of Independence, I can see the events that led me to contemplating a discussion of heroes and Jim Bowie. I had been working at collecting stories and letters about Bowie for a few years. Strange, that while I had been told dozens of stories and met Bigfoot Wallace, that remarkable frontiersman who showed me Bowie's rifle and told me stories, I still did not know Jim Bowie. Who was he? A brawler? Gentleman? Patriot? Land swindler? I had no idea.

In 1862, I went to Austin with my uncle and stayed at an inn called The Alamo. Just about everywhere you went in Texas those days you'd find something called The Alamo. Usually a saloon, although there were a few hotels and inns and one sporting house up near Waco named after the old mission, although few had any cottonwood trees around them to warrant the name.

This particular inn was a long, low, adobe and wood structure with a tile roof. Tile roofs had become rather commonplace in Texas by this time as people had civilized themselves right out of the old sod roofs that were home to cockroaches, scorpions, and tarantulas that had a habit of falling into someone's food or bed. Now, I wonder if that might not be one of the reasons we have so many people with bad teeth in Texas: they just got that way from grinding down on the dirt that trickled into their meat and beans.

Anyway, Austin was a new town, mostly mud or grass with a large number of newly constructed buildings stretching down Main Street, most of them still raw lumber. Some had hired old Mexicans to build them something along the lines of haciendas, but a lot of people still bristled whenever they saw anything that could be construed Mexican.

The Alamo in Austin stood a ways away from what you could call the "city proper," I guess. An adobe wall wrapped around a space in front of the building to create a sort of courtyard wide enough for a six-horse team to turn a coach around. A porch had been added onto the building where someone had scattered a bunch of wicker chairs. Double doors led inside to a common room. I remember those doors:

someone had spent a lot of time carving a picture of Samson fighting the Philistines into the oak wood.

"Andrew Jackson Sowell."

I turned and looked automatically into the deep shadow at the far end of the porch where a tall, white-haired man with a deeply lined face grinned back at us.

"Hello, Sam," my uncle said, clumping down the boards. He stretched out a hand. "You're looking well's could be expected."

"I am." Houston peered at me, then shook his huge, shaggy head. "Don't tell Houston that this is Houston's little friend from San Antonio a few years back."

"I've grown a mite," I said. I put my hand cautiously in his huge palm: meathooks, we called 'em then.

He laughed and solemnly shook my hand. Uncle Andy hawked and spat out into the thick dust. "Well, why you drinking alone, Sam?" he asked. "There something wrong with the Texicans hereabouts that they ain't buying President-Governor-by-God-Sam-Houston liquor?"

The smile slipped from Houston's face. His lips tightened for a moment, then he let out a huge sigh. "It's this war, A. J.," he said. "Houston didn't think it was necessary. He still doesn't, for that matter, but Texes is still Houston's home and he still believes in her laws—even if they're being passed by fools who bray like Balaam's Ass." He glanced around to see if anyone was listening, then hitched his chair closer to us, lowering his voice. "Now, Houston wouldn't want this to get around, but he became a teetotaler a few years ago." A heavy eyebrow quirked. "Houston's reputation was damaged a mite by that."

They laughed heartily. I chortled along with them, but I was a bit puzzled as to why old Sam wasn't revered by all Texicans. But I was too young then to see the weaknesses of men who had been caught up in the excitement of war, a last adventure in a time when many had given up the possibility for adventure. Houston had had enough of war in his time to understand its brutishness. He also believed firmly in the sanctity of the Union—especially since we had fought the Texas War for Independence so we could join that Union.

Today, a man like Houston would be laughed at, but Houston was positive that the United States had a destiny to rule everything from one ocean to the next and that internal squabbles between states should be fought out in Congress and not on the battlefield that pit brother against brother, son against father. His highly vocal opinions caused many to belittle him. Maybe that's one of the reasons that he died the next year.

Our business kept us at The Alamo for a few days. It was a great opportunity for me, although I didn't recognize it at the time. Later, I was able to piece together some of Houston's views, and jot down some of his opinions and political maneuverings. I listened to the stories people exchanged with him when they came to sit in the sun with him. I learned quite a bit in those few days about how the Texas government came about. Before that trip, I assumed everyone was a Texas patriot and that they shared the same ideas about Texas. Of course, when you're fifteen, you're positive that you have the right idea about everything and that everyone who doesn't agree with you must be either bull-headed or stayed out in the sun too long until they became hydrophobic. Maybe the reason I thought that way was because I was afraid that if too many disagreed with me, I'd have to reexamine my own thoughts, and what young man wants to do that?

When we were alone, Houston spoke long and in great detail about our history. He knew those men well who formed Texas. Maybe he was trying out his arguments on me before he voiced his opinions to those politicians who had frozen him out. Maybe they should have listened to him, because Houston sought to fulfill a dream while others simply wanted to carve great fortunes out of the Texas wilderness.

I think now that the war for Texas's Independence was a foregone conclusion from the time Santa Anna became emperor of Mexico. In a way, I supposed Santa Anna wasn't entirely wrong in trying to stop Texas from becoming Texas. The great experiment when Mexico opened its borders to people settling from the United States had gotten greatly out of hand. At the time, though, Mexico had a lot of land and too few people to put on it. The Mexicans also had a lot of money problems. It didn't take much, I expect, for Mexico to put two-and-two together and hope for six to realize the profit they could make from selling land to certain land speculators called *empresarios*. I guess they didn't figure, however, that the United States had too many people who wanted land.

Anyway, a Connecticut man, Moses Austin, applied for land from the Mexican government, but before he could come to Texas with the three hundred families he had recruited, he died of pneumonia. His son, Stephen, took over the old man's dream, though, and led those families to the two hundred thousand acres of promised land that Mexico had set aside for them. It didn't take much for others to see a profit in that, though. Men like Jim Bowie soon figured out that they didn't have to attach themselves to a man like Austin. They could become *empresarios* themselves.

Only ten years after Austin's people settled in Texas, the people from the States outnumbered the Mexicans—a subject that caused great concern to some of the political leaders of Mexico. The result was a new dike of immigration laws to stop the flood of people from the States.

One night, Houston took dinner with us. We sat in the common room, talking for quite some time. I realize now that he was laying a foundation for me to comprehend the personalities involved in the beginning of Texas's fight, but it was the next morning before I started getting the full story.

I woke early and wandered down the stairs to the little plaza. Houston was already awake, sitting under a chinaberry tree, whittling on a piece of jackpine. At first, I thought he was studying the work in his hands, but when I came closer to watch, I saw his hands were moving mechanically, his mind elsewhere.

"Come to sit with an old man, Jack," he said.

"Find me one, and I'll do it," I answered.

He laughed, pleased with my response, and moved over on the bench to make room for me. It didn't take long before we were talking about the War. I guess I steered him in that direction, though, because I wanted to pick his brains a little more about Jim Bowie, but like most adults, Houston took a roundabout way of getting to what I wanted to know. He was a natural tease, though, so maybe that had something to do with it, too.

"Well, Stephen Austin came across the Red River with three hundred families that had given most of their savings to Austin for land that Mexico gave free to Austin," he said. He stopped and reached down beside the bench for a tin cup and took a long swallow. I frowned. I thought Austin had bought the land, but here was Houston telling me different. I mentioned this to him. He shook his shaggy head and smiled.

"Yes," he said. "That's what the Austins would like most people to think. Especially now that they're trying so hard for respectability. Makes them appear rather saintly instead of opportunists. But they weren't saintly, Andy; they were just people who had figured out how to make a little money from nothing. Some would call them land pirates, Houston expects, and maybe they were. They probably had to grease the skids a little, but the Austin fortunes were greatly improved by the sale of their land. Now let's see . . . hmm. Houston was still in the States in 1821 when Austin brought all his people in, but stories from these families say that Austin was always jealous of his position." He winked at me. "Like Houston, but with less cause.

"Being fair, Houston thinks Austin always cared for his people and Texas. He had the respect of the Mexican government and many of the other settlers in Texas."

"I've always heard that Austin was a good leader," I interrupted.

"Well, he thought he was; that's for sure. To a point, he was, too. Until he wrote a letter to the Mexican government that got him arrested, he was always pretty sure his decisions were the correct ones, but two years in a Mexican prison changed a lot of his thinking." He winked and tapped a thick broad forefinger along the side of his nose. I smiled.

"The colony was a good one, wan't it?"

"Austin had good people. Most of them, anyway. He didn't bring down any of the Gone To Texas rascals that came later, but good, hardworking farmers looking to carve a living out of the land here." He peered closely at me. "Ambition is a good thing if it is coupled with a habit of hard work. The success of this country comes from people who want to do better and are willing to go out and sweat over a plow or an ax. Men who are willing to hunt up land and raise cattle and horses."

"That's good, ain't it? Isn't it?" I amended when he frowned.

He nodded. "Well, it made Austin worry about his position. He was their leader, but he was really not cut out to be a leader. He always thought he had to dictate to his people instead of leading them. There's a difference, you see?" I shook my head. He frowned and took another deep swallow from the tin cup. "Well, Andy, it's like this. There's two ways of being a leader and being a success at it. Either corrupt those following you, or make them want you because they believe in what you believe. Austin had doubts, but he couldn't bring himself to express those doubts. He couldn't stand others to see him as a human being," he said. He frowned thoughtfully. "Houston doesn't expect you to understand, but it's hard to let others see you as a human. We all want to look bigger." He laughed. "Maybe we all want to be gods." He shook his head.

"Well, Austin took over for his father, but he wasn't Moses. He snapped out orders and expected others to jump at them. But Texicans don't hop just because another man hollers 'Frog!' "

He paused for a second, then said, "Jim Bowie had cold, gray eyes. When he looked at you, you just simply had to accommodate him. If he told you to attack hell with a bucket of well water, you'd just naturally do it because you wouldn't want to tell him you couldn't. That made a big difference between Bowie and Austin. People just naturally wanted to follow Bowie. They just naturally shied away from Austin."

"Is that because Bowie corrupted them or made them want to follow him?"

He laughed and took his watch from a vest pocket, opening it. "A good question, Andy. A real good question. But Houston is a little peckish now. Let's go get something to eat."

I waited until we sat down to platters of eggs and ham. He piled his plate high, and took a few bites, chewing thoughtfully.

"Mr. Houston," I said carefully. "What can you tell me about Jim Bowie?"

He continued to chew silently for a long minute and I was afraid he wasn't going to answer. Then, a tiny grin tugged at the corner of his mouth.

"Well, now," he said softly. "That's rather hard to do. The man and this country are one. To understand one, you have to understand the other."

I groaned inwardly. I could see what he was fixing to do. Houston liked nothing better than to lecture to a captive audience. It's something about old men: when their bellies grumble and their corns ache on a regular basis, they like to remember their youth, and Houston seemed as old as the hills.

"Well, now. Let's see." He shoveled a load of ham in his mouth, chewed and swallowed. "A man named Don Augustín Iturbide, a high Spanish officer, used a half million dollars Spain had given him to start a rebellion. He hired two men, a Guerrero and Victoria, to help him set up a national congress in 1822 that elected Iturbide president, admiral of the navy and generalissimo of the army. The next year, Iturbide was named emperor by the peasants, the rabble, and the soldiers. To make it legal, he called another Congress, then surrounded the men with bayonets until they confirmed him emperor, then he dissolved the Congress and sent everybody home.

"But there was another man around them who took a dim view of what happened and in December, General López de Santa Anna revolted. Over the next few years, Mexico existed in a state of chaos until a new constitution was confirmed in 1824. But the funny thing is that once someone can see how powerful a dictator is, why, then, it's just natural to want the same things. Slavery was abolished in 1824, but they also abolished other things, too, like Masonic lodges and such. In 1830, they outlawed immigration.

"War broke out in the south and the government opened up Texas for immigration, hoping to get a fighting force on its frontiers. But when Texans outnumbered the Mexicans, why then Santa Anna just slammed the door shut and wouldn't let any more in."

"I got it," I said. "Some Mexicans gave rights to us and others took them away. Mother told me some of that, but I didn't really get it settled until now."

"Well, that's what happened," he said, pushing his empty plate away from him. He fingered a cigar from a vest, bit the end and spat it on the floor, and lighted it with a lucifer.

"We lost a lot of good men over that," he said softly, rolling the cigar around in his mouth. "Both Americans and Mexicans, Andy. Don't get to thinking that all the Mexicans followed Santa Anna. A lot of Texicans are doing that these days. That kind of thinking's going to cause a lot of problems in the years to come."

I never forgot that prophecy.

SAM HOUSTON

Sam Houston was another giant, not only in stature, but in the things that he accomplished. It is almost impossible to relate in a few lines all his achievements, nor is there space to tell of all his setbacks. He was both military man and politician. Unlike many who carved two separate careers out of a lifetime, Houston actually fought and his own blood was spilt in several encounters with his enemies.

He was governor of Tennessee and Texas, president of the Republic of Texas, and was once seriously considered as a presidential candidate for the United States. He served as a spokesman for the Indians, yet he was also responsible for killing more than most any other man.

Sam Houston also wrote about James Bowie. The two were good friends, possibly drinking companions, but always there was a trust between the two. Houston, who had habits that drove lesser men to distraction, such as referring to himself as "Houston" instead of "I," tried several times to get Bowie promotions during the Texas War for Independence, but Bowie's reputation was considered a hindrance. At least, that was the excuse Houston's political enemies gave when they blocked Bowie's promotion for his colonelcy. And yet everyone used Bowie's abilities to organize and to fight.

*Houston and Bowie traveled much together in the early 1830s. They also attended several council meetings, and they must have had similar views on the treatment of Indians, because Bowie was sent on several errands to the tribe.—*A. J. S.

Bowie? Well, there's an enigma, a walking contradiction if ever Houston saw one, half-truth and half-fiction. To understand Bowie's role in the birth of Texas, you need to understand something of the politics involved. People like Jim Bowie—and Ben Milam—were speculators, but they were also visionaries. They understood that Texas was the greatest opportunity in the New World for fabulous wealth.

Cotton, cattle, mines, lumber—all of these might be found aplenty in Texas where land was open for settling. All it took was a special person.

The Indians of Texas had never really been conquered. Houston doesn't think they ever will be, for they are like ghosts in the night, now you see them, now you don't. In the 1820s, Mexico decided that it would be best to bring in settlers from other countries to provide a buffer against its villages upon the frontier. Thousands of square miles were opened up for settlement. It was a time when the common man—yes, even the poor man—could get rich beyond his wildest dreams.

As an additional incentive to encourage settlers, Mexico arranged for no tax revenue to be levied against the property. On the surface, it appeared to be an ideal situation for a young man. But what else could Mexico do? None of their own citizens wanted to move north and face the Comanches and other Indians. Mexico then sweetened the pot by inviting the new settlers to become Mexican citizens and embrace the Catholic faith.

In 1824, Mexico established a very democratic constitution that offered the citizens of Mexico a decent form of government. Unfortunately, the presidents of Mexico demonstrated little compunction in upholding that constitution. They did find, however, that the independent, free-minded Americans they had invited into Texas were not as complacent as the *peons* they were used to dealing with in the interior.

Before Houston came down to Texas, Andrew Jackson, President

James Bowie was riding hard from South Texas to Nacogdo-ches. I know not the reason, for he did not tell Houston. Though Houston suspects it was because Santa Anna had or-dered the arrest of all the members of the Monclova council of which Bowie was one.

James Bowie's horse was lathered. It had been ridden hard and it was showing signs of becoming windbroken.

Houston was staying at an inn. There were several of the men who would become Texas Rangers with him.

James Bowie was asked to go speak to Chief Bowles of the Cherokee. He was told the mission was urgent, and he was willing, but his horse was too tired to go on.

Bowie came up to Houston. He greeted Houston and said, "I need a horse. Can I borrow yours?"

Houston replied in the negative. "I have but one horse, and I need him."

Houston did have a fine thoroughbred horse from Ten-nessee.

"I'm going to take him," Bowie said and left the room.

Houston turned to Caiaphas Ham. "Do you think it is right to give up my horse to Bowie?"

"Perhaps it would be better under the circumstances," re-plied the loyal Ham.

"Damn him, let him take the horse," Houston said. Bowie was a friend and why should something as lowly as a horse, even a fine horse, break up a friendship?

of the United States at the time, asked me to see if Texas could be a viable part of the Union. The United States was like a twenty-year-old in a ten-year-old's trousers; fitting to burst its seams what with the massive settlement of its lands within its self-imposed boundaries.

One of the first people Houston met was Jim Bowie. A great

gentleman, Jim could have been the prince of politicians had he only turned his charm into that arena. He was a natural diplomat, intelligent, fearless, with a reputation that scared the living bejesus out of his opponents.

In 1832, Jim was riding high; he had married a beautiful and charming woman at the top of the society ladder and had begun his family. He doted on that family; it meant everything to him, and he worked himself into a lather, riding back and forth between Texas and Arkansas and Louisana, speculating on land with his brothers John and Rezin.

Unfortunately, that speculation was earning him a reputation as an unsavory character. He bought many old Spanish grants and promptly resold them only to have the title claims be challenged in court. Of course, people who knew Jim's reputation were a bit reluctant to file charges against him on the off-chance that he might take offense and they would be facing the business end of a pistol or the edge of his knife.

Houston remembers once when he was in Bexar having the odd drink or two in a little *cantina* and Jim walked in. Houston called his name and Bowie peered through the gloom until he found Houston sitting in the corner. His face brightened and he came down the bar to greet Houston.

"Hello, Sam," he said. He called to the bartender to bring a bottle of Saltillo brandy. We sat and worked our way through many subjects, including politics, as we worked our way through that bottle. Houston asked him if he would be willing to help Texas move up in the world.

"You know," he said softly, his eyes disfocusing into the distance, "I love Texas. Ever since I first came here more than fifteen years ago, I've known the potential that is here. I bought land here; I sold land here; and I sold land to those people I thought would make good citizens. Good citizens make a good state."

Houston looked swiftly around the room, for to talk about statehood at this time in Texas was a bit like tempting a rattlesnake to strike.

"Lower your voice," Houston said. "But Houston agrees with you. Take a look at Tennessee. People thought nothing but riffraff lived there and now one of that riffraff is President of the United States."

"True," Jim said. He took a large swallow of brandy, washing it down in installments. "But at least those people had clear claim to their land titles."

"Ah, now, Jim, that isn't your fault. You know you bought that land fair and square from the people who were on it at the time."

"Tell that to Roane," he said dryly, mentioning the Attorney General who was trying to bring Jim to court.

"It's politics," Houston said, trying to dismiss the situation with a magnanimous wave. "Hell, everybody is getting stung by that damn Roane."

"We need a consul in Mexico City who can speak for us," Jim said, ignoring me. "My father-in-law is an honest man and could do a lot of good for us in Mexico City if we let him."

"What about Hotspurs like that one over there?" Houston said, nodding at a man by the bar who was busily damning the Mexican government.

Jim leaned back in his chair and gave the man his attention. The man looked a month from a bath; his dirty shirt hung outside his frayed trousers. Greasy hair stuck out from under a hat and he scratched constantly at his beard as if lice were nibbling at his chin.

"All we need to do is tell that bastard Veramendi that we don't want his damn government anymore, and throw all them damn greasers back across the Rio Bravo," he said garrulously.

Jim rose and crossed to the man. He leaned up against the bar and eyed him. The man obviously didn't know who Jim was for he ignored him.

"What if Veramendi doesn't want to leave?" he asked mildly.

"Then, we'll cut his black heart out and mail it back to Mexico City," the man guffawed.

"What if his family doesn't want to go?" Jim asked.

Houston could see that someone had whispered Jim's name to the people near the man. A space began to widen around him.

"What the hell?" he said. "We'll send them along the same way."

"What about that Jim Bowie?" Jim asked. "I hear he's not one to be pushed."

Houston leaned back in my chair, watching carefully. Houston was beginning to enjoy the little melodrama opening up in front of me. The man shook his head.

"Jim Bowie? Hell, he's a scoundrel and thief. Look at who he married: a greaser." The man laughed and raised his glass, draining half of it. A thin trickle of raw whiskey ran down into his beard.

Houston doesn't know how far Jim would have played it, but at that time, the door swung open and Caiaphas Ham and Ben Mc-Culloch staggered in. They spotted Jim immediately and called out to him.

"Bowie! Damn you, buy us a drink."

The man turned pale beneath his layers of dirt. His eyes swung down to Jim's side and registered on the huge knife there. He swallowed, his large Adam's apple moving up and down.

"Jim Bowie," he said. The words were a statement, but Jim answered them anyway.

"Well," he said, squaring his shoulders. "I said my piece and I won't back away from a land thief." He tried to pull his pistol from his pants, but Jim stepped in and hit him once: a short, clean shot that sounded like an axe going into oak, and the man fell backwards, out cold.

Houston decided then and there that Texas needed men like Jim Bowie and if we needed men like him, we sure as hell needed him. Houston spent the rest of the evening and two bottles of whiskey convincing him to join our ranks.

Houston has never regretted that decision.

I was twenty-two when I fought the Wichita Indians as a Texas Ranger, and even though I was raised on the frontier and was almost captured by an Indian when I was only six, I had never seen the kind of violence that occurs when many men fight as in battle. It is not an easy thing to put into words. There was blood and body parts scattered throughout the battleground. Men groan in pain and it is a solemnizing change from the demonic howling that pierced the sound of your heart pounding only moments before.

Your concentration seems so intense in battle that you don't even hear the sound of your gun being discharged. Afterwards, the problem is a different one; then your ears ring in the silence. Of course, all of this has to be put into perspective since at first you are relieved at being alive and so you don't notice anything about the enemy except they are not standing and you are. You want to scream with joy, and some do, but then the shock ends and the pain strikes. Every muscle seems to be bruised, strained, or both. Some men start crying for help, others crawl off to tend themselves, still others wait patiently for someone to come look at them.

You can tell a lot about a man by the way he stoically deals with gashes that go bone deep, or those who complain at the slightest scratch. I guess that is why I have always been fascinated by those men who are willing to go through such trials without a thought of consequences.

Every time I see an article about the Alamo, or Jim Bowie, I save it. Ever since Sam Houston got me interested in true History instead of stories. I have tried to keep notes about those things that happened in the early days of Texas, and in Bowie's case, what happened in Louisiana and Arkansas.

In 1870 I met a man who called himself Pierre Douchet. He claimed to have been a member of Jean Lafitte's crew in Galveston. I clearly remember the day I met this garrulous old man. I was twenty-two years old and assigned to a company of Texas Rangers. This information about Bowie came to me when I and several of my company rode into a sleepy little town in August of that year.

It was baking hot outside, somewhere around 100 degrees, and we wanted to cut the dust from our mummified throats. We saw the cantina and with a whoop descended on it. We hitched our horses to the rail and sauntered into the cool darkness. No one who hasn't been horseback in mid-summer can possibly imagine what we felt when we stepped into that cool adobe building.

A round-faced Mexican bartender stood behind a plank bar while a small, weather-beaten, gray-headed old man sat in one of the chairs. The bartender showed only a hint of a smile when he asked what we wanted to drink. I ordered a beer and as I waited, I considered the other man, dressed in canvas pants and a striped shirt, with a broad leather belt from which a bone-handled knife hung on his right side. The old man was complaining about the quality of the "grog," as he called the whiskey.

"Lafitte would have strapped you over a cannon for serving such piss to real men," he complained. He looked at us, his eyes wavering, slightly out of focus.

"Rangers," I said quickly.

The old man grinned, and mumbled to himself.

"What?" Jimmy Jones, our youngest recruit, asked. He leaned towards the old man. "What did you say?"

"I said that you need real whiskey to face the Indians, not so?"

"You claiming we need barley courage?" Jimmy asked.

"No, no. Just real whiskey. Not this . . ." the old man spluttered as he searched for the right word.

"Here, here," the bartender said hurriedly. He reached beneath the bar and brought out a dusty bottle. "There's no need for trouble, now. Right? Is this not so? There, now. All friends. Right?"

A nervous tic began in his cheek as he handed the bottle to me and gestured that I should take it to the old man. I grinned and crossed the dirt floor and pulled out a chair opposite the old man.

As we drank, I mentioned Bowie's name and, much to my surprise, I discovered that Douchet had been present the night when Bowie fought a duel sitting down and nailed to a log by his britches.

"But," Douchet said, "the fight was not over a slave as has been told. No, no. It was over a woman. Bowie cut his man to ribbons before he kill him. Lafitte was so pleased that he sell Bowie slaves at good price. But," he shook his head, "that man! Lafitte was right to make the quick deal and get rid of him."

"How so?" I asked.

Douchet closed one eye in a slow wink, squinting at me. Finally, he nodded his head and said, "All right. I tell you. He is the only man who frightened me."

"Why?"

"His eyes. Gray, but cold like the sea. He was . . . hmm . . . death."

I put our conversation down to the drink that Douchet had been pouring down his gullet. Later, after he told other stories about Bowie's "blackbirding" days, I wondered why he was so reluctant to talk about Bowie. The man had been dead for many years, by then. How could Bowie have generated so much fear in an old pirate? Was it because of the cruelty that he saw in Bowie when Bowie used his knife to slice up his challenger before killing him? Somehow, I doubted that, for surely the old pirate had seen many other cruel tortures performed by others during his long career. But somehow, there must have been something unusual enough about Bowie to make the old pirate fear him even now.

"No," Douchet said, when I brought the question up to him again. "No, it is really very simple. Too many people try to find hidden meanings behind the man. But men are not hard to understand. Especially Bowie. He was easy to understand. He was Death. That is all. That is enough."

He shrugged and reached for another drink.

On October 6, 1835, Sam Houston was appointed Commander-in-Chief of the Nacogdoches Department. This empowered him to raise troops, organize forces, and do whatever pertained to the carrying out of his duties in that office. Soon, news came to the Texans in Bexar that General Cós was leading four hundred men to confiscate goods from the citizens, who promptly elected Stephen F. Austin Commander-in-Chief of the Gonzales forces on October 19.

Stephen Austin was the son of Moses Austin, an empresario who received 200,000 acres to parcel out to three hundred families. Stephen Austin gathered five hundred troops and prepared to march on Cós in order to defend Texas property. One volunteer was James Bowie, who arrived on a small gray mare with six men from Louisiana, his famous knife secured in his sash and a rifle slung from his saddle.

On October 22, Bowie and Captain Fannin, who attended the United States Military Academy at West Point for two years, were assigned a scout-

ing expedition. They were to reconnoiter the missions of San Francisco de la Espada and San José de Miguel de Aguayo and gather supplies for the army. Juan Seguín, whose ranch was south, had offered provisions to the army.

On October 24, Colonel Bowie asked for more men to guard the large stretch of road. Though Austin was to refer to Bowie as Colonel, he never actually gave Bowie a commission, a sore point that was never reconciled.—A. J. S.

Early morning, 22 October

General Austin has ordered Jim Bowie and myself on a scout. We have three duties to perform: establish friendly contact with Texas Mexicans, send back food for the troops, discover where the Mexicans are keeping their horse herd, and choose a mission that will serve as a fortified position to control the Goliad Road.

Late afternoon

We have just sent a message to General Austin. Colonel Bowie also has suggested we point out a campsite for the army that will be most strategic. Colonel Bowie seems to have a natural aptitude for organization that translates well to command. Although he has not received his command from Austin, his men elected him to that rank when he led a company of rangers against the savages who inhabit the wilder portions of the country in the West.

Tomorrow we head for the missions San José and San Juan.

23 October

We had a hot dusty ride and found little of interest. Little food and less of military importance. I am even more impressed with Bowie. He maintained our pace, yet still looks the gentleman. His command of Spanish and the sheer magnitude of his knowledge of both the land and the people of the area have made the trip much less tedious than otherwise.

24 October

Jim and I are taking our ninety men on a scout. There seems to be a strain between General Austin and Jim. I do not understand why, yet I have been in enough councils now to see the harsh looks between them. Where does that leave me if I must some day have to decide which leader to follow? What happens if I have conflicting orders?

27 October

Jim and I were sent to find a good campsite for the army so that Austin can move into a good defensive position. We found the perfect campsite only one-fourth mile from Mission Concepción.

Bowie has broken our command down into four companies to be commanded by Captains Andrew Briscoe, Robert Coleman, Michael Goheen, and Valentine Bennet. Additionally, he has placed our men in pickets that can provide early warning if the Mexican Army travels up the road from Goliad. It also puts Cós's troops between our troops if he attacks.

We were reminded of our deadly position when we bedded down for the night. A cannon roared in the distance and a cannon ball landed near. Altogether, six huge chunks of iron were fired at us. There is no damage—except to our peace of mind.

29 October

I have just discovered that Jim and I were expected back the same day. Austin has written a document that states any order not followed to the last detail will be grounds for court-martial. It seems as though he is aiming this directly at Jim. The men are not happy with Austin's proclamation. They believe that during a war there must be some room for initiative. I also believe that some of them suspect that Austin is baiting Jim, and Jim is an extremely popular man with the army.

31 October

Austin has received reinforcements and supplies. We now have almost the same number of men as General Cós. The town of Bexar is surrounded. We have kept our position and Austin has placed troops around the city.

Colonel Bowie has, under his own authority, sent a message to General Cós offering to discuss a peaceful solution to the situation. But he received no answer. Instead, we received orders from Austin to move to a more forward position.

1 November

Austin had received word that two companies of Mexican cavalry were willing to desert if given the opportunity. We are that opportunity. We received no answer.

2 November

Austin has called a council of war to determine a course of action. There were twenty-six officers. The question was whether or not to attack the town since we now had more men and supplies. Major Benjamin Smith was the leader of the group who want an immediate attack. He lost.

Bowie returned to our command. He delivered the decision to his own officers of which there were twenty-one. They voted fourteen to seven in favor of this decision and then voted to join Austin's group north of town.

Bowie took this as a sign of unrest in his leadership, and resigned his command of the division.

Austin accepted gladly.

4 November

Bowie was right. Our troops are down to 450 and morale is poor. Many troops have simply gone home.

I rode with Jim Bowie. Many times. I was a Young Lion, and I was with him on 26 November 1835 when Deaf Smith told Jim about a troop of Mexican cavalry a few miles from where the army was camped.

We attacked the Mexicans and a sharp battle ensued. What I mean is we shot about fifty of them and lost two of our own men. We tried to grab up the horse and find out what kind of supplies they were bringing into San Antonio, which we called "bear" then.

The bundles were filled with grass. Can you imagine that? More'n fifty men killed for a bunch of grass to feed their livestock in the city. There were two battles fought before we could try to take San Antonio, and Jim Bowie won both of them, and it was because he won the grass fight that we were able to take San Antonio.

Andrew J. Sowell,
grandfather to the writer

22 November

We have been waiting for almost one month. The attack on Bexar has been discussed and postponed so many times it is now impossible to generate enthusiasm for the attack.

26 November

Deaf Smith galloped up to the commander and reported a Mexican cavalry column five miles away. Bowie led a force to scout them.

ORDER FROM AUSTIN
TO JAMES BOWIE,
27 OCTOBER 1835

Col James Bowie, Volunteer Aid:

You will proceed with the first division of Captain Fannin's company and others attached to that division and select the best and most secure position that can be had on the river, as near Bejar as practicable to encamp the army tonight, keeping in view in the selection of this position pasturage and the security of the horses, and the army from night attacks of the enemy.

You will also reconnoiter, so far as time and circumstances will permit, the situation of the outskirts of the town and the approaches to it, whether the houses have been destroyed on the outside, so as to leave every approach exposed to the raking of the cannon.

You will make your report with *as little delay as possible*, so as to give time to the army to march and take up its position before night. Should you be attacked by a large force, send expresses *immediately* with the particulars.

By order P W Grayson, Aid-de-camp

S. F. Austin.

The self-styled Colonel Bowie has asked constantly for more men, first fifty, then one hundred and fifty. It seems that he fancies himself more than just a bravo, but also a full-fledged soldier. I placed him in co-command with Captain Fannin who should be able to keep Bowie in line. I think, though, that he has taken command away from Fannin.

I intend to send a message to Bowie asking for a quick reconnoiter and report of enemy movement to which I will bring the army. I have also written a proclamation that will give me the power to court-martial any man who does not follow my orders.

Bowie's long reconnoiter is splitting my force while Mexican troops constantly move closer.

**Excerpt from a Letter to A. J. Sowell
from Noah Smithwick**

The Texian victory at Concepcion happened because of Jim
Bowie. Jim Bowie was a natural born leader: he never need-
lessly spent a bullet or imperiled a life. His choice of ground
was excellent. He was able to use that riverbank to cover our
movement until we were right up on them. We suffered only
one killed and one wounded, the enemy lost over 100 close to
one-third of their entire force.

28 October

Morning found us surrounded by fog filtering out the sun. This,
however, did not stop Mexican troop movement which began about
7:30 or 8:00. About three hundred soldiers advanced upon our position. Henry Karnes was standing picket when the Mexican cavalry
saw him and fired upon him. The first shot caused him to yell, "The
damned rascals have shot out the bottom of my powder horn." Another soldier was hit by a bullet that deflected off his knife. He now
has a black and purple imprint of the knife on his side.

Skirmishing lasted about two hours. The Mexican infantry and
artillery practically encircled us. Bowie shouted, "Keep under cover,
boys, and reserve your fire. We haven't a man to spare."

Grapeshot and canister rattled in the pecan trees overhead, but
we were dug in behind a ditch and the shot did very little damage.

The Mexicans advanced to about three hundred yards, and Bowie
calmly commanded, "Call your targets and fire." He then sighted on
a sergeant who was overseeing the charging of the cannons. "The
fat sergeant—bet you two-bits I'll hit him."

Noah Smithwick took the bet and lost.

Fire became very effective. Mexican soldiers were dropping too
regularly for them to maintain their position. Their commander ordered a charge and Bowie ordered Coleman's company to reinforce
the point of attack. All the movement was accomplished while staying

under the cover of the bank so the men were able to inflict heavy casualties while sustaining few.

Twice and then three times the enemy charged and each time they were seriously damaged. When they withdrew, we crept closer to the cannon.

Only about thirty minutes of this intense battle passed when Bowie saw the opportunity and charged with his men, crying, "The cannon and victory."

Such is Bowie's charisma that all the Texans yelled the same and leaped up to join him. Bowie was first at the cannon and with another man turned it around and fired upon the fleeing Mexicans.

When I asked him why he did not follow the Mexicans, he said, "Had it been possible to have communicated with you, General Austin, and brought you up earlier, the victory would have been conclusive and Bexar would have been ours before sundown."

Undated Entry in Austin's Journal

Bowie is a hero. He has won the battle of Concepción. But, he has done it by disobeying my orders. Now, my own men are refusing my orders after Bowie complained the fortifications at Bexar were too strong. I have encamped and am now preparing for a siege.

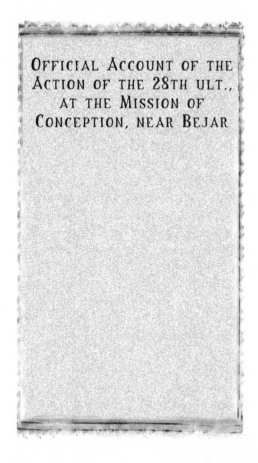

Dear Sir,—In conformity with your order of the 27th inst., we proceeded with the division composed of ninety-two men, rank and file, under our joint command, to examine the Missions above Espada, and select the most eligible situation near Bejar, for the encampment of the main army of Texas. After carefully examining that of San José (having previously visited San Juan) we marched to that of Conception, and selected our ground in a bend of the river San Antonio, within about five hundred yards of the old Mission Conception. The face of the plain in our front was nearly level, and the timbered land adjoining it formed two sides of a triangle, both of which were as nearly equal as possible; and, with the exception of two places, a considerable bluff of from six to ten feet sudden fall in our rear, and a bottom of fifty to one hundred yards to the river.

We divided the command into divisions, and occupied each

one side of the triangle, for the encampment on the night of the 27th, Captain Fannin's company being under cover of the south side, forming the first division, and Captains Coleman, Goheen, and Bennet's companies (making in all only forty-one, rank and file) occupied the north side, under the immediate command of myself (James Bowie, aide-de-camp).

Thus the men were posted, and lay on their arms during the night of the 27th, having out strong picket guards, and one of seven men in the cupola of the Mission-house, which overlooked the whole country, the horses being all tied up.

The night passed quietly off, without the least alarm; and at dawn of day, every object was obscured by a heavy, dense fog, which entirely prevented our guard, or look-out from the Mission, seeing the approach of the enemy.

At about half an hour by sun, an advanced guard of their cavalry rode upon our line, and fired at a sentinel who had just been relieved, who returned the fire, and caused one platoon to retire; but another charged on him (Henry Karnes), and he discharged a pistol at them, which had the same effect.

The men were called to arms; but were for some time unable to discover their foes, who had entirely surrounded the position, and kept up a constant firing, at a distance, with no other effect than a waste of ammunition on their part. When the fog rose, it was apparent to all that we were surrounded, and a desperate fight was inevitable, all communications with the main army being cut off. Immediate preparation was made, by extending our right flank (first division) to the south, and placing the second division on the left, on the same side, so that they might be enabled to rake the enemy's, should they charge into the angle, and prevent the effects of a cross-fire of our own men; and, at the same time, be in a compact body, contiguous to each other, that either might reinforce the other, at the shortest notice, without crossing the angle, in an exposed and uncovered ground, where certain loss must have resulted. The men, in the mean time, were ordered to clear away bushes and vines, under the hill and along the margin, and at the steepest places to cut steps for foot-hold, in order to afford them space to form and pass, and at suitable places ascend the bluff, discharge their rifles, and fall back to reload. The work was not completed to our wish, before the infantry were seen to advance, with arms trailed, to the right of the first division, and form the line of battle at about two hundred yards distance from the right flank. Five companies of their cavalry supported them, covering our whole front and flanks. Their infantry was also supported by a large force of cavalry.

In this manner, the engagement commenced at about the hour of eight o'clock, A.M., on Wednesday, 28th of October, by the deadly crack of a rifle from the extreme right. The engagement was immediately general. The discharge from the enemy was one continued blaze of fire, whilst that from our lines, was more slowly delivered, but with good aim and deadly effect, each man retiring under cover of the hill and timber, to give place to others, whilst he re-loaded. The battle had not lasted more than ten minutes, before a brass double fortified four-pounder was opened on our line with a heavy discharge of grape and canister, at the distance of about eighty yards from the right flank of the first division, and a charge sounded. But the cannon was cleared, as if by magic, and a check put to the charge. The same experiment was resorted to, with like success, three times, the division advancing under the hill at each fire, and thus approximating near the cannon and victory. "The cannon and victory" was truly the war-cry, and they only fired it five times, and it had been three times cleared, and their charge as often broken, before a disorderly and precipitate retreat was sounded, and most readily obeyed, leaving to the victors their cannon. Thus a small detachment of ninety-two men gained a most decisive victory over the main army of the central government, being at least four to one, with only the loss of one brave soldier (Richard Andrews), and none wounded: whilst the enemy suffered in killed and wounded near one hundred, from the best information we can obtain, which is entitled to credit; say sixty-seven killed, among them many promising officers. Not one man of the artillery company escaped unhurt.

No insidious distinction can be drawn between any officer or private, on this occasion. Every man was a soldier, and did his duty, agreeably to the situation and circumstances under which he was placed.

It may not be amiss here to say, that near the close of the engagement another heavy piece of artillery was brought up, and fired thrice, but at a distance; and by a reinforcement of another company of cavalry, aided by six mules, ready harnessed, they got it off. The main army reached us in about one hour after the enemy's retreat. Had it been possible to communicate with you, and brought you up earlier, the victory would have been decisive, and Bejar ours before twelve o'clock.

With sentiments of high consideration, we subscribe ourselves,

Yours, most respectfully,

James Bowie, Aid-de-Camp. [RUBRIC]

J. W. Fannin, Commandant, first division. [RUBRIC]

General S. F. Austin

DEATH OF THE LION

The Texas leadership during the Texas War for Independence was fractured. It is hard to discuss because these men have become heroes to the country and especially to their fellow Texans.

On November 3, 1835, fifty-five delegates from the thirteen municipalities of Texas elected a provisional government. Stephen F. Austin lost by nine votes. He resigned his commission as Commander-in-Chief of the army and was replaced by Sam Houston.

The powers of the provisional government were so poorly defined that no one really knew what the limits were, or for that matter, their jobs. This, then, became a free-for-all with everyone trying to gain power for themselves without really thinking about the responsibility that went with the power they craved.—A.J.S.

Sam Houston

James Bowie came before the government to plead for a battlefield commission. Houston has never heard such a brilliant oratory. Bowie, who never spoke about himself, gave all his qualifications. He spoke of the Battle of Concepción, and the Grass Fight. He explained his tactics and strategy. He described battles with Indians and Bandits.

For one hour there was not one person who could not see Bowie battling the enemies of Texas with intellect as well as great natural fighting ability. Yet, they turned him down. Jim Bowie received no commission.

Captain Fannin, his co-commander, received a colonelcy, and that boastful bombastic Travis got himself a lieutenant-colonel's rank, but Bowie was only offered thanks.

Houston had no openings himself for field command, but to keep Jim Bowie's talents Houston said, "Jim, Houston can put you on his staff. You'll be a full colonel of Texas and not just a colonel of rangers."

"No thanks, Sam. My brothers have always done the paperwork. I travel ... I fight ... I kill." His voice was husky with emotion. "Sam, I've lost my family, my biggest land deal was lost in the courts, and now the thing I want to do most is prove myself. I've never talked about myself, or what I've done. My father told me a gentleman never does. I just did, and they rejected me."

"Jim, if you don't blow the bugle about yourself, no one will ever do it for you ..." I looked into his eyes, saw the hurt there, and knew that I couldn't let my tendency for showmanship hurt my friend further. "Except maybe Houston. Maybe Houston could talk to them, but that damn Wyatt Hanks, the Chairman of Military Affairs, hates Houston, and will do his best to stop Houston from getting the good men."

"I appreciate Houston's good will. If my friend Sam and his *amigo* Houston would walk over to the tavern, Jim Bowie, he, himself, and I will buy those two big-talking sons of Texas a few drinks."

Bowie turned his head, coughing, his face cording from the effort. He swallowed and grinned. Houston accepted with alacrity. Houston may be a showman and a big talker, but he is most certainly not a fool.

SAM DOCKER

Sam Docker was a sickly young man who came to Texas for his health on the advice of his doctors. He was one of the secretaries at the Brazos meeting when Bowie pleaded his case for a colonelcy in the Texas Army. Bowie spoke long and eloquently and although no official record of his speech remains, Docker jotted down as much of it as he could. Docker later died of consumption while traveling from Austin to Waco.—A.J.S.

Esteemed sirs. I have never pleaded for justice in my life, preferring, instead, to let justice serve blindfolded to pomp and circumstance. Lately, I have been the recipient of scurrilous speculation in regards to my loyalty to Texas. My detractors have repeatedly used my Mexican citizenship as proof of my loyalty and where my sympathies lie.

Gentlemen, nothing could be further from the truth. I place my record beside any man's in Texas from Stephen Austin's record to any present in this august body. None here can say that James Bowie has led a double life. None here can accuse me of treasonous acts against the state.

I know what some latecomers to Texas have said about James Bowie. Pirate, blackbirder, knife-fighter, adventurer, confidence man, gambler. I do not pretend that my life has been one of piety and passivity. I am cut from the same mold like Achilles and like Achilles I have chosen a short but adventurous life, if the Fates allow choice, to that of more platonic bends.

I do not pretend to be anything more than what I am, and I am what Texas desperately needs at this moment. You may detest the life that I have lived, yet you cannot but recognize the value that such a life has to Texas now. I do not ask for anything that is not in your power to grant: only the rank that will allow me the right to recruit more people like me to make a battalion of men willing to fight for their independence.

Many of you are aware that while you were raising children and crops, I, along with several friends who were wifeless and childless, formed a company of men to keep the frontier safe from attack by the savages. We stood between many a settler and annihilation time and time again.

Many of you are aware of my holdings of which I have oft been accused of turning to profit, yet the same number of you are aware that upon much of that land I have allowed people to settle and work, taking a pittance for the price of the land in exchange for giving them homes.

Many of you are aware that I have fought renegades and given money to help those who have been wiped out by the disasters of God and His horsemen without the slightest hesitation or equivocation whatsoever, knowing only that here was a man in need.

Yes, of this you are aware, yet many of you have also taken sides with those detractors of mine who swish through salons, bearing their honor in words instead of deeds, curling their lips at the mention of my name and repeatedly stating their opinion of my character. I do not choose to answer them with words, but am willing to meet any upon a field of honor.

Here, there appears to be a large gap in time.—**A. J. S.**

... although this body has seen fit to place such honors upon men such as William Travis, whose own character could be held to question and proven by his doctor.

Gentlemen, my blood is in the soil of Texas ...

A rather lengthy passage here has been rendered unreadable by water.
—A. J. S.

I therefore beg of you, sirs, to grant my petition for appointment to the rank of Colonel without pay in order that I may use that rank in the fight for the independence of Texas and freedom. Thank you.

JOHN HENRY BROWN

We have to turn to John Henry Brown in order to get a feel for the full flavor of Bowie's speech. Brown was one of Bowie's friends who stayed with him through his mourning period following the death of his wife and children. That was a true test of friendship as Bowie's personality changed radically. He became sullen and morose and highly argumentative. Yet Brown, who traveled the Mississippi with Bowie in 1829 and ate and drank with him on several of his adventures, refused to give up on the man he had known. Brown was with Bowie when he made his appeal.—A. J. S.

Stepping inside the railing, hat in hand, with a dignified bow Bowie addressed the council for an hour. He reviewed the salient points of his life, hurled from him with indignation every floating allegation affecting his character as a man of peace and honor, admitted that he was an unlettered man of the Southwest, and his lot had been cast

The elected representatives who met to debate the need for a constitution and army for Texas became known as the Consultation and not the Congress in order to distinguish them from that of the United States.

in a day and among a people rendered necessarily, from political and material causes, more or less independent of law, but generous and scornful of every species of meanness and duplicity.

He said that he had cast his lot with Texas for honorable and patriotic purposes; that he had ever neglected his own affairs to serve the country in an hour of danger, had betrayed no man, deceived no man, wronged no man, and had never had a difficulty in the country, unless to protect the weak from the strong and evil-intentioned. That, yielding to the dictates of his own heart, he had taken to his bosom as a wife a true and lovely woman of a different race, the daughter of a distinguished "Coahil-Texano"; yet, as a thief in the night, death had invaded his home and taken his wife, his little ones, and his father-in-law; and now, standing alone of all his blood in Texas, all he asked was the privilege of serving it in the field, where his name, so frequently besmirched by double-dealing, unspeakable cowards, might be honorably associated with the brave and true.

Not an indecorous or undignified word fell from his lips—he made not an ungraceful movement or gesture—but stood there before the astonished council, the living exemplification of a natural orator.

He tarried not, but turned immediately and left the chamber, satisfied that he would receive generous consideration, and returned to San Antonio. In that memorable December, 1835, Bowie finally received his Colonel's commission.

There are conflicting stories as to where Bowie was during the storming of Bexar. My grandfather, however, claimed that Bowie was at the battle. None of these are clear enough to add to this account of Bowie's life, but it was true that Austin had sent Bowie to Goliad on the third, two days before the attack.—A. J. S.

Sam Houston

The council is a constant thorn in the side of the army. They have just classified a new term. Military agent is a person given rank in the army by the council. This agent can serve as a battlefield officer, but is not responsible to the military commander-in-chief. How can those fools think this will keep Santa Anna from re-taking Texas?

Proposal from John Grant of Matamoros to the Council of Texas

As is well-known to the council, Santa Anna is a tyrant who has destroyed the Constitution of 1824. In so doing he has left himself and Mexico open to brave-hearted individuals who would free the land and the people of other parts of Mexico.

There is nothing as beautiful, nor as rich as the Coahuila. The spoils that could come from the towns of Nuevo León, Tamaulipas, and San Luis Potosí would greatly enrich the coffers of the new Republic you have begun.

An attack on Matamoros would be the beginning of a financially secure Texas.

From Sam Houston's Diary

After tremendous and futile argument, Houston has been ordered to take Matamoros. Houston cannot refuse any more if he expects any cooperation from the council in the future, and so he must choose an able commander.

The only choice is Jim Bowie. There is no one who can touch him for promptitude and manliness. Above all he is valued by Houston for his forecast, prudence and valor. Houston will draft orders for Bowie and give him his rank.

Houston does hope that his cough has cleared up. Texas cannot afford a sick Jim Bowie.

Bowie never received the letter, or at least received it too late. Frank Johnson led the army toward Matamoros, and Bowie on January 12 was told in no uncertain tones that he was not an officer of the government nor of the army.—A. J. S.

Sam Houston

Houston was telling Bowie of his problems with the Alamo. When Johnson left to attack Mexico, thus turning our rebellion into an outright theft, he stripped the garrison of every blanket, horse, most of the shot and powder, and left eighty sick or wounded to protect the city we spent so much blood to take.

Lieutenant-Colonel Neill has asked for men. Houston told Bowie about this when he found him, trying to staunch his cough with sips of whiskey.

"Houston has no extra men, so he will send orders to Neill to destroy the fortification. That damn Johnson and his raid . . ."

"I'll go, Sam," Bowie said. "Give me a chance to ask for volunteers, and we'll go see what we can do."

On 17 January, Jim Bowie left Goliad with thirty volunteers to deliver orders to destroy the Alamo.

Lieutenant-Colonel Neill

I do not believe that Houston wants to give up the fort without a fight. Though we are short of cannon, men and supplies, we are Texans and we can hold this fort against any force of Mexicans.

James Bonham

We will pass a resolution to Governor Smith. We will hold the Alamo. James Bowie concurs and will be the second to sign the resolution.

The men have demanded $500 from the council. Bowie knows without a doubt that they will not send the money quickly, if at all, so he will arrange a loan for the sake of the rebellion.

Citizens and Soldiers of San Antonio de Béxar to Council, San Felipe

At a large and respectable meeting of the citizens and soldiers of this place, held this 26th day of January 1836, to take into consideration the recent movements at San Felipe, James C. Neill was called to

Much speculation has been held about the generous benefactor who loaned Bowie the five hundred dollars. A scrap of a letter from Noah Smithwick to A. J. Sowell names the man as Juan Seguín.

the chair, and H. J. Williamson appointed secretary. The object of the meeting having been stated by the chair, on motion of Col. J. B. Bonham, a committee of seven was appointed to draft a preamble and resolutions for the consideration of the meeting; whereupon the following were appointed by the chair. Chairman of Committee J. B. Bonham. Jas Bowie, G. B. Jameson, Doctor Pollard, Jesse Badgett, J. W. Seguín, Don Gasper Flores.

Preamble

Whereas we have been informed from an undoubted messenger that the Executive Council and its President, a subordinate and the auxiliary department of the government, have usurped the right of impeaching the governor who, (if we would imitate the wise institutions of the land of Washington) can only be impeached by a body set forth in the constitution which constitution must have been established by the people through their representatives assembled in general convention. Moreover, the said council and its president, whose powers are defined to aid the governor fulfilling the measures and objects adopted by the general consultation, have taken it upon themselves to annul the measures of the said general consultation. They are about to open the land offices, which were temporarily closed until a general convention of the people should take place, thereby opening a door to private speculation, at the expense of the men who are serving their country in the field. Moreover the said council have improperly used, and appropriated to their own purposes a FIVE HUNDRED DOLLAR LOAN, from a generous and patriotic citizen of the United States intended to pay the soldiers in the garrison of Bexar. Moreover, that private and designing men are, and have been embarrassing the governor, the legitimate officer of the government, by usurping, contrary to all notions of order and good government, the right of publicly and formally instructing and advising the governor and the people on political, civil and institutional matters subject. Moreover that a particular individual has gone so far as to issue a proclamation on the site of public affairs, and to invite volunteers to join him as the commander of the Matamoros expedition, when that particular individual must have known that General Houston the commander in chief of all the land forces in the service of Texas has been ordered by the government to take command of that expedition. This particular individual is also fully aware, that all officers under the commander in chief are elected by the volunteers themselves, and that therefore there was neither room nor necessity for another appointment by the council. Still in the possession of these facts, he has issued his proclamation, and continues to aid all those who are embarrassing the executive.

Therefore, be it resolved 1st That we will support his excellency Governor Smith in his unyielding and patriotic efforts to fulfill the duties, and to preserve the dignity of his office, while promoting the best interests of the country and people, against all usurpations and the designs of selfish and interested individuals.

Resolved 2nd That all attempts of the president and members of the executive council, to annul the acts of, or to embarrass the officers appointed by the general convention are deemed by this meeting as anarchical assumptions of power to which we will not submit.

Resolved 3rd That we invite a similar expression of sentiment from the army under Genl Houston, and throughout the country generally.

Resolved 4th That the conduct of the president and members of the Executive Council in relation to the FIVE HUNDRED DOLLAR LOAN, for the liquidation of the claims of the soldiers of Bexar, is in the highest degree criminal and unjust. Yet under treatment however illiberal and ungrateful, we cannot be driven from the Post of Honor and the sacred cause of freedom.

Resolved 5th That we do not recognize the illegal appointments of agents and officers, made by the president and members of the Executive council in relation to the Matamoros Expedition; since their power does not extend further than to take measures and to make appointments for the public service with the sanction of the governor.

Resolved 6th That the Governor Henry Smith will please to accept the gratitude of the army at this Station, for his firmness in the execution of his trust, as well as for his patriotic exertions in our behalf.

Resolved 7th That the Editors of the *Brazoria Gazette*, the *Nacogdoches Telegraph* and the *San Felipe Telegraph* be requested, and they are hereby requested to publish the proceedings of this meeting.

Lieutenant–Colonel
Neill

Colonel James Bowie has been of vast help. Since he has been here he has been able to gain supplies and much valuable information from the Mexican populace. They seem to love him. A day does not go by when someone comes to see Don Jaime, and the troop movements of the Mexican army are somehow brought into the conversation.

JAMES BOWIE TO
GOVERNOR HENRY SMITH

BEXAR: Sir: In pursuance of your orders, I proceeded from San
Felipe to La Bahia and whilst there employed my whole time
in trying to effect the objects of my mission. You are aware
that Genl Houston came to La Bahia soon after I did, this is
the reason why I did not make a report to you from that post.
The Comdr. in Chf. has before this communicated to you all
matters in relation to our military affairs at La Bahia, this
makes it wholly unnecessary for me to say any thing on the
subject. Whilst at La Bahia General Houston received dispatches from col Comdt. Neill that good reasons were enter-
tained that an attack would soon be made by a numerous
Mexican army on our important post at Bexar. It was forthwith
determined that I should go instantly to Bexar; accordingly I
left Genl Houston and with a few very efficient volunteers
came on to this place about 2 weeks since. I was received by

Col Neill with great cordiality, and the men under my command entered at once into active service. All I can say of the soldiers stationed here is complimentary to both their courage and their patience. But it is the truth and your Excellency must know it, that great and just dissatisfaction is felt for the want of a little money to pay the small but necessary expenses of our men. I cannot eulogize the conduct & character of Col Neill too highly: no other man in the army could have kept men at this post, under the neglect they have experienced. Both he & myself have done all that we could; we have industriously tried all expedients to raise funds; but hitherto it has been to no purpose. We are still laboring night and day laying up provisions for a siege, encouraging our men, and calling on the government for relief.

Relief at this post in men, money, and provisions is of vital importance and is wanted instantly. So this is the real reason of my letter. The salvation of Texas depends in great measure in keeping Bejar out of the hands of the enemy. It serves as the frontier piquet guard and if it were in the possession of Santa Anna there is no strong hold from which to repel him in his march towards the Sabine. There is no doubt but very large forces are being gathered in several of the towns beyond the Rio Grande, and the late information through Senr. Cassiana & others, worthy of credit, is positive in the fact that 16 hundred or two thousand troops with good officers, well armed and plenty of provisions, were on the point of marching, (the provisions being cooked &c). A detachment of active young men from the volunteers under my command have been sent to the Rio Frio; they returned yesterday without information and we remain yet in doubt whether they intend to attack on this place or go to reenforce Matamoros. It does, however, seem certain that an attack is shortly to be made on this place, and I think it is the general opinion that the enemy will come by land. The citizens of Bexar have behaved well. Colonel Neill and myself have come to the solemn resolution that we will rather die in these ditches than give up this post to the enemy. These citizens deserve our protection and the public safety demands our lives rather than to evacuate this post to the enemy.—again we call aloud for relief; the weakness of our post will at any rate bring the enemy on, some volunteers are expected: Capt Patton with 5 or 6 has come in. But a large reinforcement with provisions is what we need.

James Bowie [RUBRIC]

P.S. I have information just now from a friend whom I believe that the force at the Rio Grande (Presidia) is two thousand complete; he states further that five thousand are a little back and marching on, perhaps the 2 thousand will wait for a junction with the 5 thousand. This information is corroborated with all that we have heard. The informant says that they intend to make a decent on this place in particular, and there is no doubt of it.

Our force is very small, the returns this day to the Comdt. is only one hundred and twenty officers & men. It would be a waste of men to put our brave little band against thousands.

We have no interesting news to communicate. The army have elected two gentlemen to represent the Army & trust they will be received.

James Bowie [RUBRIC]

ENRIQUE ESPARZA

My mother sold beef, tamales and beans to the Texans. I helped her to carry the earthen jars full of food. It was a heavy task at times. One day I was carrying a jar along the log that made a footbridge over the San Antonio River, I slipped and fell into the deep water. Señor Bowie jumped in and brought me out. I could swim from the time I was four years old. This day I think I struck the log in falling, as I was very bloody. I was very fond of Señor Bowie after this. Señor Bowie had no family. Why? Sra. Veramendi and her two children had died. He was a very sad man.

Andrew J. Sowell
(My Grandfather)

I was walking with Jim Bowie one day close to the San Antonio River. Jim was in a curious mood. He was organizing the defense of the Alamo, and there wasn't much of anything to defend with. Jim did have a temper, though he hid it most of the time, and this made it just that much worse when it finally exploded. Kind of like a big old Dutch boiler without a steam release valve.

Because he was thinking so hard, I was just quietly walking with him. We stopped for a moment by the footbridge. One of the little Mexican boys was trying to cross while carrying a big old pot of water.

It was somewhat comical watching this little boy, no mor'n three feet tall, wrestling the pot that was probably two foot or two and a half. Then, he fell. I laughed knowing these boys could swim almost from the time they could walk, but the boy wasn't swimming.

Jim tossed his hat down, ripped off his jacket and hit the water.

He found the boy and dragged him out. The boy must have hit his head, cause it was bleeding freely from the scalp as Jim pulled him to shore.

Jim started coughing, but he turned around and hit the river again and dived for that darned pot.

"What are you doing?" I asked him, being a little upset at him being in that cold water a second time.

"The boy'll get in trouble if he don't bring home the pot," Jim said. "His folks work hard, but they don't have much."

"Jim, you've already got a cough. We'd best get you a drink to warm you from the inside out."

And after we got the boy home, that's just what we did.

JAMES BONHAM,
17 FEBRUARY 1836

Lt.-Col. Neill has left for a furlough. Lt.-Col. Travis has taken his place. Bowie and Travis argue.

THE PRIVATE JOURNAL OF W. BARRET TRAVIS

Bowie is insufferable. The ass believes that his Colonelcy in the Texas Rangers a group formed without any official sanction makes him my superior. When Col Neill left due to an illness in his family, he left me in charge, at which point Bowie, fresh from his bottle, said, "Now hear me, Col Neill, I'm not taking any orders from a 26 year old kid." Several of Bowie's men shouted angrily that they concurred with this at which point I ordered an election, under the impression that any wise individual would not elect to be led by a drunkard and buffoon.

. . .

The election has been held, and I have been ousted from my command. This is truly incomprehensible. That drunken knifefighter has done the impossible and stolen my command. But I should not have been surprised. When Colonel Neill left, he made the announcement that "due to illness in my family, I find it necessary to return home. Therefore, I am transferring command of this fort to Lieutenant Colonel Travis." A great silence followed his announcement, then Bowie, fired well with his morning drink, shouted, "Now hear me, Colonel Neill, I'm not taking any orders from a twenty-six year old kid!"

The rest of Bowie's men raised their own voice in indignation. At last, I stepped in and said that a vote had to be taken. My fault. I should have known that the men would prefer the drunken Bowie to me. As he left, Colonel Neill said, "Very well, gentlemen, all regular army troops will be under Lieutenant Colonel Travis, and all volunteers will be under the command of Jim Bowie, except for the Tennessee Volunteers. They will be under Colonel Crockett."

Three commanders. This must be how Rome fell.

. . .

I have sent a missive to the council. Bowie in a drunken folly has freed all the prisoners in town. He has threatened the duly constituted law and even threatened to destroy the jail because one prisoner was returned to his incarceration. The council must act and this loudmouthed bully must be removed if I am to save this fortress for Texas.

WILLIAM B. TRAVIS TO HIS EXCELLENCY HENRY SMITH

BEJAR: I wrote you an official letter last night as Comdt. of this post in the absence of Col Neill & if you had taken the trouble to answer my letter from Burnam's I should not now have been under the necessity of troubling you—My situation is truly awkward & delicate—Col Neill left me in the command—but wishing to give satisfaction to the volunteers here & not wishing to assume any command over them I issued an order for the election of an officer to command them with the exception of one under me. Bowie was elected by two small company's & since his election he has been roaring drunk all the time; has assumed all command & is proceeding in a most disorderly & irregular manner—interfering with private property, releasing prisoners sentenced by court-martial & by the civil court & turning everything topsy turvey—If I did not feel my honor & that of my country compromised I would leave here instantly for some other point with the troops under my command—as I am unwilling to be responsible for the drunken irregularities of any man. I hope you will immediately order some regular troops to this place—as it is more important to occupy this Post than I imagined when I last saw you— It is the key of Texas from the Interior without a footing here the enemy can do nothing against us in the colonies now that our coast is guarded by armed vessels—I do not solicit the command of this post but as Col Neill has applied to the commander in chief to be relieved and is anxious for me to take command, I will do it by your order for a time until an artillery officer can be sent here. The citizens here have every confidence in me, & they have shown every disposition to aid me with all they have—we much need money—can you not send us some? I read your letter to the troops & made a speech & they received it with acclamation—our spies have just returned from the Rio Grande—the enemy is there one thousand strong & is making every preparation to invade us. By the 15th of March I think Texas will be invaded & every preparation should be made to receive them. E. Smith will call on you & give you all the news—so will Mr Williams the Bearer of this—

In conclusion, allow me to beg that you will give me definite orders—immediately—
W. Barret Travis [RUBRIC]

P.S. This is a private letter & is to Nibbs for fear it may fall into bad hands.

The Private Journal of
W. Barret Travis

The council will waver, and the difficulty between myself and Bowie
will not be resolved. This will cause too many insurmountable problems if the Mexicans attack. We have agreed on a compromise that
will give him the volunteers and me the regulars and the cavalry. We
will sign orders for the command jointly and so the defense of the
Alamo will continue.

Antonio López de Santa Anna

Santa Anna was born in Jalapa, Mexico. He entered the military when he was sixteen and by 1833, twenty-three years later, he was president of Mexico. Once in power, Santa Anna quickly revealed himself to be a despot. When Texas proclaimed itself as a Republic, Santa Anna installed Gómez Pedraza as president to serve until January 1833 when national elections would again be held. He then quickly gathered an army and, placing himself in charge, led it into Texas. Vain and arrogant, he called himself the "Napoleon of the West" and adopted Napoleon's mannerisms and dress. One of Santa Anna's hidden secrets was that he was related to Bowie through marriage. He was, in effect, and according to Mexican custom and law, Bowie's second cousin.—A. J. S.

On the 23rd of this month [February] I occupied this city [San Antonio], after some forced marches from Rio Grande, with General

D. Joaquin Ramírez y Sesma's division composed of the permanent battalions of Matamoros and Jiménez, the active battalion of San Luis Potosí, the regiment of Dolores, and eight pieces of artillery.

With the speed in which this meritorious division executed its marches in eighty leagues of road, it was believed that the rebel settlers would not have known of our proximity until we should have been within rifleshot of them; as it was they only had time to hurriedly entrench themselves in Fort Alamo, which they had well fortified, and with a sufficient food supply. My objective had been to surprise them early in the morning of the day before, but a heavy rain prevented it.

Notwithstanding their artillery fire, which they began immediately from the indicated fort, the national troops took possession of this city with the utmost order, which the traitors shall never again occupy; on our part we lost a corporal and a scout, dead, and eight wounded.

When I was quartering the corps of the division a bearer of the flag of truce presented himself with a paper, a copy of which I am enclosing, and becoming indignant of its contents I ordered my nearest aide to answer it.

Fifty rifles of the rebel traitors of the North fell into our hands and I ordered their delivery to the general commissary of the army.

From the moment of my arrival, I was kept busy hostilizing the enemy in its position, so much so that they were not even allowed to raise their heads over the walls, preparing everything for the assault which I had determined would take place when the first brigade arrived. At the time, it was sixty leagues away.

As to the matter of James Bowie, I took great pains to make sure that our relationship did not become known. I had vehemently opposed his marriage into the family, so much so that after the wedding, I received a letter from Ursula's father forbidding me to visit in San Antonio. I was shocked that Señor Veramendi would cast me out of the family in favor of this *gringo* and outraged that I would be forbidden to even visit the city in which they resided.

I dashed off a quick letter to Juan Martín, my cousin by marriage, complaining of this harsh treatment. But he never returned an answer to me.

Yes, I knew Bowie was in the Alamo, and yes, I must admit that I took great pleasure in knowing that I had him within my grasp and that I controlled his destiny.

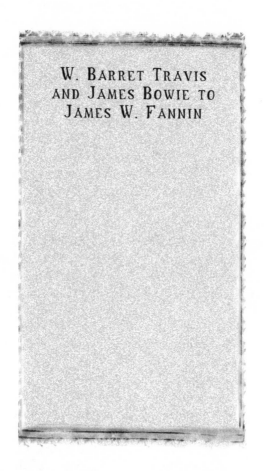

W. BARRET TRAVIS AND JAMES BOWIE TO JAMES W. FANNIN

COMMANDANCY OF BEXAR: We have removed all the men to the Alamo where we make such resistance as is due our honor, and that of the country, until we can get assistance from you, which we expect you to forward immediately. In this extremity, we hope you will send us all the men you can spare promptly. We have one hundred and forty six men, who are determined never to retreat. We have but little provisions, but enough to serve us till you and your men arrive. We deem it unnecessary to repeat to a brave officer, who knows his duty, that we call on him for assistance.

JAMES BOWIE TO
COMMANDER OF THE ARMY
OF TEXAS [MEXICAN]

Commander of the Army of Texas:

Because a shot was fired from a cannon of this fort at the time a red flag was raised over the tower, and a little afterward they told me that a part of your army had sounded a parley, which was not heard before the firing of the shot. I wish, Sir, to ascertain if it be true that a parley was called, for which reason I send my second aid, Benito Jameson, under guarantee of a white flag, which I believe will be respected by you and your forces. God and Texas.

Fortress of the Alamo, February 23, 1836

James Bowie

Commander of the volunteers of Bexar to the Commander of the invading forces below Bexar

JOSÉ BATRES TO JAMES BOWIE

As the Aide-de Camp of his Excellency, the President of the Republic, I reply to you, according to the order of his Excellency, that the Mexican army cannot come to terms under any conditions with rebellious foreigners to whom there is no other recourse left, if they wish to save their lives, than to place themselves immediately at the disposal of the Supreme Government from whom alone they may expect clemency after some considerations are taken up. God and Liberty!
José Batres to James Bowie
General Headquarters of San Antonio de Béxar.
Feb. 23, 1836

DR. JOHN SUTHERLAND

Dr. Amos Pollard, the doctor in the Alamo, called me in for a consultation on Jim Bowie shortly before Santa Anna got there with his men. Bowie had been coughing up blood for quite some time. He tried to stem it with alcohol, a prodigious amount of alcohol, I must say, but that only gave him temporary relief. When I examined him, Bowie's eyes had a dangerous yellow cast to them of a peculiar nature. I could see that whatever ailed him would not be cured by an ordinary course of treatment. Frankly, I believe Bowie had an advanced case of consumption complicated with pneumonia he contracted after leading some of the volunteers across a river on a raiding party. Whatever it was, I knew he would not last long and I think Bowie knew it, too. He gave me a bitter smile and shook his head, saying, "Never mind. I'll keep the medicine I've got for now. I don't think I'll be needing it long." I have often thought this was a peculiar if ghastly prophecy. I think Bowie knew his end. It would be within the man to have that knowledge. Death was a familiar *compadre* to him.

ANDREW J. SOWELL

On 21 Feb. Jim and some of the boys were trying to set a cannon. Jim had been getting sicker and sicker. He was coughing and drinking to stop the cough. He shouldn't have been trying to manhandle that cannon into position, but Jim always was pig-headed that way.

The damn breastwork collapsed on Jim. He broke some ribs and his hip. Along with his cough and general weakness from that cold he caught in the river that day he saved the boy, he was no good as an active soldier. We confined him to his bed. Madame Candelaria agreed to do for him until he was well again.

On 2 March I saw Jim Bowie for the last time. I was headed out on a cattle drive. I went into Jim's room. He was burning up with fever, but people kept coming in and out, and Jim was working on pure guts.

JUAN SEGUÍN

I, as captain of Cavalry and scouts, went by to see Don Jaime. I was being sent as courier with Bowie's request for more men and supplies. Pero, my horse, was windbroken, and Jaime had a fine horse that was not doing anything important while my friend was sick.

He smiled as he saw me. *"Juan, bien de verte."* The great man was sunken to a shadow.

"I travel with your requests, and my horse is not in the best of shape."

"Take my horse. He needs a good run. Just don't let the Mexican troops take him. He is good for little, but I have grown fond of him." He looked at me for a second and then continued, "I have sent my niece and her family away, Juan."

"Porqué?"

"I don't think I can defend this place. Or them."

He fumbled beside his bed and picked up a knife from among

those there and handed it to me. It is a thing of beauty. I no longer carry it, but display it with honor, but then all I could do was blink away the salty tears from my eyes. "Jamie . . ."

"Take it, Juan," he said faintly. "I have not forgotten the loan you made, the five hundred dollars. I regret that I cannot repay you nor honor Texas's debt to you, but . . ." He coughed and I turned away so that I would not see his weakness. When I turned back, there were no more words to be spoken between us. The debt, he knew, had been settled as far as I was concerned. He shook hands, but the strength that was once there was gone. I never saw my good friend again, and as I left his room, I heard the sickening sound of his lungs bursting from him as he coughed so hard his breathing halted and the gasps were so weak I thought he might expire even as I left.

This was not the way I wanted to remember my friend from *Los Leoncitos*.

JOE, SLAVE OF TRAVIS WHO ACCOMPANIED TRAVIS INTO THE ALAMO

Much controversy surrounds Bowie's death. The following is a report given by Joe, who survived the battle, to George C. Childress, the editor of the Nashville Banner. *Childress was present at Washington-on-the-Brazos when Joe delivered his account of the final battle to Houston and his staff. I do not know if Joe could read or write, but I do know that he would not have delivered the following in as florid a style as it appears. That style undoubtedly belongs to Childress. We must also be careful to remember that Childress was an editor and probably took great editorial leeway with the account, honing it to serve his own purposes, whatever they were at the time.*—A. J. S.

Well, sir, the Honorable Davy Crockett died like a hero, surrounded by heaps of the enemy slain. Colonel James Bowie was sick and unable to rise. He was slain in his bed: the enemy allowed him a grave—

probably in consideration of his having been married to a Mexican lady, a daughter of the late Governor Veramendi. The enemy had made daily and nightly attacks upon the place for ten days. The garrison was exhausted by incessant watching; at last the enemy made a final assault with 4000 men, half an hour before daylight, on the morning of the 6th instant. It was dark, and the enemy were undiscovered until they were close to the walls, and before the sentinels had aroused the garrison, the enemy had gained possession of a part of the ramparts. The garrison fought like men who knew there was but a brief space left them in which to avenge the wrongs of their country's possession. When driven from the walls by overwhelming numbers, they retired to the barracks, and fought hand to hand and man to man until the last man was slain—no, there was a man yet left; a little man named Warner had secreted himself among the dead bodies, and was found when the battle was over, and the dead men being removed without the walls of the fort. He asked for quarters; the soldiers took him to Santa Anna, who ordered him to be shot. The order was executed, and the body was taken out and burnt with the heroes who deserve as bright a remembrance as those who died on the pass of Thermopylae.

William Fairfax Gray, later associated with the Fredericksburg Arena, *was also present when Joe gave his report. The following is his account of Joe's narrative.*—A. J. S.

The Garrison was much exhausted by hard labor and incessant watching and fighting for thirteen days. The day and night previous to the attack, the Mexican bombardment had been suspended. On Saturday night, March 5, the little Garrison had worked hard, in repairing and strengthening their position, until a late hour. And when the attack was made, which was just before daybreak, sentinels and all were asleep, except the officer of the day who was just starting on his round. There were three picket guards without the Fort; but they too, it is supposed, were asleep, and were run upon and bayonetted, for they gave no alarm that was heard. The first Joe knew of it was the entrance of Adjutant Baugh, the officer of the day, into Travis' quarters, who roused him with the cry—"The Mexicans are coming." They were running at full speed with their scaling ladders, towards the Fort, and were under the guns, and had their ladders against the wall before the Garrison were aroused to resistance.

Travis sprung up, and seizing his rifle and sword, called to Joe to take his gun and follow. He mounted the wall and called out to his men—"Come on Boys, the Mexicans are upon us, and we'll give them Hell." He immediately fired his rifle—Joe followed his example. The fire was returned by several shots, and Travis fell, wounded, within the wall, on the sloping ground that had recently been thrown up to strengthen the wall. There he sat, unable to rise. Joe, seeing his master fall, and the Mexicans coming near the wall, and thinking with Falstaff that the better part of valor is discretion, ran and ensconced himself in a house, from the loop holes of which he says, he fired on them several times after they had come in.

Here Joe's narrative becomes somewhat interrupted; but Mrs. Dickinson, the wife of Lt. D., who was in the Fort at the time, and is now at San Felipe, has supplied some particulars, which Joe's state of retirement prevented him from knowing with perfect accuracy. The enemy three times applied their scaling ladders to the wall; twice they were beaten back. But numbers and discipline prevailed over valor and desperation. On the third attempt they succeeded, and then they came over "like sheep." As Travis sat wounded, but cheering his men, where he first fell, General Mora, in passing, aimed a blow with his sword to despatch him—Travis rallied his failing strength, struck up the descending weapon, and ran his assailant through the body. This was poor Travis' last effort. Both fell and expired on the spot. The battle now became a complete *melee*. Every man fought "for his own hand," with gun-butts, swords, pistols and knives, as best he could. The handful of Americans, not 150 effective men, retreated to such cover as they had, and continued the battle, until only one man, a little weakly body, named Warner, was left alive. He, and he only, asked for quarter. He was spared by the soldiery; but on being conducted to Santa Anna, he ordered him to be shot, which was promptly done. So that not one white man of that devoted band was left to tell the tale.

Crockett, the kind hearted, brave David Crockett, and a few of the devoted friends who entered the Fort with him, were found lying together, with 21 of the slain enemy around them. Bowie is said to have fired through the door of his room, from his sick bed. He was found dead and mutilated where he had lain. The body of Travis, too, was pierced with many bayonet stabs. The despicable Col. Cós, fleshed his dastard sword in the dead body. Indeed, Joe says, the soldiers continued to stab the fallen Americans, until all possibility of life was extinct. Capt. Barragan was the only Mexican officer who showed any disposition to spare the Americans. He saved Joe, and interceded for poor Warner, but in vain. There were several Negroes and some Mexican women in the Fort. They were all spared. One only of the Negroes was killed—a woman—who was found lying dead between two guns. Joe supposes she ran out in her fright, and was killed by a chance shot. Lieut. Dickinson's child was not killed, as was first reported. The mother and child were both spared and sent home. The wife of Dr. Alsbury and her sister, Miss Navarro, were also spared and restored to their father, who lives in Bejar.

. . .

The slain were collected in a pile and burnt.

SUSANNA DICKINSON

Susanna Dickinson was the wife of Almeron Dickinson, who served as an artillery officer at the Alamo. She survived the final battle along with her infant daughter, Angelina. When the Mexican soldiers came over the walls, she fled into Bowie's room for protection, huddled in a corner opposite the door. This is her account sent to me shortly before her death in 1883. Her memory had dimmed somewhat over the years, but is still one of the few accounts we have of Bowie's last hour. I do not know if she actually was in the room with Bowie when the Mexican soldiers broke in, but according to Juana Navarro Alsbury, a niece of Governor Veramendi and a cousin to Bowie's wife, she was. The reader must decide if this account of Mrs. Dickinson is the true one or an earlier one in which she claimed to have been taken prisoner while in the chapel. Frankly, I would believe this to be the true account for Bowie, as sick as he was, had the formidable reputation as a fighter. I believe instinct for survival would have driven Mrs. Dickinson to seek him out for protection when she saw the Alamo being captured and all of its defenders massacred.—**A. J. S.**

Yes, I remember James Bowie. I remember him well as I remember Travis and Crockett who often performed on the violin for us to take our minds off the siege. Bowie was always a gentleman, even at the end when his sickness often made him feverish and sent him out of his mind. I remember listening to him rave about Ursula, calling out to her from his feverish hell for water. At last, Madame Candelaria was brought in to care for him and that account is best left to her.

I remember when the Mexicans, numbering well into the thousands, poured over the wall to kill the one hundred and eighty-two Texan defenders. My husband rushed into the church where I was staying with our child and exclaimed, "Great God, Sue, the Mexicans are inside our walls! All is lost! If they spare you, save our child!"

Then he took his sword and plunged back into the fray, leaving me with three unarmed gunners, one of them named Walker who spoke to me several times during the siege about his wife and four children.

As the Mexicans drew closer to us, two of the gunners found weapons and charged them, fighting desperately to keep them away from us. I picked up my child and told Walker that I was going to Bowie's room. Walker followed me there. So did Juana Alsbury, her eight-year-old son and thirteen-year-old sister.

Bowie was near death when I burst into his room, crying for his help. I remember a faint smile creased his lips, then he turned and said something to Madame Candelaria, but I no longer remember what that was. I huddled in the corner opposite him with Walker in front of me.

When the Mexicans burst into the room, Bowie killed two of them with his pistols and more with his knife before they killed him. Walker tried to keep them from me, but they caught him up on their bayonets and tossed him around like a sheaf of wheat before an officer came in and, addressing me in English, asked: "Are you Mrs. Dickinson?" I answered "Yes." Then said he, "If you wish to save your life, follow me."

He took me to Santa Anna who questioned me about Bowie and Travis. He took great delight when I told him about Bowie's death, but I could tell he would have liked it better if Bowie would have been taken prisoner. I do not know what ever made him think that Bowie would allow that to happen. That just shows the vanity of the man, I guess.

ANTONIO LÓPEZ DE SANTA
ANNA, MARCH 6, 1836

*This is the letter that Santa Anna sent back to Mexico City following the
final assault on the Alamo. Perhaps it is only fitting that I include it here
in order to throw a little light on the complete contempt that Santa Anna
had for Bowie and the rest of the defenders of the Alamo by claiming to have
killed more defenders than were actually present and severely lowering his
number of casualties. The flag to which he makes reference was the Mexican
flag with 1823 outline in charcoal and blacking in the middle of the white
band. It was made by Mrs. Dickinson and flew over the Alamo until the
bitter end.*—**A. J. S.**

Victory belongs to the army, which at this very moment, 8 o'clock
A.M., achieved a complete and glorious triumph that will render its
memory imperishable.

As I had stated in my report to Your Excellency of the taking of this city, on the 27th of last month, I awaited the arrival of the 1st Brigade of Infantry to commence active operations against the Fortress of the Alamo. However, the whole Brigade having been delayed beyond my expectation, I ordered that three of its Battalions, viz: the Engineers—Aldama and Toluca—should force their march to join me. These troops, together with the Battalions of Matamoros, Jiménez, and San Luis Potosí, brought the force at my disposal, recruits excluded, up to 1400 Infantry. This force, divided into four columns of attack and a reserve, commenced the attack at 5 o'clock A.M. They met with a stubborn resistance, the combat lasting more than one hour and a half, and the reserve having to be brought into action.

The scene offered by this engagement was extraordinary. The men fought individually, vying with each other in heroism. Twenty-one pieces of artillery, used by the enemy with most perfect accuracy, the brisk fire of musketry, which illuminated the interior of the Fortress and its walls and ditches—could not check our dauntless soldiers, who are entitled to the consideration of the Supreme Government and to the gratitude of the nation.

The Fortress is now in our power, with its artillery, stores, &c. More than 600 corpses of foreigners were buried in the ditches and entrenchments, and a great many who had escaped the bayonet of the infantry, fell in the vicinity under the sabres of the cavalry. I can assure Your Excellency that few are those who bore to their associates the tidings of their disaster.

Among the corpses are those of Bowie and Travis, who styled themselves Colonels, and also that of Crockett, and several leading men, who had entered the Fortress with dispatches from their Convention. We lost 70 men killed and 300 wounded, among whom are 25 officers. The cause for which they fell renders their loss less painful, as it is the duty of the Mexican soldier to die for the defense of the rights of the nation; and all of us were ready for any sacrifice to promote this fond object; nor will we, hereafter, suffer any foreigners, whatever their origin may be, to insult our country and to pollute its soils.

I shall, in due time, send to Your Excellency a circumstantial report of this glorious triumph. Now I have only time to congratulate the nation and the President, *ad interim*, to whom I request you to submit this report.

The bearer takes with him one of the flags of the enemy's Battalions, captured today. The inspection of it will show plainly the true intentions of the treacherous colonists, and of their abettors, who came from parts of the United States of the North. God and Liberty!

MADAME CANDELARIA

We must turn to one of the most colorful individuals to emerge from the Texas Revolution, a Mexican woman named Madame Candelaria, who attended James Bowie during his illness in the final days at the Alamo, to find the truth of what happened in the tiny room where Bowie was taken on his deathbed prior to the final assault. Although no records exist that establish her presence at the Alamo on the thirteenth day when Santa Anna's troops stormed the mission walls, no records exist that refute it either. No detractor, however, can take away her fierce and compassionate dedication to the cause of freedom.

Madame Candelaria was born on November 30, 1785, in Presidio de Rio Grande and moved with her family to San Antonio de Béxar when she was twenty-five, where she was employed as a servant for the wife of Don Manuel Antonio Cordero y Bustamante, the Spanish governor of Texas from 1805 to 1810. Sometime in the 1830s, she married Candelario Villanueva and became known as Madame Candelaria when she opened a small hotel near Alamo Plaza and quickly earned fame for cooking the best Mexican food in town. Her hotel quickly became the meeting place for many, among them David Crockett, Sam Houston, José Antonio Navarro, Placido Benavides, and William B. Travis.

Madame Candelaria hated the Mexican government and Antonio López de Santa Anna with good cause as Santa Anna had been a lieutenant in Joaquín de Arredondo's army of Spanish royalists at the Battle of Medina in 1813 where her then husband, Silberio Flores y Abrigo, a revolutionary who supported the ideologies of Father Miguel Hidalgo, was killed.

Shortly before Santa Anna's army of three thousand arrived at the Alamo, Madame Candelaria received a letter from Sam Houston, asking her to go to the Alamo to care for his sick friend, James Bowie. Houston was unaware of the extent of Bowie's illness, the symptoms resembling those of pleurisy, tuberculosis, or pneumonia.

Madame Candelaria found Bowie lying upon a narrow cot in a small room in the fort, his body wasted from his fever, his breath rattling in his lungs agonizingly slow. Beside him lay a rifle and two pistols given him by Crockett and upon his belly on top of his blanket, his knife.

She stayed by his side day and night throughout the thirteen-day siege, raising his head for sips of water and bathing his forehead in a vain attempt to bring down the fever. She was with him at the end.—A. J. S.

And then the thunder stopped and the bugle blowing the *degüello* stopped. In the distance I heard a few pops like a children's firecracker. The friar's cell felt cold and clammy and I smelled the sickness of Señor Bowie. His eyes looked brightly at the door, his tongue flickering out to wet his cracked lips.

"Come," he whispered. "Come."

He reached out to pick up his pistols, but they were too heavy for his hands and fell back upon the table beside him. He fell back against the cot, groaning from the effort of raising himself for his pistols. He touched a small portrait of his wife, Ursula, that he kept constantly by his bedside, his fingers running over her face. He lifted it, and gently kissed it.

Suddenly, the door flew open and two Mexican soldiers entered. Señor Bowie lunged and grabbed his pistols and shot them. They fell in the doorway and Señor Bowie cried out in pain and fell back on his cot, the pistols falling to the floor. His hands dropped limply upon his blanket, upon his knife.

"Old friend," he said. A ghost of a smile traced his lips. I wiped his forehead with a cold rag. Señora Alsbury ran across the room, pulled the soldiers into the room, and threw the door shut. Suddenly, a great silence fell and I knew we were the last alive in the mission.

"Old friend," he said again. Had the guns not been silent, I would not have been able to hear his words. He rolled his head, facing the doorway, clutching his knife in his hand. He raised the knife, looking at it. The dim light glittered down the edge of the blade. His hand closed tightly upon the wire-wrapped handle.

"Old friend," he whispered, and I heard the words spoken like the words he spoke to his wife and two children the day before when he did not know he was speaking them.

I heard more Mexican soldiers moving down the hall, doors banging open. His eyes glowed brightly, his lips spreading in a smile.

"Hurry," he gasped. His eyes rolled to me, pleading. "Lift . . . me . . . please . . ."

I put my arm under his shoulders and easily lifted him, so wasted was he by sickness. A gout of blood burst from his lips. I turned to get the cloth and wipe them clean.

"Ah . . . You have come . . . *mi compadre* . . . At last," he said.

I turned back, but we were alone in the room. He fell back against the cot. One long, shuddering breath rattled from his lungs.

And he was dead.

The door burst open again and Mexican soldiers crowded cautiously into the room, looking at Señor Bowie upon the bed. A slight smile still hung upon his lips.

"*Es el León,*" someone whispered.

"*Es el Diablo,*" another said. "*El Cuchillo feral.*"

"It is only a dead man," yet a third said. He looked down at the knife still clutched in Señor Bowie's hand. "At least, this will be mine."

He tried to pull it from Señor Bowie's hand, but could not. He swore and propped his rifle between his legs to use both hands. Others crowded into the room, bumping him. He lost his grip and Señor Bowie's hand fell back to the blanket, the knife slicing deeply through the man's hand, nearly severing his thumb.

"Ah!" he screamed. "He lives! He lives!"

The others lifted their rifles with the long bayonets upon the end. I threw myself across Señor Bowie, trying to keep his body from being savaged. A bayonet sliced through my upper arm, another through the flesh of my chin. I bear the scars to this day.

Someone pulled me off Señor Bowie's body and threw me into

the corner of the cell. They began stabbing him, lifting him finally from his cot and throwing his body up into the air upon their bayonets. Then, they threw him back upon the cot.

"His wounds," someone breathed. "They do not bleed."

"He is not a man," another said.

"*El Diablo!*" a hushed voice exclaimed.

Some turned and ran from the room. Others crossed themselves and backed away, staring at the dead one upon the cot.

An officer came into the cell and saw me huddled in the corner. He looked at Señor Bowie and shook his head.

"Animals," he said. He turned to those standing back against the wall. "Bring him out with the others." No one moved. "Bring him!" he shouted.

The soldiers moved timidly forward and carried him from the cell. The officer looked down at me.

"Come with me," he ordered. I rose and walked from the room ahead of him.

All was silent now. I heard the bells of San Fernando ringing. The massacre had ended. One hundred and seventy-six of the bravest men the world ever saw had fallen and not one asked for mercy. I walked out of the cell, and when I stepped on the floor of the Alamo, the blood ran into my shoes.

EPILOGUE

The story is not quite complete with Madame Candelaria's words. After Bowie's death, an auction was held of his belongings. An inventory revealed a Masonic apron of lambskin valued at $4.00, a pair of "crape" pants valued at 50 cents, a blue cloth coat at 13 cents, a blue cloth jacket at 25 cents, a black cloth dress at $2.00, a cotton hunting dress at $1.50, a pair of blue cloth pants at 12 cents, a "casonet" vest at 25 cents, a woman's apron at 25 cents, a pocket wallet at 6 cents, two pocket books at $1.00, a trunk at 25 cents, a "whipsaw" at $6.00, a cross-cut saw at $4.00, two mill saws at $2.00, and 640 acres of land. The auction brought $99.50.

What happened to the rest of Bowie's property is unknown, but without a doubt, Bowie had been one of the richest men in Texas at the time. Surprisingly, deeds to all his Texas land vanished. Some say that John and Rezin Bowie took them, but more than likely Bowie's enemies finally got a piece of him.

I do not believe the account of Bowie's death as given by Apolinario Sal-

digna, a young Mexican fifer, who claimed that Bowie was captured and taken out to a Captain who ordered Bowie's tongue cut out and had Bowie thrown still alive on top of the funeral pyre. It was not within the man to be taken alive to be ridiculed by his captors. He had too much honor in his soul to allow that to happen.

*And so, we come at last to the end of the story of Jim Bowie, not knowing any more than what we had at the beginning. Perhaps that is the way it should be, for to know too much of a man is to eliminate the legend and discover the earth, the clay, in which his feet are mired. We do not need the common man; we need the legend, and the legend exists only in the enigma of what was Jim Bowie. Yes, it is much better this way, for we can all invent what we need from the man.—*A. J. S.